Relinquish

M. N. FORGY

RELINQUISH
Copyright © 2015 M.N. Forgy

Edited by Hot Tree Editing
Proofread by Julie Deaton
Cover by LM Creations
Formatted by Max Effect

To every *woman* who looks in the mirror

and wonders where she went wrong.

To every *man* who is on a mission that seems pointless.

I dedicate this book to *you.*

Know that no matter how bad things get,

or how broken you may feel,

there is light at the end of the tunnel.

That light could be your *soulmate.*

A soulmate who's on the same path of discovery.

Prologue

CHARLIE

Nine Years Old

The air is thick and hot, and it smells bad. Similar to the smell of rotting flesh, and pennies. I try to cover my nose with my dirty shirt, but I can't move from this spot to see what's causing the disgusting smell. Mommy told me to hide under this table and not to come out until she said so. That was two days ago. I'm hungry, and blood has crawled from the other side of the kitchen and under the table, painting my feet in a staining of red. I've peed myself a few times, and I'm starting to shiver, but I'm not sure if it's from being wet and cold or from fear. I've called for Mommy, begged for her to come to me, but my cries go unanswered. I should disobey her, get up and look for her, but I'm too scared. Terrified something has happened to her. All I can seem to do is sit under this table and rock back and forth, replaying snippets of what happened just days before. But the images are getting foggier, the sounds of voices fading.

I close my eyes, trying to remember. There are legs blocking my view, legs wearing black pants along with black shiny shoes. A loud bang erupts, followed by a man growling and yelling. Then I hear Mommy screaming. All in that order. I squeeze my eyes closed harder, trying to make out what the man was yelling about, but my brain washes it out. The growl that came from the man sounded like that green guy on TV who gets stronger when he's angry. My mommy's scream terrifies me to the point I plug my ears and freeze. The man attached to the legs and black shiny shoes leaves, slamming the door behind him.

Closing my eyes, I try to remember the faces I saw from when I peeked from under the tablecloth, but all I get are blurred images. Was there more than one face? How many people were there? All I see are wings behind my eyelids. Wings that make my stomach fall, my teeth chatter and my body quiver. Is it a drawing? Is it a painting? I can't tell. Tears slip down my cheeks, and a sob escapes my mouth.

"MOM?"

"Charlotte, can you tell me what you see?" Dr. Tesser asks, pushing his wired glasses up on his nose firmly. I gasp for air, my fingers clawing into the white pleather chair. My back is covered in sweat, and my head is throbbing with unbearable pain from trying to remember. I've been here two weeks. Every day, I'm brought to this room that is nothing but white: white couch, white pillows, and white walls. The only color in the room is from the carpet, which is gray, and Dr. Tesser's black shoes. The doctor is an older man, with white hair and a white mustache, so he fits perfectly with the room. He has wrinkles on his forehead and around his mouth, giving him a permanent scowl.

"I saw nothing," I mutter, looking down at the carpet. I tell him the same thing every time we do this crap. Truth is, I don't want to remember that day. Every time we have one of these sessions and he tries to pry me to remember more, it just hurts. I can't remember much, honestly, but the things I *do* remember can only point to devastation. So I tell him I see nothing. If I don't speak of it, it's like it never happened. Right? Eventually, this fear that rattles my brain when I think about it will disappear. At least, I hope it does.

Dr. Tesser sighs, tossing the clipboard to the side in frustration.

"As usual. Maybe we should double your meds, make sure you're sleeping better." He pulls his glasses off his face, pinching his nose in frustration. More meds don't sound so bad, considering they make me feel nothing. Like a puffy cloud just passing through Hell.

"Charlotte, dear, you're never going to get better until you start telling us what happened that day. What you saw, what you heard, what you're feeling. Something other than silence," he informs roughly. "You're not even trying the exercises to help jog your memory. Don't you want to remember?"

I shrug and look out the window. "Not really."

CHARLIE

Now

Looking at my pale complexion in the mirror, I turn and glance at my small breasts, flat stomach and barely-there ass. I groan in frustration and finger my long, curly brown hair. I turn eighteen today, and I look the same as I did when I was fifteen: small. Sighing, I lean down and grab my black frayed shirt off my suitcase and pull it on. My tits being so tiny, I don't really have to wear a bra if I don't want to. Not that I could find a good bra around here if I wanted to. In foster care, you're given only hand-me-downs, which are usually in the worst condition. Sure, the state supposedly gives us money every so often for clothes, but that shit's pocketed by the foster care parents. If we're lucky, they'll take us to a thrift shop to get clothes, but the pickings are slim.

Foster care. I snort at the thought of it. Supposedly, the system helps by bringing in children from the worst situations and putting them into a home full of hope and love, until they can find the right couple for adoption. It's all bullshit. It's a façade. I'm not saying there isn't a good foster home out there, with loving, caring providers, giving kids who have nobody a little hope that things will get better. I just haven't seen one.

Sometimes, I feel like a butterfly trapped in a Mason jar. The world is moving and happening on the other side of the glass, while I'm stuck inside. But today, the lid comes off this hopeless jar and I escape. Flying free, with endless possibilities.

I open the black, torn suitcase and grab a pair of distressed shorts. Shimmying them on quickly, hues of red and blue paint my legs from the sun shining through the ratty quilt hanging over the window, acting as a curtain.

I grab some magazines by the bunk bed, which usually holds more kids than there is mattress, when the door slams open to my room.

"Charlie, you need to hurry downstairs and do Tee's hair before the school bus pulls up. Get a move on," Aneta grumbles, jostling a small baby on her large hip. I smirk and toss the magazines in the suitcase before zipping it up, having to push and step on the damn thing to zip it up.

Aneta sighs loudly, making sure I hear her irritation. I blow out a breath from the exertion of closing my suitcase and look toward a pissed-off Aneta.

Her caramel-colored, frizzy hair is pulled into a tangled pony-tail, which shows she hasn't seen a brush in a couple days. Her overly large, white shirt is stained and torn in multiple places, hanging off her large frame loosely. And oh, God, she has no pants on, exposing her thick thighs. *I hope she has underwear on today.* Aneta is the foster parent of this fine establishment, which is a two-story house with more kids than beds. I couldn't even tell you the name of the child she's switching from hip to hip, because we have so many kids coming in and out of here, it's hard to keep track. I'm sick of this fucking place—of all foster care homes, to be exact—and today being my eighteenth birthday...I'm fucking out of here.

"Not happening," I sing, pulling on my worn flip-flops. I'm the one who does all the kids' hair, makes sure they're bathed—hell, I even have to cook for them. It can be difficult at times, but it's even more frustrating with the ones who require special care. Most of the foster care homes take in kids who have special needs, because the foster parents receive a bigger paycheck in return. The temporary parents find themselves in over their heads, and make the foster kids do the work by taking care of each other. During my years of high school, I skipped out on the fun, crazy things kids do 'cause all I could think about was one of the toddlers not being fed. But those kids, the cute, squishy-face ones... they get adopted quickly, thankfully. But today, I'm only thinking of myself. Otherwise, I'll never leave.

"What do you mean it's 'not happening'?" Aneta snaps. "And what the hell do you think you're doing with that?" She points at the suitcase on the floor, a look of despair splintered across her greasy face as her eyes widen.

"I'm eighteen. My sentence as a ward of the state is done," I explain, pulling the busted-ass suitcase off the floor. "You're the one who signs up for all these kids then hides in your room behind your computer for me to take care of them. I'm done. Find another victim of the state to be at your beck and call."

"It don't work like that, I'm afraid," she huffs, rolling her eyes and pursing her lips.

I stop, my heart beating faster than my lungs can take in air.

6

The thought of staying in this piss-smelling prison causes a mini panic attack to combust in my chest. I can't stay here. More than most of the time, there's hardly any food. Bugs and mice the size of house cats share the tight living space, and the so-called 'disciplinary actions' of the foster care system can cause more mental damage than most can handle. When one of the kids acts out, their punishment is taking visits away from those who have loved ones, and cleaning up the fecal matter of those who can't control themselves and expel wherever they're sitting. I've witnessed enough suicide attempts, seen enough breakdowns of those who are mere children because they can't handle the Division of Family Services (DFS) system. I have fallen off the path of sanity more often than I can count through the years. My morals surely could be tested as the acts of a juvenile delinquent. Not every child who walks in the door of the system is bad, but it's what foster parents like Aneta try and accomplish.

My face scowls with determination toward Aneta. "I don't care if you send the damn police after my ass. *Nothing* is stopping me from leaving today."

"Charlie, you're not going anywhere."

"Try and stop me," I threaten, pushing past her.

"Charlotte Evans, you cannot leave until your social worker has a judge sign off on your release. If you step a damn foot out that door, I'm obligated to call the police," Aneta screeches, using my whole name to emphasize her point. The house shakes from her feet pounding against the stained linoleum floor as she chases me toward the staircase. The walls, marked and scuffed from children sliding their hands down them instead of the railing, pass by as I descend the steps.

"Then call them! I'll even wait a few minutes to give them a

head start," I sass, struggling with my suitcase down the steep stairs. She'll call them. I know she will. She loves calling the police on me. Every time she and I get into an argument, she does just that, telling them I'm violent and out of control. It's always a lie. She's just a drama queen.

"Where will you go? You have no job, no money, no family." She snorts the last part, causing my head to snap in her direction. She knows how much not having a family bothers me, so of course she would make it obvious I have nobody to run to in my darkest hour. I never had weekends away from this hellhole, a family fighting with all their might to get me back home, or some cute little couple who couldn't have kids to come see me. I'm utterly alone, and it's the worst feeling ever.

"Well, this for sure isn't my fucking family. I'm leaving, and I don't care if I have to sleep on a park bench. Anything out there is better than what's going on in here," I explain, my brown eyes staring at her dull green ones fiercely.

"I'm coming with!" My gaze follows the voice up the stairs, finding the new girl Jayden staring back. She just arrived last week and has been locked in her room most of the time. I took her under my wing as much as I could, but she has a mind of her own. I would take food to her room, but she wouldn't eat it. I tried to talk to her, but she only responded some of the time. I get it, though; it's hard being pushed into a new home. The first couple weeks, you don't want anything to do with anyone. I respected that, but I also let her know I was here for her. Jayden smirks, looking down at us and scratching her head, which is covered in kinky curls. Jayden is one of the prettiest girls I've seen come through here. Her race is mixed, giving her a glowing tan, and her thick frame gives her a body full of sexy curves. I bet she receives a ton of male attention.

"NO!" Aneta yells, pointing at Jayden with a sturdy finger. "Charlie is one thing, but you, Jayden? You're only seventeen and underage." Aneta's acne-scarred forehead wrinkles with annoyance as she waits for Jayden's reply.

"Watch me," Jayden clips. She pulls her brown suitcase behind her, the wheels thumping against each step as she makes her way down the first couple. My eyes fall on her suitcase, the only possession an orphan is guaranteed to have.

Jayden's blue shirt, which looks like it used to have writing across the front of it, rides up from her white torn shorts, causing a sliver of skin to show as she wrestles the luggage down the steps.

"That's it, I'm calling DFS!" Aneta yells. She sets the baby on the floor and throws her hands in the air as if she's had enough. I knew she would call DFS, and the cops will be next. I expected it. I should be out before they get here, though.

"Where're we going?" Jayden asks, out of breath, her curls spiraled out every which way.

"*We* aren't going anywhere," I reply sternly, my eyebrows raised to indicate just how serious I am.

Jayden frowns and looks over my shoulder. I follow her gaze and find Aneta on the phone, yelling hysterically.

"Look, the way I see it, we could join forces, use each other's street smarts and money to get the fuck away from this hellhole," Jayden explains. I *could* use the money; I only have two thousand from baby-sitting and I know it won't get me far. But Jayden is underage and that alone is a big risk. She'll make us a target for law enforcement everywhere.

"I have money, so I don't need you. Besides, you're underage. I'll have the cops all over me," I defend.

"I have money, too, and haven't you heard traveling in pairs is better than alone? What if you run across a creeper or something?" She shrugs, her gray eyes pleading for me to bring her along.

"What? You think you're going to save me?" I laugh, looking away from her puppy dog eyes.

"I've been known to kick some ass," she replies seriously. "My record alone can prove that." I stop laughing instantly. If foster care has taught me anything, it's you have to learn to fight if you want to live. There have been many occasions when fighting has kept me in one piece, but it also added to my criminal record. I've come across many bad seeds being tossed from home to home over the years. Not to mention no matter how small you mess up in care, a foster parent can make a mountain out of a mole hill, because again, the more trouble a kid, the more money they're worth. I have a bunch of infractions against me because of a lying foster parent who needed a bigger paycheck.

"Jayden, I know it sucks in here, but out there could be worse." I try to reason with her, placing my hand on her shoulder. Her brows furrow, and she pushes my hand off.

"Nothin' out there can be as bad as this place," she growls, her nose scrunched in anger. I lick my lips and nod. Aneta's place is definitely one of the worst houses, that's for sure.

"The police are on the way, ladies, along with your DFS workers," Aneta interrupts, smiling like the bitch she is. If we're caught running away, Jayden will be bumped to a run case in the system, which means more money for Aneta, and a harder life for Jayden.

"Fine!" I yell, giving into Jayden's pleading. I don't have time to argue with her, and by the looks of her packed suitcase, she ain't taking no for an answer. I grab my own suitcase and all but run out of the house. There's no way I'm going to let this be a big pay-out for the half-dressed bitch now standing in the doorway, laughing at me and Jayden's frenzied state. The air outside is hot, almost to the point of suffocating, from the sun bearing down on my skin with vengeance.

I fish the keys out of my pocket and unlock the door to my purple Geo, careful to watch where I step from all the toys and trash littering the driveway. Jayden cusses at the rusty lawn chair that snags her suitcase as she passes. *This place is a dump.*

"I hope wherever we're going, it's not far." Jayden laughs, tossing her crap into the backseat of the car. The seats are ripped up with stuffing spilling out, and the headliner is pinned up with tacks to keep it from falling on your head. She's rough, but she was dirt-cheap.

"My car has never let me down before. We'll make it," I encourage, lying to her face. This piece of shit is always letting me down, but I'd like to think that this one time, fate would lean a little on my side of things.

•••

As soon as we make it into town, my car stalls and smoke bellows from the hood.

"Shit!" I scream, slamming my fists against the steering wheel. Sweat trickles down my back in my fit of anger against the dash.

"We'll have to make it on foot," Jayden prompts, hopping out of the car and collecting her luggage from the back.

I laugh mockingly. "And just where do you think we'll go?" I question, my voice laced with anger as I grab my suitcase, too. "We live in Reno, and it's the middle of the summer. This heat alone

will kill us!" I throw my hands out wildly, my eyes darting up the black street with a hazy steam of heat rising from the surface.

"Umm." Jayden hesitates, looking around us. "The bus station!" she squeals, pointing behind us. I turn and look the place over. The old, brick building has several big, black buses parked beside it.

"You really think they're going to let your ass on the bus? You're wanted, Jayden," I remind her, rolling my eyes. "Hell, I'm probably wanted now, too," I huff.

If I'm caught, who knows what shit I'll be in for taking Jayden with me. But I couldn't leave her behind. Sure, her eyes might hold this brightness, and that huge smile may fool others, but I can tell the difference between a real smile and a fake one. She's lonely and scared, like me. She needed me, and I couldn't turn my back on her. That's a weakness of mine. I can't turn away, even if I know it's good for me.

"The bus station is not like boarding a plane. All they want here is cash and for you to get out of their face. It's worth a shot, Charlie." Jayden doesn't even wait for me to respond before she walks across the street toward the bus station, leaving me gawking behind her. She can't venture off alone; who knows what could happen to her. It's one thing for me to sleep on a park bench, but my conscience wouldn't sit well with me if I let Jayden do the same.

"Fine! Wait up!" I yell, running after her and abandoning my car on the side of the road. It's such a pile of junk. I'm betting that, based on that loud knocking and smoke bellowing out of the hood, it would cost more to fix the car than I paid for the piece of shit.

Entering the bus station, my body rises with goose bumps from all the eyes on us. The smell of exhaust fumes and sweaty bodies fills the space, and nothing but dirt and grime coats every surface it can find.

"Everyone is staring at us," I whisper to Jayden, my body vibrating with paranoia that everyone knows we're running away.

"No, they're not. Chill," she hisses, standing in line. "Where should we go?" She stands on her tiptoes trying to see the billboard that lists the locations of the loading buses. "The further we go, the more it'll cost," she states.

I search the billboard for future departures, and Vegas is what catches my eye out of all of them. That's where I was born, although I don't know a lot about myself before I was placed into care. I know my mother's name, Maria Evans, and that I was born in Las Vegas, but not much more. I sometimes have small memories of my mother from time to time, but nothing significant. Getting ice cream with her, her smile. Simple things.

"I'm from Las Vegas," I whisper, my eyes never leaving the sign as a feeling of despair rushes up my spine.

"Oh, yeah?" Jayden laughs. "What? You wanna go find your parents or something?" She giggles, but I don't. Truth is, I don't even know where my mother is, or if she's even alive. I was placed in care at the age of nine, and I've been told many things about my mother growing up. I was told she left me in an abandoned home, that she killed herself, that she overdosed. The list goes on. I was never told anything about a father, though, and I don't remember one.

Jayden looks over her shoulder at me, her bright smile fading quickly as she notices I'm not finding any humor in her questioning.

"Shit. I'm sorry, Charlie." She tilts her head to the side, and a look of sympathy wrinkles her beautiful face.

"Nah, it's okay," I respond, mustering a smile and stepping up next in line.

Waiting to get tickets, I can feel Jayden looking at me, wanting to ask me what happened to my parents and why I was placed in care. My story. It's like going to prison, the whole 'what are you in for'. It applies to jail as well as foster care sadly. I hate it and avoid it.

"Next!" the man yells, grabbing Jayden's attention and causing me to jump.

I quickly step up and walk in front of Jayden. With her being underage and possibly on every cops' radar in the city, she needs to lay low. Not that I being a fucking kidnapper is any better, but I can't help the side of me that wants to protect Jayden from coming forth.

"Two tickets to Vegas, please," I request, digging in my suitcase for money. The guy eyes Jayden and me, a toothpick swirling in the corner of his mouth. He looks like he's in his fifties, but I can't really tell. His face is severely sunburnt, and his head is covered with a black ball cap.

"You got some ID?" he questions, staring at us. His cheeks jiggle as he moves his jaw to talk.

"I do, but my sister doesn't. We're supposed to meet our uncle in Vegas," I lie. He rolls his eyes and nods, as if my ID will do, so I pull it out and hand it to him.

He gives it back and takes the cash from the counter. My heart literally skips a beat in my chest that he believes us and is letting us on the bus. I can taste freedom it's so close, causing me to want to piss myself with excitement.

"Enjoy your ride, ladies," he mumbles.

Jayden and I find our seats on the hot bus and throw our crap in the seats next to us, noticing the bus isn't nearly as full as some of the others. The seats are covered in a black fabric with streaks of rainbow stitched along them.

Sitting next to the window, I watch cars drive by, praying a police car doesn't pull up. I keep wishing everyone would hurry and get on the bus so we can get out of here.

"So, how'd you wind up in care?" Jayden asks, sitting next to me. I sigh. *I knew she was going to ask.*

"I don't know," I reply truthfully.

"You don't know? Where's your parents?" she continues to question.

"Not sure. Well, I mean, I never knew my father, but I know I had a mother. But things before being placed in care are just... fuzzy. It's like my mind has blocked them out. Maybe it's because I was only nine when I was placed in foster care that I can't remember anything from before," I mumble, still looking out the window.

"Yeah, maybe. So, are you going to go look for your mom?" Jayden prods.

"I'm not sure what would be worse: finding out my mother didn't want me and left me for the wolves to devour, or that she's dead. Either way, she'd be dead to me, so I would ultimately be chasing a ghost," I mutter.

I take my gaze from the window and look at Jayden, her bronzed skin glistening from sweat and her gray eyes staring at me strongly.

"Why were you in care?" I ask. *If she's going to ask me, I'm going to ask her.*

"My mom died from a heroin overdose, and my dad just wasn't equipped to raise a little girl on his own. He got DFS called on him for leaving me unattended one night when he went out with his buddies. DFS, of course, gave him rules and guidelines after that, and they would show up for unexpected visits to inspect our house, which always failed. I was eventually taken from him and placed in care." She takes a big breath, releasing with a heavy sigh. So much hurt and despair was let out with that breath it causes goose bumps to plaster my skin. *That right there is why I don't want to remember my past.*

"Where is your dad now?" I interrogate further.

"In Hell for all I fucking care." She shrugs, pursing her lips. I wince from her harsh words, curious why she feels such ill toward him. "He would come by and see me every other weekend at first, but eventually, he stopped showing up. When DFS tried to contact him, he was nowhere to be found."

I nod and shimmy myself closer so I can wrap my arms around her in comfort. If Jayden's anything like me, she doesn't want pity for her life. Nor does she want anyone to give her a sympathetic look and say they understand what she's going through, because nobody knows a damn thing about how it feels or what you've been through. I don't know Jayden, but I know we've both been through more devastation than either of us deserved.

"Fuck them all," I whisper. "We're free now." I laugh, giving her a squeeze. The words leaving my mouth give me an ultimate high of happiness.

"Fuck yeah, we are." She giggles, laying her head on my shoulder as the driver starts the bus. *Finally.*

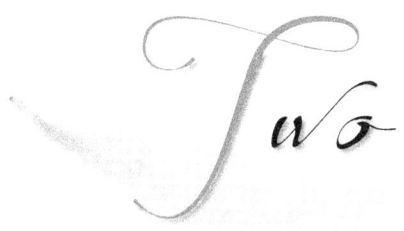

CHARLIE

Behind my eyes, I see it: the intricate etching of dark ink, each feather given such malicious detail my body instantly chills from fear. My heart picks up a pace so hostile I feel it may combust behind my ribcage any minute. My eyes clench, trying to wake myself up from the nightmare that's in full-force, but it won't work. It never does.

My eyes travel up the rigid back holding dark wings that haunt my dreams. I don't know what they mean, but I know I fear them. A piece inside me knows they're from the day I lost my mother. A day of dread, filled with terror, desperately wanting to escape... But I want none of it.

The dark wings suddenly pull from the skin, sweeping off the toned back and surrounding me like a million little blood-seeking bats. I shake my head, jerking from side to side to get away from the death they seek—mine—but I can't escape the ravenous hold they have on me. Surrounding me one by one, until I see nothing but pure

black.

"NO!" I scream. My eyes snap open and find the bus driver clutching his chest and falling into the seat next to us with a startled look across his face.

"What the fuck?" Jayden startles, nearly falling from her seat next to me.

"I'm- I'm sorry," I stutter, out of breath, my heart beating hard against my chest.

"We're here, ladies. Please gather your things and get off," the driver instructs, shaking his head. Irritated, he makes his way back up the aisle.

"Dude, what the fuck was that about?" Jayden's brows narrow with concern.

"Nightmares. I get them a lot," I whisper, standing from my seat which is damp from sweat.

"Umm, Charlie? Did you leave your bag unzipped?" Jayden asks, looking across the aisle at the seats holding our luggage.

"No," I answer hesitantly. I crawl over her, seeing my suitcase unzipped and my things spilled from it.

"No. No. No," I whisper, shuffling through the clothes to find the envelope that contained my cash gone.

"What?" Jayden asks, looking from my bag to me.

"My money is gone," I grit with disbelief. I look around the seat as if it had fallen out, but I know as well as anyone that someone stole it. *How could I be so stupid to just leave it unattended?*

"Shit," Jayden whispers angrily. "Did you see anyone over here?" Jayden hollers to the front of the bus at the driver. The man runs his hand over his bald head and shrugs before looking out the front of the windshield.

"What are we going to do?" My voice cracks with emotion.

"Shit!"

Jayden shoves her hand down her shirt and pulls out a wad of cash.

"I always keep my money close. We'll use mine to find a place." She shrugs, stuffing it back in her bra.

"I worked so hard. Not only did I save that money, but I also kept it hidden from bratty little shits who lived with us, only to have it stolen in a matter of minutes," I mutter under my breath, running my hands through my hair in distress. "How much do you have?" I look at her with weary eyes, nervous at the number she's going to say.

"About seven hundred." She shrugs.

I close my eyes, my bottom lip trembling. *Fuck!*

"How are we going to live? That money was…" I pause, emotional. "Our everything," I cry.

"We can find something for seven hundred, even if it's a shitty hotel for a couple nights," Jayden suggests, reaching over and giving my arm a reassuring squeeze.

Tears fall from my eyes as I glance over at Jayden. We have to figure out a way, have to stay strong and keep moving forward, because going backwards is *not* an option. I worked too hard to get here to turn back now. Most importantly, I need to stay strong for Jayden. If she sees how fucked we could possibly be, she may panic. And having us both panic will only detour us from finding a solution. I straighten my back and wipe my tear-stained cheeks.

"We'll just have to find jobs quickly," I reassure.

"Right," Jayden agrees, a big smile etched across her face. I nod, taking a big breath to calm my racing heart.

We travel down sidewalk after sidewalk, the blistering heat causing a stream of steady sweat to cascade down my back and

between my breasts. And don't get me started on the swamp ass I got going on downstairs. We pass casinos, little stores, and some streets even have men with hot dog carts. Even with the unbearable heat, the smell of the hot dogs makes me want to throw myself over the cart and scarf as many as I can into my mouth. It wouldn't be pretty, but I'm not one for class.

"Charlie, what's the plan?" Jayden yells out, her voice giving away how exhausted she is.

"I need to get a newspaper," I explain, looking every which way for one of those machines that holds them. *Do they even make those anymore?*

"So just go into a store and buy one," she complains. Jayden hands me a few bills from her bra and purses her lips. The heat is making us irritated. *Hopefully, we find something soon.* I side-step off the sidewalk into a little dumpy convenience store that doesn't have air conditioning. I grab a water and newspaper then meet Jayden outside.

"Here, see if you can find something." I hand her the paper while I chug the cool water down. I literally moan from the cold spring liquid splashing down my dry throat.

"Ah-hah!" Jayden exclaims, poking the newspaper. "I found a place that's only charging six hundred a month. Hopefully it's still available."

"Is there anything cheaper?" My eyebrows rise. *That amount's high considering we still need food and furniture.*

"That's the cheapest by a landslide, and it says partially furnished." She scrunches her nose, eyeing the paper.

"All right, let's do it then." *What other choice do we have?*

"I'm going inside to pee and ask the store clerk where this address is. Then we can go," Jayden explains, folding the paper and handing it to me.

I lean against the hot brick making up the small convenience store, watching the sun dissipate behind the large buildings. Their vibrant lights flicker on to light the way for the life that stalks through the night.

"Let's go. We head this way." Jayden points to the left, away from the lights and down some back alley.

"This looks promising," I sneer, following Jayden with my suitcase trailing behind me.

Eight blocks later, I start finding more and more people walking by with college logos on their shirt.

"We must be close," Jayden pants, out of breath. "The clerk said it is near the college."

"This bag is getting heavier, I swear!" I complain, shuffling it from hand to hand.

"I think this is the last block, right across this street," Jayden replies, pointing toward some rundown buildings. Between us and the buildings sits a little café. It's small and painted white, the roof flat. It's cute, but it's like the stepping stone into the ghetto. On this side of the café, the blocks are made up of little businesses and stores that eventually lead off to the heart of Vegas. The other side, which Jayden is pointing to, has grimy rundown buildings with graffiti sprayed on the sides.

Following Jayden across the way, I skim the crowd at the café and land on a pair of handsome eyes. So handsome, I stop walking.

Sitting at a table full of sexy men is a short, blond-haired guy, his face hard and chiseled. My God, his arms are pumped with muscle as his hands flex around a brown football. My core blossoms with incredible need as I eye his toned arms, and what I assume is a matching hard chest beneath his jersey.

Relinquish

"Charlie, let's go!" Jayden yells, making me realize I've been standing here like an idiot, staring at a sexy stranger in a café. The guy smirks at me and tosses the football in the air, breaking eye contact.

I tuck my hair behind my ear, giving a small smile in return before walking forward. I suddenly crash into something, the impact throwing me back on my ass hard.

"Shit!" I shout with pain.

"Fuck!" roars a male voice standing above me. My eyes jolt upward to find a broad-shouldered man in a black suit, holding a broken plastic cup in one hand with coffee spilled all down his front. My stomach tangles into a bundle of tight knots, and my hands tremble from the strength and power this man radiates. *Oh, shit.*

"I am *so* sorry!" I stand up and start frantically brushing at the man's very expensive-looking suit. *My God, it's like rubbing a rock.* His body is so toned and strong beneath my palms, which isn't helping me get a grip on myself. My eyes skirt up his arms, finding the fabric stretched tight around his biceps and causing me to swallow the lump forming in my throat. The knots in my stomach crawl into a fit of butterflies, and my heart races. He's handsome—intimidating, really. The way his toned body and squared shoulders take up the space takes my breath away. His jaw is chiseled to perfection with scruff claiming it perfectly. I bite my bottom lip to keep from moaning.

"It's fine, really," he states, his voice deep as he grabs my wrists to stop me from slapping at his stained shirt pathetically. My body sparks with electricity where he grips me firmly. My mouth parts and my breathing shallows as I slowly trail my eyes from his hold on my wrist to his eyes. They're green with little brown flecks thrown around them. They're captivating. His jawline is strong and defined, his nose broad, and his dark hair is smoothed back with just a trail hanging loosely out of place on the front of his forehead from our sudden run-in. He's fucking gorgeous, and I can't look away.

"Are you all right?" he questions, raising an eyebrow. His voice is low and rough, making my eyes focus on his mouth.

"I-" I stutter, completely lost in the thought of his luscious lips on mine. These lips are not like any belonging to the guys at my high school, that's for sure. When you look at them, his lips look like they're made to make love to a woman's body. The thoughts of the glorious pleasure they could bring make my cheeks warm, my chest ache.

"Charlie, let's go!" Jayden hollers, catching mine and Sexy Man In a Suit's attention.

"That your friend?" he asks, his lips that hold the perfect cupid's bow turn into a slight smirk.

I open my mouth to speak but a wild hiccup noise escapes instead, caused from the wild beat of my heart against my chest. I close my eyes, humiliated.

He chuckles, releasing his hold of my wrists. The way he laughs causes my skin to rise with goose bumps.

"I gotta go," I whisper nervously. I look down and stride quickly toward Jayden, praying I don't bump into any more hot men on the way.

"Lord, give me strength. Vegas is already becoming a bad influence," I mutter, catching up with Jayden.

She takes us down a dark alley between old brick buildings, fire escapes climbing up the side of them. In the distance, a dog barks angrily. *Yeah... this is the ghetto.*

"Here it is," Jayden chimes, looking up at a building plastered with spray paint and posters.

"How do we get in?" I ask, looking at the door which is barricaded with metal fencing.

"Fuck if I know. Let's knock," she suggests.

She steps up the cement blocks and knocks against the door with a rusted cage at the front of it.

Nothing.

She continues to knock and knock, knowing we have nowhere else to go.

A light flickers on behind the caged door, and the door swings open with haste.

"What the fuck is your problem?" a man with dark brown, curly hair mopped over his ears hollers, standing in his boxers.

"Um, are you renting out an apartment?" Jayden questions, her tone soft. I scowl at the man for talking to her so harshly.

"Yeah, I am." He crosses his arms, sticking his chin outward.

"Can we rent it?" I ask annoyed.

"I need six hundred now in cash, and it's yours." He gurgles in the back of his throat before hawking a big wad of spit right onto the sidewalk. *Gross.*

Jayden reaches in her breast and thumbs out the cash, handing it to him.

"Great. Follow me," the man says without emotion.

Jayden and I follow the man inside and up a set of dusty stairs. They're made out of old wood, splinters and nails sticking out of them everywhere. There's only one light showing the way, swinging from a long electrical wire, above the stairs.

"My name is Henry. I expect rent at the end of every month or you're out," he explains, opening a door to the left. "I'll get you keys in the morning."

Jayden and I head inside the apartment as Henry leaves and retreats back to wherever he crawled out of. The room is dark, so I feel along the gritty wall looking for a light switch. I hear a click and the space fills with a dull light.

"Found it," Jayden laughs, standing next to a light switch that has wires hanging from it.

The apartment is one big open space. There are two small beds on each side of the room, and a kitchen along the back wall that contains a pea green fridge and matching stove. There's also a busted island with two bar stools, which look to be rusted and lopsided, sitting in front of it.

Walking along the untreated wood floor, I make my way to the only door in the apartment, hoping it contains a bathroom.

"Please tell me that's the bathroom," Jayden mutters, echoing my thoughts while walking behind me.

Opening the door, I find an old, rusted green tub with a matching toilet and sink. A little window with bars sits right above the tub.

"Yeah, it's a bathroom," I grumble, looking up at the water-stained ceiling.

"It's not too bad. At least we have somewhere to sleep," Jayden states.

I shrug, and head back into main area, looking around the dump.

"We could do worse in Vegas, I'm sure," I point out.

"I mean, look at these bars along the windows. They're a blessing 'cause now we don't have to buy curtains," Jayden jokes, making me laugh as she looks at the three windows lining one of the walls.

"And we don't have to worry about keeping up with the paint, either. Very nice!" I join in, pointing at the cement walls, the windows the only void in the sea of gray.

Jayden falls onto a bed laughing, her face red. Although, I'm not sure if it's from lack of breath or the sun that graced us with its presence while searching for a place to stay this evening.

Heading over to the opposite bed, I collapse on my back against the mattress, dust lifting from the blankets as I land. I look up at the ceiling which holds rusted metal beams.

"But you know what the best part is?" I question Jayden.

"We're free," Jayden whispers, and I smile. Nobody telling us what to fucking do. Not having to worry about what will happen if you don't obey the foster parent. Not having that gut-wrenching feeling of possibly being taken to a new place with new rules and strangers tomorrow. Not having to worry about anyone but myself. Well, I have Jayden, but I actually *want* to look after her. It's something I want to do rather than feeling obligated to. We're free to do what we want.

"Yup, we're free," I repeat blissfully.

CHARLIE

"What are you doing up?" Jayden grumbles, pulling the thread-bare sheet up over her face. We only had to beat the crap out of the sheets twenty times to get the dust out of them last night.

"I'm looking for a job today, as you should be," I scold, pulling on my worn KISS shirt. Hopefully after finding a job, I'll finally be able to buy some decent clothes. I've saved every penny I received over the last couple years, preparing for this epic runaway. If I knew who stole my money, I'd kick their ass.

"I should probably not throw my name and social security down on job applications if I don't want to get caught as a runaway," she informs.

"Shit, I didn't think about that. I could be wanted, too. But I have to find *something* that'll pay the bills. I'll stick to small, family-owned businesses or something," I mutter, worrying my bottom lip with my teeth.

Jayden stretches, causing her perky breasts to pop out from

under the sheet, revealing dark little nipples.

"What the hell, Jayden? Are you naked?" I laugh, pulling on some jeans. Her breasts are much bigger than mine. *If I had tits like that, I'd probably throw them around every chance I got, too.*

She nods and smiles.

"I always wondered what it would be like to sleep naked and not have to worry about purvey old men or horny teenage boys sleeping in the next room," she explains, fluffing her head of curls and pulling the sheet over her chest.

"So, what's the verdict?" I laugh, pulling on my ripped black and white shoes. I think they're a knockoff of Chucks, but they're comfy as hell and were free, so who cares what brand they are.

"Fucking epic. I may never sleep in clothes again," she answers seriously, her voice groggy with sleep.

I shake my head and laugh. Jayden is a mess, but I would be so fucking lonely if she weren't here with me. I can tell she hasn't had much direction growing up. After taking on the role of a mother over the years at Aneta's, I'm sure I can handle one rambunctious girl, though.

"When do you turn eighteen?"

"In six months." She yawns.

"Well, I'll get a job and hold us until then," I offer. It's the least I can do, considering we're living off her saved money right now, or what's left anyway.

"Just try and clean up around here, and stay out of trouble," I state.

Jayden nods and closes her eyes, falling back asleep. I inhale deeply, relieved she isn't going to resist trying to help out.

•••

The sun is already blistering the sidewalk with unbearable heat as I make my way down the side alley, and it's only nine in the morning. The smell of coffee and eggs from the café is strong as the small breeze wafts down the street.

The small café comes into view after I turn the block, the little outside tables already holding a bunch of college kids. A spinning football tossed in the air above the crowd catches my attention as I continue to walk by. My eyes follow the ball, and the hot, blond guy from yesterday catches it. He laughs as if the guy sitting next to him just told him something funny, causing his head to look away from the sky where he was tossing his ball, his piercing eyes landing on me. *Shit, don't make a fool of yourself.* I flick my hair over my shoulder and pretend not to notice him as I quicken my pace.

"Hey!" I slightly look over my shoulder, finding the football player jumping over the small fence that holds all the tables within the patio.

"Hey, yourself," I reply, turning back around and crossing my arms.

"You're new," he observes, rubbing the back of his neck nervously.

"I am," I laugh.

"You off to class or something?" He tilts his head to the side, looking me up and down, a smirk lifting at the corner of his mouth.

"No, looking for a job." I stick my tongue out in distaste, making him chuckle.

"Well, I'll see you around...," he pauses, waiting for me to say my name.

"Charlie," I add.

"Well, I'll see you around, *Charlie.*"

"And what should I call you?" I question, laughing and sounding like a bimbo. I grit my teeth, trying to get a hold of myself.

"Chasen." He jerks his chin out proudly.

"See you around, *Chasen*." I give a little wave before trotting down the sidewalk in looks of a 'for hire' sign.

Hours later, I call defeat and head back to the apartment pissed-off. Who knew getting a job in Vegas would be so hard?

Not only are my options limited, but my record doesn't help, either. I was tried as an adult with my last fight. Some chick who was at the foster home temporarily was in my room, stealing my clothes. When I confronted her about it, she punched me, splitting my eyebrow. I, of course, defended myself, but because she was Aneta's brown mouse, they called the cops, telling them I started it and threatened the girl's life. They arrested me right there. The court tried me as an adult and I got probation with community service. It was all bullshit.

"Someone looks pissed-off." I look over and see Chasen leaning against the fence to the café, staring at me like dessert. "I take it the job hunting didn't go too well."

"Wow, you don't miss a thing," I sneer, walking past. The idea of flirting is not near as appealing now that starvation and being homeless are a big possibility. I need to take care of Jayden, not just myself. And not getting a job is going the opposite direction of taking care of us.

"Wait up," he hollers, jumping over the fence.

I slowly turn, my hands on my hips.

"I know a place you can try," he adds, pulling on his snug jersey which is sticking to his sweaty body.

"Mm, where's that?" I ask irritated.

"Try the kids' dentistry three blocks up. My bitch of a sister owns it and said they can't seem to keep a receptionist." I can't help but scowl. Where I come from, you don't offer things unless you want something in return. I tilt my head, eyeing Chasen, wondering what his angle is.

"Why are you telling me this?"

"Because, I'm a nice guy." He shrugs arrogantly, walking back to the café.

"Yeah, I'm sure you are," I mumble, heading down the road he pointed to.

"Good luck!"

•••

"Hello, Charlotte, I'm Mrs. Jennings. Thank you for your interest in our receptionist opening." Mrs. Jennings leans over the desk, shaking my hand firmly. Her manicured nails grab my attention along with the strong smell of her perfume. Her scrubs with little cartoons fit her toned body snugly, and the way she eyes me with a perfectly waxed, arched brow makes me shift self-consciously. I look down at what I'm wearing: my shirt is damp with sweat, and distressed. The paint on my nails is chipped, the ends jagged from chewing on them. I swallow my insecurities and lift my chin high.

"Thank you, I am very happy to—"

"Look, the truth is I need someone to fill the spot quickly, and you're the third girl in here today to fill out an application. Get back here at seven in the morning and the job is yours," she interrupts, using a pen to scratch her head. Her black hair, placed perfectly into a bun, frays from the snag of the pen.

"Really! Thank you so—"

"Not a minute before, and not a minute after. Seven," she inter-

rupts again, tossing my papers into a drawer. I raise an eyebrow, annoyed with her interrupting me. *Working with her should be peachy with her nose that high in the air.*

"Yes, I understand. I'll be here," I reply, nodding and trying my hardest not to come off like a bitch. But in reality, my hands flex with the urge to grab her perfect hair and slam her head into the desk.

"I hope you're right. See you in the morning." She stands, quickly leaving the office.

She's a bitch, but I can learn to deal with her. I just got a job!

I all but skip out of the dentist's office, my emotions and mind on cloud fucking nine! *Finally, something is working in mine and Jayden's favor.*

Walking up to the café, I see Chasen and a bunch of his football buddies just entering the little restaurant, all hooting and hollering. My eyes catch a guy in a black suit, standing out like a sore thumb amongst the college kids, sitting at a table along the back of the patio. *Oh, my God, it's the sexy guy I bumped into yesterday.* My stomach clenches at the recognition. He gives Chasen and his buddies an irritated look and stands to leave.

"Did you get the job?" My eyes tear away from Sexy Suit and find Chasen leaning over a table, his forehead covered in sweat as he stares at me intently.

"I did. I start first thing in the morning. Thank you. I owe you one," I inform him, smiling big.

"Hmm, I might take you up on that offer." He winks, making my belly flutter with butterflies.

I tuck some stray hair behind my ear and bite my bottom lip to keep from laughing like a bimbo.

"Chasen, what do you want to drink?" one of his football

buddies yell behind him.

"See you around, Charlie."

"Yeah, see ya," I offer.

Walking around the patio towards my street, Sexy Suit charges out of the café, nearly running into me.

"This is becoming a nasty habit of yours," he states, his deep voice coming out like silk as he runs his hand through his dark hair. Little strands defy staying in place and fall just below his ear. His hair is longer than I thought, and it looks fucking sexy messy.

"I—" I've lost my words, I can't speak. There's something about this man that has me dumbfounded yet completely aroused. The feeling I get around him is so foreign. The bimbo state I seem to fall in around cute guys like Chasen could never compare to the surreal feeling I get around this guy.

"What's your name?" he questions, rubbing his chin thoughtfully.

"Charlie," I reply meekly.

"Charlie," he repeats. My name slipping from his perfect lips makes my knees tremble it sounds so erotic. "Charlie, I'm Landon. I'd watch yourself around those dumb fucks." Like someone snapped their fingers, my lusty haze vanishes, the cool demeanor of Landon fading with his sudden use of profanity.

"Excuse me?" I question, startled by his outburst.

"Just make sure you're all in when you're around them." He leans in, tucking a strand of hair sticking to my sweaty face behind my ear. His touch causes that glaze of desire to resurface instantly. I close my eyes and blow out a steady breath, trying to gain some self-control.

"All in? What is that, like a gambling term?" I question with a half-laugh.

Landon smirks, his eyes squinted as he looks me over.

"It means you're in it one-hundred percent. You bet everything you have on it. There's no going back, no regrets. You're all in."

I bite my inner cheek, 'cause when I think of Chasen, I don't get the feeling of being 'all in'. It feels more like... having fun.

"Just be careful, yeah?" he rasps, drawing me out of my thinking spot.

"Yeah," I reply softly. "I can take care of myself."

His lips curve to the side and he nods. "See you around, Charlie."

CHARLIE

"What the fuck, Jayden? Did you turn the alarm off?" I frantically question, falling out of the bed. The unforgiving floor slams against my kneecaps as I land, tangled in the sheets.

"You kept hitting snooze, and I was trying to sleep," she grumbles into her pillow.

"Nice. Well, you sleep while I rush to get a job so we can afford food!" I don't hold back my sarcasm. I fling on the only decent thing I can find in my closet. It's a little black dress which cuffs my shoulders and falls to my thighs. I got it at the thrift store, hence the little holes here and there, and the tatters along the hem. I glance at my poor shoe collection, wondering what I should wear with it.

"Flip-flops?" I question out loud with distaste.

"Use mine," Jayden mumbles, sitting up in her bed and pointing at her addiction of shoes. Her hair consists of little curls spiked up everywhere. "I think we're the same size, or close at least."

I run over to her shoes and find some shiny, black high heels.

"These are nice!" I admire, turning them every which way. They're not from a thrift store, for sure; there's not a scuff on them.

"Thanks. I got them at a five-finger discount." I raise my eye at her as she rolls over on her bed, pulling the sheet over her naked ass.

"With me getting this job, you won't have to steal," I inform her, but she doesn't respond. I'm not a hypocrite—I've stolen my fair share of shit, of course—but Jayden deserves better than that. *We* deserve better than that.

Slipping my feet into the heels, they fit perfectly. *Hopefully, I don't break my neck in them.*

"Well, they look hot on my feet, even if they *are* stolen," I giggle. I look at the shitty alarm clock, noticing it's 6:50 a.m. *Shit, I'm never going to make it.*

"I'll be back!" I yell, running toward the door.

"Open this fucking door!" sounds from the outside of our apartment door, along with a loud thumping of a fist against wood.

I stop in my tracks and look back at Jayden, sitting straight up in her bed, fully alert.

"What the fuck?" I ask Jayden in a hushed voice.

"You stiffed me two hundred dollars, you little bitches!"

I glare at Jayden, her eyes wide with alarm.

"You what?" I hiss.

"We needed food, Charlie!" Jayden whisper-yells. I look over at the counter, the ramen noodles and off-brand soda empty. We have no more money, not for rent or food. My stomach particularly growling for eggs and bacon is not helping any.

I tangle my hands in my hair, stressed more than I already was.

36

"Fuck."

"Take the fire escape," Jayden suggests, pointing at the window and flinging the blankets off her.

My eyes light up and I scamper over to the window.

"I can hear you in there, damn it!" rumbles against the front door, along with continuous knocking.

I slide the window up and shimmy my way out, tripping from the huge-ass heels on my feet as I fall head-first out the window.

"Good luck!" Jayden whispers, pushing my leg the rest of the way out.

"Yeah, thanks."

I make my way down the rusty metal stairs in a rush, the heels of my shoes sticking in the grates of the fire escape. After reaching the sidewalk, I take off the heels, holding them in my hand as I run with all I have.

After making it a block up, my hair sticks to my face from my sweating, and my feet burn from the brutal asphalt cutting into the bottom of them. I stop. *I'll never make it.*

"You need a ride?"

Looking over out of breath, I spot Chasen in a shiny green truck.

"I don't have any money to give you for gas," I pant, my calves burning from my running.

Chasen slides his tongue along his bottom lip, looking out the windshield before looking back at me.

"I'm sure we can figure something out."

I wince and raise a brow. "What's that supposed to mean?"

"I'm just saying. We're two adults. You're attractive, I'm attract-tive." He shrugs, hanging one of his arms over the steering wheel.

I tilt my head back and look up at the sky. *See, everyone wants something in return for a favor.*

"I'm not having sex with you for a fucking ride," I sneer, eyeing him with a vengeance.

He chuckles, leans over the seat and opens the door.

"Get in. We'll talk about it after I get you where you're going," he insists.

I look up the street, conflicted. I need this job. We need money like we need air or we'll be homeless. *Fuck!* I peer at Chasen from under my lashes, his strong jaw and plumped lips carved into a smirk. I sigh heavily. *What choice do I have?*

"Fine," I grit, climbing into the leather seat. The truck smells new, and it's detailed to perfection. It looks expensive with all the leather and gadgets.

"Take me to the dentist's office," I demand, slamming the door shut.

●●●

"It's 7:05. I said 7:00, remember?" Mrs. Jennings clips with a smirk, tapping the shiny watch on her wrist with a perfectly manicured nail. She's wearing colorful scrubs, her hair in some uptight-looking hairdo. Just from the way she's looking at me, I can tell she thinks she's better than me.

"Please! My alarm, it—"

"I'm sorry, but the position has been filled," she interrupts, turning away and dismissing me.

"Shit!" I yell, making the other people working eye me with concern.

I scowl at their reaction. The way their faces are twisted in disapproval, angers me.

"What the hell are you looking at?" I throw at all of them, causing them to resume what they're doing quickly. I flip them all the middle finger and walk out of the office, rage and defeat drumming through my body. I'm not sure what the hell I'm going to do now that I'm back at square one.

"Did you get the job?" Chasen asks as I open the passenger door.

"No," I snap. "I was late." Snatching the heels off my aching feet, I throw them into the floorboard. I look up under my lashes, my eyes stinging with the urge to cry. "Do you think you can talk to your sister for me?"

Chasen shakes his head and twists his mouth. "It won't do any good. She won't listen to me," he replies. I clench my eyes and blow out a steady breath to calm myself. That doesn't surprise me; she looks like a total bitch.

"Can you just take me home?" I ask, opening my eyes.

He scowls and shakes his head. "No. We had a deal, job or no job." His tone is dry and humorless.

"Are you kidding me?" I question, my mouth gaped open.

"Hardly," he states. "Nothing in this world is free, Charlie." I squint and nod in knowing. *Ain't that the truth.* I turn my head and raise an eyebrow.

"Why me? I seriously doubt you have a hard time getting girls to mess around with." I laugh nervously, pointing at his arms which are taut with muscle.

He shakes his head as if I'm not understanding.

"For one, we had a deal. You get a ride, I get something in return. But no, I don't have a problem getting girls; you're right about that. But girls around here want love and shit, and I'm not looking for anything serious. You're hot and look fun," he responds arrogantly.

I take a deep breath, trying to calm my heart beating wildly. I know accepting his offer is wrong, but when have I ever done what's right? I should smack him and gasp in horror. But the throb between my legs and the erect nipples against my dress have me nodding in acceptance.

"All right," I whisper weakly. "But no sex."

Chasen smiles like the devil as he starts his truck, while my mind and body battle a war of lust over logic.

He drives down the road, turning between two tall buildings that lead into an alley, driving up to a dirty green dumpster. The fit is so tight I couldn't open my door if I wanted to without it slamming into the brick building.

"Well, this is fancy," I respond sarcastically, watching a large rat scamper across a green dumpster. Chasen laughs, scratching his blond hair.

"It's not fancy, huh?" He glances at me from the corner of his eye, his chest lifting as he does so. "I think I should start calling you that. Fancy." He chuckles, turning the truck off.

"Yeah, no," I clip seriously, making him laugh harder. I swipe at the sweat trickling down my leg slowly, the heat inside the truck becoming unbearable from the lack of air conditioning.

"So, you said no sex," he states, resting his arm along the back of the seat.

"Yeah, not happening," I respond, shifting in my dress nervously.

"What about a blow job then?" he questions. My head whips in his direction from his forwardness. *He doesn't hold back, does he?*

His head tilts to the side, making him look sexy. I smirk, peering out the window and debating if I should do it or not.

My skin sprouts with little bumps of unease, but my sex throbs with excitement. I close my eyes, conflicted with my thoughts. *It's just a blow job.* He's sexy at least, and if anything, I *do* owe him. My cheeks flush with longing, and my heart beats sporadically when I realize... I want this. I want to feel desired. All my life, I've been pushed to the side by pretty girls whose parents had money. Caring for kids of the foster system kept me from being scandalous and venturous. But there's a part of me, the sexual part of me, I've never experienced before because of it.

"I mean, I've never—"

"It's simple. Open your mouth as wide as you can and suck my dick as hard as you can." He chuckles and I bite my inner cheek, embarrassed.

He pushes his ass off the seat, using his feet in the floorboard and his back against the seat to hold his weight. He undoes his torn jeans and slides them down to his knees, pulling his cock through the hole of his black boxers.

"Holy shit," I mumble, eyeing the long, pinkish shaft and swollen head completing his package. He slides his hand up and down himself, causing it to grow harder. My cheeks warm with the way my body ignites with arousal, shadowing any thought that giving head in an alleyway might be wrong. In fact... it's hot. I mean, we could be caught at any second.

"Come here, Charlie," he whispers huskily.

My breathing spikes with his words, my mouth watering to taste him. My legs tighten to try and smother the pulsing vibrating in my core. I slide across the seat, getting closer to him, my thighs sticking to the leather seat from the heat.

"That'a girl," he mutters, slipping his hand into the back of my hair. I slide my finger up his length; it's silky and veiny beneath the pad of my finger. I've never touched a penis before. There's

something about touching it that has my body warming and my panties wet. I hover my face over the tip of his dick, preparing myself. I'm so turned on I might just give in and have sex with him.

"Fuck me with your mouth, Charlie." He anchors his hand on the back of my neck and plows my face into his crotch. I have no choice but to open my mouth and take him whole.

My tongue thrashes against the bottom of his cock, taking in the taste of musk and salt. It's not bad, though. In fact, I like it. I tilt my head to the side and slide my tongue along the ridge of the head, my eyes peering up at Chasen. His head is resting against the back glass of the truck, looking down at me with a haze of pleasure fogging his eyes. I sheath my teeth with my lips, not wanting to nip him, and take the top of his head into my mouth, sucking it in with force.

"Suck me harder," he whispers, thrusting his hips upward. I hold him at the base of his length and perch my lips over the head of his cock. I suck as hard as I can, taking him to the back of my throat. I bob my head slowly, not rushing the experience. He hisses between his teeth, pushing my head down every time I come upward.

"Just like that," he moans, clenching his hands into my hair painfully. My jaw begins to ache, and my gag reflex starts to quiver with the urge to puke as he continues to fuck my mouth. You'd think I would hate this, that I would plead for him to stop. But to see him so undone, at my complete mercy just by something as simple as my mouth... it's empowering. I love it.

Drool escapes the sides of my mouth and my sex pulses with tingling waves. I hear Chasen moan, and his head hit the truck's back window from falling backwards. He suddenly tenses, stilling my head in place. His body trembles beneath me and warm, salty fluid spills into the back of my throat. Loud, guttural groans fill the cab of the truck with his release as he stiffens beneath me. He untangles his fingers from my hair, letting me up. As I sit up, I notice a big, wet circle soaking his boxers around his cock from my spit.

"Fuck, Charlie," he pants. I wipe my mouth with the back of my hand and notice how sore it is. I work my aching jaw back and forth as I eye him.

"Good?" My voice is muffled with lust.

He lifts his head off the back of the glass and exhales loudly.

"I have never come in a girl's mouth before. Like ever. So, yeah, it was good." He chuckles, sweat slipping off his forehead.

"Really?" I question, shocked.

"Yeah. They always complain their mouth is hurting and stop, or they bite the shit out of me," he replies. "You're something else, you know that?" A smile creeps across my face and my cheeks warm. I'm not sure how to respond.

He pulls up his pants, zipping his fly, and my eyes widen. *That's it? He's not even going to touch me?* At first I didn't want him to, but after just experiencing him come in my mouth, how lost he was in what I was doing, my body demands to be explored.

I slide back over to my side of the seat and situate myself, my body aching with the need to be unraveled.

"So, what are you going to do about not getting the job?" he asks, starting the truck. My high plummets. *I forgot all about not getting the job. Shit.*

"I'm not sure. I can't seem to find anything, and we need the money badly." I shake my head, completely at a loss for what Jayden and I are going to do. The air conditioning blasts against my face, causing me to sigh with relief.

Pulling up to my apartment, Chasen turns the truck off. I almost whine from the loss of cool air.

I look at him, curious if he wants to come up. *Please, come up with me, touch me, grab me, kiss me. God, my inner vixen sounds pathetic.*

He leans over, and my body weeps with gratitude that he's finally going to touch me. Just as I'm about to plow myself into him, he thrusts a handful of cash between us.

"What the fuck is that?" I ask angrily, my body instantly losing its lustful state.

"Get yourself something pretty, pay your rent, whatever," he responds, dropping the cash in my lap.

"What is this for?" I tilt my head to the side and look at him warily.

"Just take it." His tone is suddenly laced with anger.

I start chewing on my thumbnail, looking the money over. It's only fifty dollars, and it's not like I didn't work for it. I exhale a breath of despair and grab it, my fingers fiddling with the edges.

"See you around, Charlie." I look up, seeing Chasen grinning wolfishly. I grimace, looking back at the money in my hand.

"See you around, Chasen," I mumble. Fisting the money in one hand, I use the other to open the door and get out.

CHARLIE

It's been three days since my ride home with Chasen. Jayden and I still have no jobs, but I managed to keep the landlord at bay with the money I got from Chasen. It won't hold him off for long, though.

"Look what I got!" Jayden exclaims, walking through our apartment door.

Glancing up from my outdated magazine, I notice Jayden holding a plastic card in her hand. Her hair is frizzier today than usual, and her green tank top is disheveled, hanging off her shoulder.

"You look like shit, and what's that?" I question, sitting up as she huffs and lowers her hand.

"It's an ID," she explains, looking it over.

"How did you get that?" I narrow my brows with concern.

"Don't worry, I didn't apply for one or anything. It's fake." She smiles proudly. My face turns into a grimace, my bottom lip tucked between my teeth in anger.

"How the hell did you pay for that, Jayden?"

She shrugs, sticking it in the back pocket of her torn-up white shorts. "I have my ways. Don't worry, I didn't use our cash."

"You have your ways?" I twist my face in question, not sure what the hell that's supposed to mean.

Jayden rolls her eyes and falls back on her bed. "I stole some sandwiches from the college's cafeteria," she states, changing the subject. My mouth instantly waters; I haven't had anything to eat all day.

"You did?" My attention is completely on her, curious where she stuffed the delectable stolen goods. I should be angry that she did it, telling her it's not something she should be doing, but the growl in my stomach couldn't care less right now. Our food rations have been next to none with our lack of money. I'd be a liar if I said the thought of stealing food hasn't crossed my mind.

A loud knock sounds at the door, drawing our attention.

"Shit, you think it's the landlord?" Jayden whispers, sitting up. We stay perfectly still, making sure not to make a sound, waiting for the person behind the door to speak or go away.

"Charlie, you there? It's Chasen."

"It's for me," I mutter, releasing the breath I was holding, relieved it's not the landlord.

I glance down at myself, making sure what I have on is presentable. I'm wearing a white stretched-out tank top with my black sports bra showing, along with my blue-jean skirt.

"You look great, don't worry," Jayden whispers, smiling big.

I nod and open the door.

"Fancy!" Chasen chimes, looking me up and down. I roll my eyes at his stupid nickname for me. "Damn, you look good," he groans, making my cheeks flush crimson.

"Chasen," I greet, holding the door open.

He looks over my shoulder, noticing Jayden.

"Sup?" he questions, jerking his chin upward.

"Sup yourself? I'm Jayden," Jayden coos over my shoulder.

"Chasen," he responds. His eyes trail back to me, a smile playing across his face. "Wanna get out of here?"

I can't help the goofy-ass grin that splits my face. Lustful thoughts bring a flame to my sex, and I forget about my hunger.

"I take that as a yes." He laughs. "Let's bolt." He grabs my hand, pulling me from the doorway. "I'm parked up at the café. I didn't want to park here." He quirks an eyebrow up and shrugs. "No offense."

I laugh and flip my hair over my shoulder. "Nah, I get it. It'd probably be on bricks and stripped if you left your truck parked out front." He laughs and leads the way toward the café.

"That your roommate?" Chasen questions, walking a step ahead of me.

"Who, Jayden? Yeah," I respond, trying to keep up. We round the café and Landon charges out of the building, nearly knocking into Chasen.

"Watch it, ass-wipe!" Chasen hollers, puffing his chest out. My breath catches in my throat. I'm at a complete loss as to why Chasen is being so rude.

Landon's face turns into a scowl that has me scared as he steps up to Chasen. My breathing shallows and I watch in terror at the two handsome men giving death stares at each other. It's like watching two tigers circle each other with preying eyes.

"Watch where *you're* walking," Landon responds, his tone low and menacing. I clear my throat, trying to get rid of the sudden

lump forming, and Landon slowly draws his attention from Chasen to me. My chest constricts, and my stomach falls.

"Charlie," he mutters. His eyes shine, and the way he says my name sounds like a prayer slipping from his lips. He winks, and my panties go damp. My chest nearly explodes with admiration. *His face is so perfect. Even the way he talks is perfect.*

"Hi," I reply weakly.

Chasen's chest begins to rise and fall rapidly with rage, his eyes darting between Landon and me.

He steps over and grabs my hand. "Let's get out of here, Charlie." He drags me toward his truck and away from Landon. I can't help but look over my shoulder to get one more glimpse at Landon, the way his dark hair shifts in the wind, and how he jerks his tie angrily. It's a sight that would make any woman fall to her knees. I wonder what the hell happened between Landon and Chasen. Clearly, there's some tension between the two.

"So, where are we going?" I ask, searching for my seatbelt.

"Somewhere quiet," he mutters, pulling out onto the street. I peer under my lashes at Chasen, who's clearly upset. His face is red, his jaw clenched. He has one hand over the steering wheel, and we're going way over the speed limit. I fiddle with my hands nervously, the question I want to ask dangling in the air between us like bait waiting for a shark. I blow a steady breath and go for it.

"What was all that about?" I furrow my brows and watch his reaction.

Chasen scoffs and rubs at his chin.

"That ol' man just has it out for me. Because he has money, he thinks he can just do whatever he wants," he replies, his face even redder by the end. I bite my inner cheek and look out the window. I don't know Landon, but the couple of times I met him, I didn't get the impression he was some rich asshole. Rich, yes, but not an asshole.

Riding in the truck, the windows down and a warm breeze blowing through, Chasen grasps my hand resting on the seat. I peer up at him as he focuses on the road. Butterflies swarm in my stomach, making me fidget in my seat. I have never had a boy-friend before, never had a guy interested in me who looked as sexy as Chasen. It all feels too surreal. Living in foster care, not having the nicest of things, not many boys looked my way.

Chasen pulls onto a dirt road, the sun resting on the horizon warning us of its departure.

Passing a 'closed' sign, I give Chasen a concerned look.

"It says closed," I point out.

"Yeah, so?" he replies, shrugging. I smirk at his rebel behavior and shrug myself, sitting back in the seat.

He pulls over and turns the truck off. Looking out the window, I notice a small lake with palm trees planted nicely around it, and little picnic benches scattered here and there. There's yellow caution tape around areas, with small yellow tractors parked nearby. It looks like this place is still under construction.

"Come on," Chasen mumbles, getting out of the truck. I hop out and shut the door, the sound of it closing echoes through the deserted area.

Chasen walks up behind me, placing both of his hands on my hips possessively. He nips my shoulder with his teeth, causing my body to drum with that delicious ache from when I gave him head for the first time.

"Come on, let's check it out." He pushes on my back, urging me forward.

We make our way up the lake, the smell of dirty water strong.

"Got a big game tomorrow," Chasen explains, looking out across the distance. "Scouts coming in, my father on my ass. It's fucking stressful," he mutters.

"I bet," I reply, resting against one of the yellow tractors. I actually have no idea what kind of stress he's under. To have a parent believe in you so much it stresses you out, I've never experienced it. Chasen turns, looking at me with a mischievous grin.

"You're sexy as hell, do you know that?"

"Do you tell all the girls that line?" I sass. Chasen laughs and runs his hand over his chin. He walks toward me, grabs my backside and pulls me in close. My eyes widen, my mouth parting with a thirst of longing.

He runs a hand between my thighs, making my legs part and my head fall back against the large tire belonging to the machine behind me.

He rubs his fingers back and forth over the material of my underwear, causing me to pant with the incredible pressure building.

"You like that?" he whispers roughly. I nod, fevering myself onto his fingers. The intensity climbs, turning into a warmth that envelops my whole lower half.

"Yeah?" he pants arrogantly, rubbing harder. His other hand comes up and grabs my tit hard, causing me to moan.

My body shudders and stiffens with an incredible sensation that drives through my core. It tingles and is almost too much to handle, but I can't help but want to keep pushing myself on his hands for more of it. Sparks ignite behind my eyes, my body riding a wave of indescribable ecstasy. But as soon as it came... it vanishes, leaving me a panting mess. Chasen turns away as I'm gasping against the wheel.

"Come here, Charlie," he demands, unbuttoning his jeans. I close my mouth, my tongue sticking to the roof from my heavy breathing.

I pull myself off the tractor and stride toward him. His jeans are wrapped around his ankles as he fists his cock.

"Still won't fuck me?" he questions with a salacious smirk. My eyebrows narrow inward, telling him no. "Then suck me. Give me that beautiful mouth of yours," he pants, sliding his hand up and down his shaft.

I lower myself to my knees, the desert sand burning them. My eyes never leaving his, I grab the base of his cock and slowly cover the head with my tongue.

"You fucking tease," he grunts, grabbing the back of my head and pushing my mouth all the way onto his dick. I smile around his length; the control I have is a high. I have never had control of anything in my life. But when it comes to this, using my body, I have control not only of myself, but the man who wants it, as well. I suck, and bob, and suck some more before I feel his cock tighten and pulse against my tongue. I close my eyes, preparing myself for the warmth about to spill into my mouth, but he pulls out instead. As soon as I open my eyes, I'm sprayed in the face with warm semen. Chasen grunts as he strokes himself, releasing little beads of sticky cum onto my face. I turn away and get it in my hair, causing him to chuckle, an arrogant smirk covering his face.

"It's not fucking funny," I respond angry, shoving him away from me. "Seriously?" I growl, trying to wipe the mess off my face.

"I'm sorry, babe. I was just messing around." Chasen laughs, pushing my hair from my face.

After I wipe my face clean of what I could with my hands,

Chasen pulls me up and lifts my face toward his.

"I gotta get home. I need my focus for tomorrow," he explains.

"Yeah, okay. I understand," I reply, still irritated.

We walk back to his truck and get in. The air conditioning caresses my sweaty body as he starts the engine.

Chasen pulls up to my apartment and parks. The sky is dark from the sun setting; the only thing I can see is the small glow from the café in the distance.

"You wanna come up?" I ask, looking over at him stretched out in his seat.

"Can't, babe," he responds, lifting up in his seat and messing with something in his back pocket.

"Your shoes," he mentions, jerking his head toward my feet. I look down, noticing my worn-out flip-flops.

"Yeah, what about them?" I ask, confused.

Chasen pulls some cash out, throwing it on the seat. "Get you some better ones or something." My mouth falls open at the eighty bucks sitting on the leather seat.

"You deserve something better," he mutters, leaning over and kissing my forehead. I shut my mouth and look up at him, curious why he cares so much about my fucking shoes.

"My flip-flops are fine," I assure.

"Then get something else," he responds, giving me a wink and putting the truck into drive.

I haven't been one to know much about what boyfriends and girlfriends do in a relationship. Hell, I don't know what the hell you would even call Chasen and me, but I had a friend in high school who was always dating older guys. The men she went with would shower her in the finest jewelry and always gave her cash for spending. But who am I kidding? Jayden and I need the money so badly, who cares why Chasen's giving it to me? I look at it and see food rather than shoes. With that, I grab the cash and stuff it down my shirt.

"See you around, Charlie." I look up and find Chasen flashing a menacing smile.

I blink rapidly, his smile taking me aback, and shut the cab door.

•••

Chasen showed up a couple times a week after that. He would take me somewhere, and before I knew what was happening, I was either giving him head or a hand job. Not every time, but most of the time he would return the favor, rubbing on me just right to make me obliterate into nothing but pleasure. He has asked me several times if I was ready to have sex, and every time, I told him no. I just wanted more than some quickie in the back of a truck. I wanted what you see in the movies. The unmistaken sparks that fly from touching one another, and a more romantic place than public. But realistically, I'm not fooling myself. I know that kind of romance doesn't exist. What I need is to not be alone anymore. I want to be a part of something whole, and not broken.

He has bought me clothes, shoes, a cell phone, and even helped me with my rent. Jayden and I actually have some food in our fridge. We'd be starving or out on the streets without him. The next time we go out, I think I may give myself to him fully. Maybe. I don't know.

My stomach falls with the thought, excitement and confusion racing through me like a source of adrenaline. I want to want to have sex with Chasen, but for some reason, my head isn't as

convinced. *Get a grip. It'll be like taking off a Band-Aid; just get it over with.* Chasen is the only guy who's showed any interest in me since... ever.

I'm thinking way too much about it. I blow an irritated breath. *It's just sex. Nothing more.* Besides, it's not like I have a line of suitors lined up at my door. Maybe sex is exactly what I need to fill this aching hole in my chest. It's like a black hole that's been there since I can remember, and it sucks the life out of me.

"I'll be back tomorrow, babe," Jayden informs, walking out the door.

"Where are you going?" I question, all motherly and whatnot. Jayden sighs and rolls her eyes.

"There's a frat party. I'm just going to go check it out. Chill," she huffs, slamming the door before leaving.

I reach over and grab some pink fingernail polish as my phone vibrates. It's just a cheapy pay-as-you-go, but it's the only cell phone I've ever had. I reach over and grab it.

I got something just for you, babe. Meet me outside in ten.

"He has something for me?" I mutter, a smile creeping across my face. My heart skips a beat in excitement. I've never been given a gift before.

I run over to the closet and find that black dress, grabbing Jayden's black heels that match it. I look in my suitcase for some clean panties, but come up short. I need to go to the dry cleaners bad. *Looks like I'm going commando. Jayden would be proud.*

I finger my hair, trying to tame the bed-head look I've got going on, and quickly apply some light makeup. My heart beats against my chest anxiously, curious at what Chasen has for me. I'm excited and nearly trip on my heels exiting the apartment.

Walking out, it's hot and muggy, even when the sun has gone

down. The street is deserted and the café up the street just turned its lights off, making the area pitch-black. The eerie darkness conceals the alleys and sidewalk, a sense of unease rushing in my veins. I swallow the sudden lump in my throat. A bunch of deep laughter echoes down the way, causing me to look toward the street heading toward the college.

"Fancy!" Chasen hollers. Hearing his voice, I relax a little, knowing he's there. As he gets closer, I notice a couple of buff guys walking beside him. I look at the bunch in confusion. I thought Chasen would be alone. Heading toward them, I hear music blaring from the college dorms, Eminem and Sia's, "Beautiful Disaster".

"This her?" a guy with a low buzz-cut and what looks like a college football jersey that matches Chasen's asks. His eyes rake over my frame unforgivingly, and he licks his bottom lip. I curl my own in reaction.

"Damn, man," another guy with dark, short-spiked hair re-marks. My spine stiffens and my body chills. I'm not sure why I react with such high-alert, but my instincts are telling me I should run. Growing up in such a hostile environment, my gut has never been wrong. *But Chasen is with them. He won't let anything happen to me.*

"Yep, best head I've had, I'm telling you," Chasen adds, looking up at the sky like my mouth is God's gift to Earth. A menacing smile stretches across his face. *Did he always smile like that? Am I just now noticing it?* Shame fills the pit of my stomach.

My eyes widen and my mouth parts to allow my harsh breath-ing to escape. My brows furrow in confusion as to why he would say such a personal thing to his friends. Trusting my gut, I turn on my heel, ready to run back to my apartment, but a rock-hard hand grasps my upper arm and stops me, pulling me back with force.

Looking over my shoulder, I see a smiling buzz-cut glowering at me. I tear my arm from his hold, tripping over my high heels, and glare at him.

"So, Chasen said he can't get you to go all the way with him. How much more do we gotta pay to get between those legs?" Buzz-cut asks, reaching out and sliding his hand up my dress uninvited.

"Don't fucking touch me." I raise my fist back in a threatening manner, ready to fight my way through three men if I have to. But if they look closely, they could see my fist shake with fear. I can't help the wave of vulnerability and hurt coursing through me. I'm confused. *Why would Chasen tell his friends that, and why do his friends think I would sleep with them?*

"Fuck, she ain't wearing any panties," Buzz-cut laughs, looking back at Chasen and the other guys, his eyes hard with determination. My cheeks flush with humiliation as I look at Chasen with rage. *Why in the fuck isn't he coming to my defense? He should punch his friend for touching me. SOMETHING.* But Chasen just nods, his eyes looking at me with an animalistic flare. He's clearly not the guy I thought he was. He isn't going to protect me at all. In fact, he's throwing me to his frat buddies like I'm fresh meat.

"Is this what you were talking about when you said you had something for me, Chasen?" I scowl and point at his two dipshit friends. "'Cause if it was, all three of you can fuck off!" My voice echoes down the street.

"Come on, baby," Spiked hair coos, strutting forward and slapping my ass, hard. My backside burns from the unsought connection, the sting racing up my spine.

"Stop it!" I scream, jerking away from him. My voice echoes up the street, but nobody is around to hear my cries. My hands shake with anger, and my eyes well with unshed tears. My hands fist by my sides in fury. I want to deck every one of their asses. But looking at them, I'm starting to second-guess my impulse to take them on. They're all built, probably working the weight room daily for football. My fight here is pointless. *I'm fucked.*

"Chasen, brother, get your whore in check," Buzz scolds, pointing at me.

"I'm not a whore!" I seethe, tears spilling down my cheeks.

They all laugh, making me vibrate with rage and choke with emotion.

"I'm not," I mutter angrily.

The feelings I had for Chasen were nothing but clueless emotions. Trying to live a teenage dream of love and lust. I thought Chasen was giving me money because he cared, but no.

"I'm pretty sure when someone pays you after they blow their load, that makes you a dirty whore," Chasen chuckles, the sound vindictive. My body chills and my heart snaps in two. He was paying me for my sordid behavior. I close my eyes, my mind telling me I knew exactly why he was giving me the money. *Oh, my God, I have been a whore. And the worst part? I enjoyed it.* The dirty journeys behind tractors and in alleyways, and I got paid every time. And I liked it all. Being in control and having the comfort from a man was a high I enjoyed.

I'm. A. Whore.

I shake my head, not believing such a notion.

"No, I am Chasen's girlfriend," I defend, tears rolling over my lips. Just saying the word 'girlfriend' comes out feeling wrong.

"Chasen *has* a girlfriend." Buzz-cut laughs, making my head snap in Chasen's direction.

"What?" I whisper in disbelief.

"True." Chasen shrugs. "What – you thought I would be with the

likes of you?" He chuckles, staring at me with a raised brow. I look down at myself, my second-hand dress and stolen shoes making me feel like trash.

"Your dad would kill you." Spiked hair bellows with laughter, catching my attention. I shake my head again, not wanting to believe what I'm hearing. My chest feels shallow from the self-respect being ripped out of my chest.

"I came to you because my girlfriend won't put out. She's saving herself for marriage, and girls around here like to blab," Chasen remarks, tucking a bit of hair behind my ear. I shove him in the chest, completely and utterly pissed-off.

"Fuck you! Don't touch me!" I shriek. *How could I make myself believe this was anything more than being used by Chasen? I'm so stupid.*

"You used me," I seethe, my jaw clenched with anger. Chasen gives a weak attempt at a laugh and cups the back of my head harshly, pulling me forward. He rests his forehead against mine, looking me right in the eye. I try to resist his hold, but he clenches his hand in my hair, making me wince.

"Like you didn't use me? You took that money without any problem," he whispers, his breath feathering my face. "Just like a greedy little whore." He grins wildly. My eyes widen, realization setting in. *I am a gluttonous whore. There's no denying it.* The idea of having food and rent was more important than my morals, the high of doing something risqué shadowing over any thought of honor.

Living in care, we didn't get the love kids grow up with. We didn't get cuddles on Christmas morning, or kisses on boo-boos when we fell. So to say I'm desperate for that connection is obviously an understatement.

"Come on, baby. Give it up, you fucking tease," Spiked hair grunts, grabbing my wrists and yanking me from Chasen's hold. I twist and pull, trying to get away, but it does no good. He turns us and shoves me against a rusty fence placed between two apartment buildings.

"No! Please, stop!" I scream, trying to pull away, but he's too strong. My attempt of trying to free myself is pointless. My heart drives against my chest in fear, and tears fill my eyes to the point I can barely see. A vision of a woman who looks like me flashes behind my eyes, my mother. Her telling me to hide and not to scream echoes in my head. I close my eyes and shake my head to clear the noise. But my body responds in a way that has me clamping my mouth shut and obeying.

I feel a hand slide through my legs, causing me to clench them together tightly.

"That won't help you," a voice whispers into my ear, making the hair on my neck stand up.

Fingers touch the bare skin of my butt cheeks, making me jump and whimper with desperation.

"Shhh," Chasen soothes, brushing my hair from my face.

Fingertips edge closer to my most intimate spot, causing me to buck and attempt to pull away from the intrusion. I look up and down the street, not finding anybody. I'm alone and about to be gang-raped. I close my eyes, spilling tears of shame. I hold my thighs tighter, feeling hands try to tear them apart, bruising the skin painfully.

"You've already whored yourself out, so why fight who you are?" The words begin to swirl and echo in my head as I clench my eyes shut and cry harder. Hands pull at my dress, lifting it upward, and greedy palms grasp at my chest uninvited. My breathing

becomes so harsh my head starts to spin. Just as I'm about to give in, knowing I can't fight all three of them, hands which were once intruding are suddenly ripped from my body. Voices which were taunting me turn to ones of painful grunts. I throw my eyes open, curious where Chasen and his friends went, and turn my head. I find a shadowed figure holding Chasen and Buzz-cut by the throat against a brick wall, his foot holding Spiked hair on the ground and pushing his head into the concrete. Chasen and Buzz-cut are both bleeding from the face profusely, and the guy on the ground looks to have his nose completely broken.

"Apologize *now*!" The shadowed figure roars, making me jump. My fingers clench the rusty fence like a lifeline.

"Sorry," pant Chasen and his buddy simultaneously. I nod and turn the other way. My emotions so up and down I'm not sure what to feel or think at the bloody sight.

"I will fucking *bury* you if you ever look at her again. If you so much as walk up this street again, I will murder you in your sleep. Do you understand?" the shadowed man seethes, his words holding venom as he threatens. *That voice. It sounds familiar.*

"You got it, man," one of the guys cries.

I watch Chasen and his buddies start limping away back toward the college. Chasen stops, turns around and grabs his crotch, blood spilling from his nose and lip.

"You were a lousy whore anyway!" he sneers, turning to run. I wince from his harsh words.

"Are you okay?"

I blink tears away, my fingers still hooked into the fence. The smell of spice and manliness caressing my senses makes me wake from my state of terror.

"I was just trying to survive. I didn't know I was becoming a whore," I whisper gravely. Even if I didn't have sex with him, I still did things that were immoral in exchange for money. I close my eyes, wetness clinging to my lashes. *Jayden and I needed the money, though. We needed food. We needed to pay our rent.*

"What?" the voice asks.

I open my eyes, and it's Landon from the café, looking at me with concern. His brows are raised, mouth parted, as he lowers my dress over my backside gently.

"Charlie, are you okay?" he questions again, lifting my chin with his thick finger. He looks me over as if he's searching for injury. The fact he even cares is overwhelming.

"You," I whisper, my body instantly flooding with a sense of comfort.

He chuckles. "You can call me Landon, remember?"

"L—" I choke on my words. "Landon, you saved me," I mutter, pulling myself from the fence. My knees wobble from the adrenaline rush spiking my bloodstream, and I grab the fence again to steady myself.

"I was in the neighborhood." He shrugs and straightens his tie. "Come on, you look like you could use a drink," he invites, his voice smooth yet rough at the same time. He holds his hand out, waiting for me to take it. I bite my lip, unsure, and look back up at Landon. His face is sincere as he waits.

Even after everything that just happened, my body responds to him in a way that doesn't make sense. I should be running to the cops, or at least be crying it out with Jayden in our apartment, drowning my sorrows in a tub of ice cream. Instead, I hold my hand out and take Landon's.

I take a step toward him and my knees give out. Landon quickly grabs ahold of my waist and picks me up, holding me like a princess. My eyes connect with his, and my chest aches with desire. The cold that was once there blossoms with a caring warmth.

"You sure you're okay?" he asks, his voice low and sexy.

I shake my head and furrow my brows. "Um, yeah. I'm fine. Put me down," I instruct, wiggling from his strong grasp. The smell of spice and freshness is clouding my train of thought.

He sighs and slowly lowers me.

"I can walk by myself," I state, slowly standing on my own two feet.

He places his hand along the small of my back, his large frame cordial next to mine. "That might be, but I'm still helping you to my car whether you like it or not," he demands. His alpha ego takes my breath away, and I don't argue. I *can't*, actually. The idea that someone cares about my safety has me speechless. I'm consumed in the strong vortex that is Landon.

"O-okay," I mumble.

CHARLIE

Landon walks us to a fancy black car and opens the side door for me to get in. I slip into the luxury leather seat and notice the vehicle is loaded with dials and buttons. A small screen sets in the dash. This car puts Chasen's truck to shame.

"Wow," I whisper.

Landon climbs into his seat, the smell of sweat and cologne filling the space as he starts it. He's wearing a gray dress shirt and black slacks—sexy and sophisticated, as usual. Tove Lo's "Talking Bodies" starts blasting through the speakers. The lyrics of the song have me biting my lip and looking at Landon from the corner of my eye.

He looks over, his face empathic.

"Are you sure you're okay?"

I inhale a deep breath, and smile softly. "Yeah, I'll survive." I've had to push pervy men off me before. I once woke up to an old guy standing over my bed, fondling himself. I kicked him in the nuts and ran to the phone to call my social worker. The guy's name was Mr. Jenkens, and he was my foster parent at the time. He told everyone he must have been sleep-walking. That he ran out of his sleep aid and it made him do things in his sleep. Needless to say, nothing was done. *I was* moved to another home, but not before I was told I couldn't seem to live anywhere without having a problem of some kind.

Life's a bitch that keeps dishing out free life lessons. I clearly fail most of these lessons, but it doesn't mean I give up. I push back and make my way through it, every time.

"Those boys won't be coming near you again."

I turn my head, shocked at the danger and promise laced in his voice. A primal need rushes through my bloodstream, a craving that has me holding my breath as I stare at Landon's bright green eyes. My body sways toward him on its own accord, Chasen and his buddies' acts of aggression soon forgotten. Landon smiles a boyish grin, little dimples popping up on each side of his mouth. I close my eyes and turn my head to stare out the window.

The pull I have toward Landon is strong. I feel like a precious metal, and he's the strong element that draws me toward him, even when I know it's wrong... like now.

Landon takes us to a very upscale bar which sits just beneath an elegant hotel. A man in a red vest opens my door, helping me out as soon as we arrive.

"She's with me, Franco," Landon informs the man standing outside the glass double doors to the bar. Franco is wearing a black tux, sunglasses on his face even though it's nighttime. Once inside, the place isn't what I expected for a bar. Small tables with red cloths draped over them are dotted around the room, little candles sitting in the center of each one. A man plays a piano at the front of the room, and a bar sits at the back with people wearing suits and cocktail dresses drinking along the counter. I've never been in a bar, but whenever I thought of one, I imagined grimy floors, the smell of booze and vomit, and music so loud you had to shout to one another.

"Sit," Landon commands, pulling a chair out. I comply, taking a seat and crossing my legs.

"This is *not* what I expected for a bar." I laugh nervously, looking the place over.

Landon raises an eyebrow, rolling the cuffs of his sleeves up to his elbows. The candlelight shines off his distinguished jawline, and I notice dark stubble growing along his face, his sharp cheekbones fierce as he looks at me with hard eyes. I stir in my seat; the way Landon looks at me could be compared to a caveman witnessing a female for the very first time.

An initial glance at Landon and your first thought would be he's handsome and sophisticated, but really looking at him up close, you can see the small sliver of a scar slicing the cupid bow of his upper lip. It's small, but there. Landon's not as clean-cut as he wants the world to believe. He's something darker.

"And what did you expect, exactly?" Landon grins deviously.

"I dunno." I laugh. "People drunk, singing karaoke. Something dive-y."

Landon chuckles, running his large hand over his cheeks.

"How old are you, Charlie?" Landon lowers his head, his green eyes pinning me in my seat. I shift my legs, an unbearable throb heightening in my core.

"Old enough," I reply, lifting an eyebrow.

"Right," Landon responds, not giving anything away with his tone or body language.

"What can I get you, sir?" a waiter questions, breaking Landon's severe gaze toward me.

"I'd like a Manhattan, and a martini for the lady," Landon orders. The waiter bows and walks away. Silence falls between us, the man playing the piano a filler for the awkwardness.

"I told you those boys were trouble," Landon reminds me, sitting back in his seat.

I sigh and nod. I knew he was going to say that, eventually. "Yes, you did," I clip, looking at the flame of the candle and desperately hoping he drops the subject.

"Some of Chasen's buddies were on the news some time back for drugging a college girl. The news showed a group photo of the guys at the party where the event took place, and Chasen was named among them. They were cleared, but still, if Chasen is hanging around those kinds of guys, what does that say about him?"

I frown at the information, angry with myself for not digging deeper into Chasen's explanation when I asked him about the tension between him and Landon. Seeing what Chasen and his friends were about to do to me, I'd say Chasen is just like them. They prey on young, clueless girls.

"Why were you with him?"

I look up, finding Landon staring at me intently. *This man is so intense; it's nerve-wracking.* I shake my head and give a small laugh.

"I was his whore," I respond matter-of-factly. Even if I wasn't one hundred percent aware of my actions with Chasen, I enjoyed it to an extent.

Landon doesn't even flinch at my words, just stares at me with those green eyes flecked with brown. I bite my lip, a little disappointed I didn't shock him with my brashness.

Giving Landon a once-over—with his expensive-looking clothes, the way he talks with such grace, and the snazzy bars he goes to—it makes me wonder why in the hell he'd be around the area where I live.

"Why do you hang out at the café? Why would you hang out in a place full of college kids?" I question.

Landon smirks and looks toward the table. "Let's just say, it's nice to get away from where I live every now and then. People I know wouldn't look in such an area for me," he explains, his voice deep and rugged.

"You mean the ghetto. Your uptight, working colleagues wouldn't find you in the shittiest place in Vegas," I clarify, my tone coming off bitchy.

"I wouldn't be so quick to judge, Charlie," he responds sternly, and I tilt my head to the side and sigh.

"I'm just telling you what I see," I mutter.

The waiter brings us our drinks, setting them down before us. I grab mine and take a big sip. My mouth is engulfed in the nasty liquid, and an expression of distaste crosses my face. I hover over the martini glass, contemplating spitting it back out. I look up, finding Landon chuckling at my reaction. I close my eyes tightly and swallow, not wanting to spit the drink all over myself and the table. The disgusting taste causes me to nearly gag.

"I take it you don't approve?" Landon questions with a smirk.

"That was the most disgusting thing I've ever tasted," I reply while choking, wiping at the liquid slopping down my chin.

Landon looks over my shoulder with a hard stare and in seconds, the waiter is running to our table.

"Yes, sir?"

"Get us a green apple martini," Landon demands, his eyes never leaving mine. The intensity of his stare causes me to hold my breath. He's obviously a man of power and wealth, but that's not what strikes me. It's the way he looks at me, how he looks, and the way he makes me feel, like a cross between a horny teenager and a crazed, smitten woman.

"So, where are you from, Charlie?" he asks, cupping his chin. I open my mouth to respond but stop short, remembering Jayden and I are on the run.

"Around," I hesitate.

"Hmm," Landon responds, squinting at me quizzically. The waiter places my drink down and bows before leaving once again. I grab it and take a light sip, not wanting another mouthful of nastiness. After finding the green apple taste appealing, I down it.

"Another, please," I request.

Landon sips on his drink and nods at the waiter, who apparently is waiting for Landon to give him 'the look' from the back of the room.

"Another, please," I repeat to the waiter when he rushes to our table. The man looks at Landon for permission, making me roll my eyes. Landon nods once again, and the waiter takes off.

"You should slow your pace," Landon scolds, taking another sip of his drink.

"I'm a big girl. I can handle myself," I sneer, crossing my arms.

"Clearly," Landon responds dryly. Following my much-needed rescue from Chasen and his buddies even after he warned me, I'm sure I look pathetic.

He sits up, rubbing his jaw again. The sound of his whiskers against his palm causes my body to heighten from aggression to lust. I shift my legs, trying to stifle the wetness gathering between my thighs.

"I affect you," Landon points out arrogantly. My body stiffens, eyes widening.

"Excuse me?" I mutter, my heart racing with adrenaline.

"Your legs are clenched, your breathing is escalated, and the way your eyes survey my body hungrily... you're affected by me," he rasps.

I close my mouth and swallow, my eyes never leaving his. He *does* affect me. I want to punch him in the mouth, yet also tear his clothes off and run my nails over his chest.

"That doesn't mean anything," I murmur weakly.

Landon smirks and leans over the table, his broad shoulders flexing beneath his dress shirt. "Your body stacks ammo against your words. It often knows of your surroundings before you ever will. Never underestimate it, Charlie."

I nod. What else can I do? His words make sense, and the way my name leaves those lips puts me in a daze. I'd agree to anything he says.

The waiter places another martini in front me. I instantly grab it, breaking our eye contact, and down the contents, needing the distraction.

"Are you?" I question, nibbling my bottom lip nervously.

"Am I what?" he asks, running his hand over the back of his neck, making his shirt tighten against his chest.

"Are you affected by me?"

He smirks and takes a large sip of his drink, peering over the rim of the glass as he nearly drinks it all.

"You look very appealing in that black dress," Landon flirts, his eyes squinted at the corners as a smirk crosses his smug face. He's dodging my question.

I giggle, the effects of the martini beginning to take their toll on my body.

"It's from the thrift store. Still think it's *appealing*?" I laugh, pulling at the worn material of the dress. Landon chuckles and stares off, and I can't help but smile myself. There is something about his laugh that's contagious.

"I think you look ravishing nonetheless."

My laughter falters, and I swallow hard. I can't keep up with my body's reaction to this man.

"So, why are you staying in such a bad area? Where is your family?" Landon prods, taking a sip of his drink.

"I don't have any family," I mumble, the overwhelming feeling of isolation creeping its way into my chest.

"Nobody? Not even an aunt?" He looks at me with pinched brows, like I'm forgetting some long-lost uncle and just not realizing it. But the truth is, there's nobody.

"No, nobody. Not a cat, not a sister, nor a mother," I grit, the situation starting to weigh heavy.

Landon sighs and sits back in his chair. "That has to be lonely."

My eyes whip from the tablecloth to him. The word 'lonely' doesn't even compare. It's much more than the word 'lonely' can ever justify.

"It is," I whisper and he tilts his head, looking at me with admiration.

"You're a strong girl to be trying to live all on your own." He gives a genuine smile which makes me warm to my toes. It's not easy not having a mother to talk to at night, a father to speak reason into you before you do something stupid. Usually, when someone gives words of sympathy, it pisses me off. But when Landon looks at me with understanding, it feels genuine and

70

comforting.

"Come, let's go to my room," Landon demands, standing from his chair.

"What?" I question frantically, my body heating suddenly.

"You've been drinking, and at the very least you're tipsy. Come to my room, clean up and sleep it off," he instructs, running his hand through his hair.

The tone of his voice tells me I have no say in this. My legs go weak with the simple action of him swiping his hand through his hair, but goddamn if he doesn't look exotic when he ruffles it all out of place like that. I don't know why I do it, not a clue why I don't deny him, but I don't.

"Okay," I whisper, standing and accepting the offer to run off with a complete stranger.

Landon takes me to the back of the bar, punching the button on the elevator. I risk looking at him, finding him gazing at me from the corner of his eye. Tingles course through my body like a sea of ecstasy when our eyes catch. A twinge in my chest makes it difficult to breathe, causing me to draw in a slow breath. *This man affects me on levels I can't understand.*

The elevator dings, catching our attention. Landon hits the highest floor number once we're inside, and rests against the wall, still staring at me hungrily. The sexual tension is so thick I could cut it with a knife.

"So, why were you with that boy?" Landon asks, his tone serious as he emphasizes the word 'boy'. I laugh, feeling giddy from the alcohol.

"I told you, 'cause I was his whore."

Landon sighs and looks at the elevator doors while I shrug and stare at the floor. Calling myself a whore doesn't feel good, but there's no justification for what I did with Chasen other than I fooled around with him and took money more than willingly to provide for myself. Like Chasen said, I had no problem taking the money afterwards. *I was a greedy whore.* I wince at the harsh thought.

"You've mentioned that," Landon states calmly, his features calculated.

CHARLIE

After getting out of the elevator and finding his room, Landon holds the door open for me to enter. I gasp at the elegance. Walking in, I notice the huge balcony at the far end of the room that overlooks the town, with a brown leather couch and big-screen TV placed just before it. Turning to my right, a curved bar sits with a kitchen.

"There are three bedrooms, and a guest bath. Feel free to take whatever room you'd like," Landon offers, throwing his key card on the counter.

I walk over to the balcony and look out. We're so high up, I can see the strip, the vibrant lights of Sin City brilliant against the night's sky. The heat outside instantly makes my breasts and the back of my knees sweat.

"I'll shower, thank you," I finally respond.

I turn to find Landon standing right behind me, his body broad and muscular, making me feel tiny in comparison.

He slowly skims the soft skin under my arm with the pad of his finger, and I involuntarily flinch. My mouth parts and my eyes widen from my reaction.

"I'm sorry. I guess I'm just a little more shaken up than I thought," I whisper, staring at the floor.

He places his finger under my chin and firmly raises my stare to his fierce green eyes.

"I wouldn't hurt you." His words vibrate through his chest as he speaks.

I know he wouldn't by the way he looks at me, as if I'm a rare flower. It shows the delicacy he's capable of. The fact Landon rescued me from that alley and had the courtesy to bring me back to his room after drinking shows volumes. Chasen never had that care written on his face when he looked at me, and I didn't realize that till it was too late.

"I know that." My voice comes out hoarse, my eyes skimming his taut body. I'd be stupid to resist him, but to be honest, even with the trauma I just experienced... I *couldn't* resist Landon. He's good-looking, charming, and irresistible.

He slowly trails his finger over my collarbone, and a spark ignites and spreads through my limbs. I gasp, and my eyes grow heavy. He runs it over the bare flesh of my shoulder, and a moan escapes my lips. His proximity seizes the air from my lungs, and my skin flushes with want. I don't want to feel abandoned anymore; I'd do anything to just feel something other than a place of solace. It's empty there, and cold. Being this close to Landon, I feel anything *but* cold. I want the warmth his body is capable of rendering. To have the tingles that creep up my limbs when he touches me reach optimum levels and leave me breathless, wanting more.

His finger glides downward, meeting the fabric of my dress just above my breasts. A mewl escapes my mouth and my body pushes forward on its own accord, wanting more contact. I peer from under my lashes, finding hungry eyes grounding me, his mouth parted slightly as he devours me with looks alone. His eyes are hooded and hold a daydream gloss to them.

He clears his throat and retracts his hand, stepping away and breaking the haze of lust we're both under. The sweat on my body chills, and I shiver. Landon paces the floor with his head tilted back, looking up at the ceiling, his hands resting on the back of his neck. I can tell he's trying to stay away from me, but he's failing. I cross my arms and walk down the hall, searching for the shower. I'm not sure if we should indulge our cravings for each other, we're obviously from separate sides of the tracks. And, especially with what just happened with Chasen. The draw my body and mind have toward him, though, I'm not sure I can fight. I'm not sure I want to.

LANDON

My hands grip the railing, my knuckles turning white from the force of my hold. I close my eyes and clench my jaw with anger. Liquor warms my veins, warning me I've drank too much. I'm not supposed to drink excessively; it's against Blackwell rules. I smirk. *Yet here I am tossing the fucking handbook out the window.*

There's something about Charlie, something I can't seem to rein in. The way she tries to act so bold, yet her weakness shows with every flush of her cheeks and tremble of her lips. I'm losing

control, showing emotion that doesn't need to be revealed. I shake my head and open my eyes. *Vegas. This is my city. I run this place, and everyone knows it.*

I run the pad of my finger over my swollen lips. Charlie. The way my body pulls toward her - it's a fucking mystery. When I saw those punks manhandling her, I could have easily snapped their necks. The look of despair on Charlie's face tore my cold heart in two. I close my eyes, irritated. The way I'm reacting is ridiculous.

"Get a fucking hold of yourself," I chastise. It's a fucking woman, a girl. I shake my head. I just need to fuck her out of my system and get on with my life.

I replace my hand on the banister, my fingers choking it. I've had girls I wanted to fuck badly before in the past, and none of them compared to the ache I have in my dick, the burning in my chest I have right now. Looking at Charlie, she can't be more than eighteen or nineteen, yet she manages to have me at my knees. *I need to get out of here before I do something I can't undo.*

"Why do I feel so drawn to you, Charlie?" I whisper to myself.

CHARLIE

I put the shower on hot, hoping to wash any trace of Chasen and his fucking friends off me. Taking the soap between my legs, I notice bruising blemishing my skin.

"Damn," I whisper, running my hand over the tender black and blue spots like they might magically wash away. I shake my head and continue to wash my body with the lavender-scented soap.

Closing my eyes, all I can think about is how Landon swooped

76

in and saved me tonight. The way my body wants him, even if my mind can't comprehend why. Ever since the day I bumped into him, I've been at a loss of the way I respond to him. It's not like anything I've ever known. My need for him is animalistic. There's a strong possibility that Landon might use me just like Chasen, but at least this time, it'll be on my own terms.

"Landon..." escapes my mouth as I run my hands down my stomach, but stop myself from exploring any further. I turn the water off, having enough of this torture. *Screw what's right.*

I throw the shower door open and stare at the white towel sitting on the counter, contemplating if I should do what my body's telling me to do. When I'm around Landon, it's the first time I feel like I maybe have someone I can connect with and understand the real me. He's the first man who's looked my way and caused sparks to ignite from just a simple glance. It's an out-of-body experience. Regardless of whether my naive heart can handle the repercussions of what I'm about to do, my body can't handle the 'what if' if I walk away.

I step out slowly and walk past the towel, leaving the glass shower, and extravagant bathroom that matches the rest of the hotel room.

A trail of wet footprints follows me. I find Landon out on the balcony, his hands resting on the railing as he looks out. His shoulders are tense, his posture calculated and confident. My body begins to tremble, and a rush of insecurity rockets through me.

"Landon," I mutter seductively, but my voice cracks, giving away my vulnerability. *What if he turns me down again?* The thought of rejection has a trail of sweat spreading down my back.

He turns, and his mouth parts with surprise. He quickly masks his emotions, and his chest lifts as he takes in a steady breath. His

eyes go heavy as they take in my naked form. But the pulsing in my lower half has me tossing my wet hair over my shoulder and striding toward him.

I slide my hand up his chest, soaking his shirt with my wet hand. The small contact causes a delicious ache at the apex of my thighs. I notice his chest rise as he inhales deeply, his nostrils flaring as he watches me.

"I affect you," I rasp bravely, repeating the accusations he fed me at the bar. I peer up from under my wet lashes. Landon grabs my wrist roughly, stopping my hand from exploring his hard chest any further. Instantly, my stomach falls.

"You're drunk." His eyebrows narrow. The wind rushes from my chest at his harsh tone, and I pull from his grip with force.

"I'm not drunk. Tipsy, yes, but not to the point I don't know what I'm doing." I lift my head in confidence and stand on my tiptoes. "Your body can't lie to me, Landon," I whisper into his ear, flicking my tongue against his earlobe, pushing him.

He grabs hold of my waist and plows me backward into the wall surrounding the doorway. The abrasive scratch from the brick stings my backside from the blunt force. My body bolts with a trace of excitement that he's giving in.

Landon leans down so his eyes are level with mine. His stare is hard, and his face is clenched with anger. His thumbs caress circles over my hips as he takes his eyes from mine and down my body. The tender touch from his hands contradicts the ferocity in his eyes. My skin grows goose bumps, even with the heat of the night. The scrutiny of his stare causes me to shift on my feet and look away.

"Is this what you want, Charlie? You want me to treat you like a whore?" His voice is deep. One of his hands leaves my hips, a finger trailing right below my belly button. "I could bend you over that balcony, grab you by the hair and treat you like you want me to. Prove to your subconscious I *am* the bad guy you think I am, that you hope I am."

His eyes fly upward, pinning me where I stand. I shrink back, my brows slicing downward with his hostility. He leans in, his nose almost touching mine. My lips take on a sudden pout, desperate to connect with his.

"But you deserve so much better," he mutters, seizing the breath from my lugs. The way he says those words, like it pains him, has my pouting lips frowning. I don't respond, don't dignify his words with a reply. My mind is everywhere, and I blink rapidly to help clear the fog tainting my train of thought. I can't tell if he wants me or not.

A guttural growl leaves Landon's mouth as he leans down and grabs me by the ass, lifting me. His fingers dig into my butt cheeks. I moan in satisfaction, the feeling of his hands on me exhilarating. Finally getting him to lose control is a power I cherish. I wrap my arms around his neck and my legs around his strong waist, my aching nipples brushing against his hard chest.

He turns us, resting my ass on the lip of the railing, the city hundreds of feet below.

He runs his nose up my neck, his scruff burning my delicate skin. I clench my teeth, hissing from the delectable burn.

"God, you smell fucking amazing," he growls into my neck. Trailing his nose across my jawline, his lips find mine feverishly and his mouth grabs hold with force. As if his next breath depends on the air leaving my lungs, he kisses me hard.

I can't help the whimper that wracks my body as his hands slide up my back, his touch ravenous. My legs tremble with adren-

aline as they struggle to stay around his waist, and my fingers shake as they slip into his hair. He usually has it slicked back and perfectly in place. When I run my hand through it, I find it's actually longer than I thought.

His large hands take hold of my thighs, and he lifts me from the railing. He carries me into the hotel room and down the hallway into one of the bedrooms, our mouths never leaving each other. We can't stop kissing if we wanted to. It's as if our mouths have their own accord, his working with mine, our breathing in sync. We're both strangers, yet we're impatiently ready to tear each other's clothes off. Both of us ready to fill a deep-rooted desire and need within each other, so realistically, we *are* made for each other. We're both on the same playing field of sin.

The bed is massive, with white sheets and extra fluffy pillows. Doors right in front of the bed lead out to another balcony. The room is dark, the only light coming from a hotel taller than ours, giving off a soft, red glow in the room. He plops me down on the bed, the warm air of the night coming from the balcony sweeping past my body, and my nipples pebble.

He pulls his shirt apart, muscles bared, buttons popping off in every direction. I sit back on my elbows watching him. Craving him. My eyes trail down his hard chest, perfectly outlined in muscle. *He* has *to work out to have a hard body like that.*

He unbuttons his black slacks, letting them fall to the floor with his underwear. My eyes widen in fear, and my mouth parts with disbelief. His cock is thick, massively so compared to Chasen's. It's slightly longer, too. I bite my bottom lip, nervous how that's going to fit inside me, scared it's going to hurt. I second-guess if this is a good idea. *Maybe he just looks big from the dark shadows of the room.*

My eyes trail upward, finding a confident smirk on Landon's face, an arrogant glow reacting to the shock clearly written on mine.

"It'll fit, don't worry," he remarks. I inhale a nervous breath following the confidence Landon exhibits. He is the sexiest thing I've ever seen, and my body knows it. The boys at school, Chasen, hell, no male I've ever met compares to Landon. He's real. He's raw. He's fucking gorgeous.

He crawls onto the bed and slowly pulls my knees apart, adjusting himself between them. My chest burns and I realize I've been holding my breath. I inhale deeply, my heart drumming against my chest with a rush of adrenaline. His gorgeous face frowns as he scans my body.

"What?" I question nervously, but he doesn't answer. His fingers stroke firm circles on my inner thighs. I sit up to look at what he's so focused on when I find the bruising.

He slowly raises his head, his brows furrowed with anger but laced with a hint of care. Like he might actually be pissed someone did this to me.

"I'm so sorry that happened to you. I tried to warn you." He softly caresses my inner thighs once again, and I have to bite my bottom lip to keep from crying. Nobody has ever cared about me, or came to my defense before. I know right now that lying in this bed with Landon is the best decision I've ever made in my small existence of a life. *I may never find someone like him again.*

"I'm fine, really," I mumble, rubbing his arm. My breathing turns into desperate pants when I feel just how hard the muscle of his bicep is beneath my palm.

I draw in a shaky breath and lie back, and he releases a loud sigh and lays his strong body over mine. I'm quivering with nerves as he positions himself on top of me. My liquid courage has vanished, and I'm just a bundle of nerves. I spread my legs wider letting him in. My ears ring and my heart races with an unsteady rhythm.

"Jesus, I can feel your heart beating against my chest. Are you sure this is what you want?" he questions, looking me over with a touch of softness. He takes hold of my chin and makes me focus solely on him.

I swallow the lump in my throat and say, "All in, right?" Landon's eyes hold a raw emotion as he searches my face. I wrap my legs around his waist, urging him forward.

He closes his parted lips, nods, and in one swift move, grabs my wrists and pins them above my head. Leaning down, he plants kisses along my jaw, and down my neck. I arch my back, pushing my pebbled nipples into his chest, finding his heartbeat almost as rampant as mine. My body seeks the warmth of his, wanting that connection. I lean up and grab his bottom lip with my teeth, nipping it. His eyes go heavy and his breath comes out in short spurts. Seeing him unravel makes my body come alive, thoughts of second-guessing sleeping with Landon gone.

Just as I'm about to pull my mouth away, he deepens the kiss, exploring my mouth with his tongue. His taste is my kryptonite, I kiss him back passionately. He nudges my legs further apart with his knees and presses the tip of his cock against my opening. It feels huge. Scared, I close my eyes, preparing myself for the pain.

"Open your eyes, Charlie." Landon breathes heavily against my lips. I slowly peel my eyes open, finding his. The green mixed with spots of brown reminds me of a rainforest after a hostile storm. He pulls his body back and thrusts himself into me in one swift movement. I buck against him and whimper loudly with pain. The fit is tight as he pushes every inch of his length deeply inside me, filling me. My nails anchor themselves into the skin of his neck, and I inhale deeply as my body tries to accommodate his size.

Landon's eyebrows furrow as he thrusts again, a little slower this time. The pain searing through my lower half isn't any better than the first time he drove into me, and I let out a small cry. He pulls off me and looks between us, finding the evidence of my innocence staining his cock and myself.

"What the fuck, Charlie?" he growls, trying to pull off me completely. I dig my heels into his ass, pushing him back onto me.

He sighs heavily, closing his eyes.

"Do you know what you just gave me, Charlie?" he pants, his tone an edge of angry. I furrow my own brow and swallow the sudden lump in my throat.

"I didn't give you anything. It's nothing," I whisper, pushing my hips upward, encouraging him to continue. I *need* him to continue; my body demands we finish. *What's virginity anyway? It's nothing. I didn't give him anything. It's not any different than a man's first time. The blood spilt from a virgin is just evidence that she's passed from being innocent into something sinful.*

"You just gave me a piece of yourself. I'll be forever planted in your soul now, Charlie," he whispers in my ear, brushing hair from my face. "Anytime you get turned on, any partner you have sex with in the future...you will always think of me. You lost a piece of yourself and gave it to me."

He confirmed I wasn't his, that I would be elsewhere having sex with others. Not him. That should stop me from continuing this charade. Realization should flood my mind, but I'm too high on want to care. I want him to keep fucking me, to take my mind to a place of pleasure rather than pain. To take me from my fucked-up

life, even if it's temporary.

"I didn't give you anything," I repeat, contradicting my thoughts. I push his ass cheeks with my heels, wanting him to keep going. A piece of me knows he's right, though. I just sewed a piece of Landon into my soul, and now I'll never escape him.

He continues to slowly thrust in and out of me. The pain that once ripped through me finally starts to climb into a blossom of pleasure.

"You chose this. You picked me. Now, you'll never escape me," he grunts, pushing himself up on his fists as if he is doing a push-up. "I'll be rooted in the base of your memory forever." He drives his cock into me, making my breasts bounce with the force.

"Yes!" I moan, my eyes heavy with arousal. Having a piece of Landon in me forever doesn't so sound bad.

I turn my head, watching his arms flex and bulge with every drive of his hips. I can't help but reach out and hold onto his biceps as he rocks into me. He leans down and nips my earlobe, making my mouth fall open and a whimper escape from my lips.

His dick hits me just right, the head of it creating a sensation I've never felt before. It's indescribable and has my eyes rolling into the back of my head. My legs spread wider as I give him all of me.

"Oh, God," I cry, arching my hips upward, wanting more of that blissful pressure rising in my core.

He leans down, takes my nipple between his teeth and gives it a light tug. My eyes flutter, and I let out a full-body mewl when I slowly slip over an edge of ecstasy from the warmth of his mouth on my bud. The scruff of his cheeks causes a delicious burn against the sensitive flesh of my breast.

I lazily open my eyes, finding his pinning me to the spot. The way he looks at me, it's as if he can't get enough.

"Why do I feel so drawn to you?" I blurt mindlessly, my mind only feeling the pleasure Landon inflicts upon me.

He shakes his head, breaking eye contact before he thrusts into me hard, his dick hitting that spot again, and again. Like a match finding its spark, I grasp the sheets, hanging on for dear life as my body drums with an intensity that leaves me holding my breath. Warmth ignites in my abdomen, racing through my body like wildfire. My head pushes into the mattress, my body heaving as it chases that realm of ecstasy into oblivion. I scream, the feeling of him fucking me hard, the feeling of my orgasm crashing into one internal thought: euphoria.

The sensation of falling but flying at the same time slowly dissipates, allowing me to finally grab that morsel of oxygen I need so desperately. Landon roars a feral moan, stilling above me as he comes. His body suddenly relaxes and he falls on top of me. His weight nearly crushes me.

I turn my head, finding the red glow of the lights from the hotel. I yawn, my body aching and suddenly exhausted. That thought of wanting to feel or being wanted, even if it was just for a few minutes, clouded my better judgment. If I was smart, I wouldn't have slept with Landon, but how could I resist the draw between us? How could I possibly turn down a man who looks at me like I'm Heaven?

I sigh. *Landon is going to rip my heart out.* But the worst part is, I gave him way more than that. *I just gave him my mind, body, and soul. I gave it all to him.*

CHARLIE

The overwhelming feeling of being warm wakes me. With my body sweaty and sticking to the sheets beneath me, I finally open my eyes.

"Fuck," I whisper as the hotel room comes into focus. The night before rolls through my mind: Chasen and his friends and... Landon. I sigh at the thought of Landon then jerk my head up and look for him, but he's not next to me. I sit up, noticing his clothes, on the floor the night before, are gone. Frowning, I climb off the bed. I scamper into the living area still naked, my feet padding against the floor echoing through the suite. Nothing. He's not here. I nibble my bottom lip, unsure what to do, when my eyes catch a note on the kitchen island.

You need this more than I do.

-L

Looking down, I find two stacks of cash, making me gasp in shock. An uncontrollable shame bubbles through my limbs, my lungs refusing the entry of air to the point I collapse on the floor.

Money. After sex. I shake my head, and tears pour off my cheeks onto the handwritten note. I bite my bottom lip angrily, my teeth nearly piercing the skin. I knew sleeping with him would be a bad idea, but I was too high on lust to care. A small piece of me, a small juvenile piece of me, thought maybe I could be wrong, and I would wake up to him displaying a full menu of breakfast items this morning because he didn't know what I would want to eat. I thought he realized how alone and misunderstood I felt, that he would be here this morning. I've never felt more alone than I do right now. The ache in my chest never burned with such emptiness before.

I run my hand under my nose, sniffling the uncontrollable snot back, and roll my eyes. A sudden laugh escapes my mouth. Those fairy tales might exist for some people, but not me. I'm meant to be alone.

"I was so stupid to think he would want anything to do with the likes of me," I grit out loud. "Hell, he probably has a stuck-up wife back home, or at the very least dozens of girls throwing themselves at him."

If the Lord ever tried to tell me anything before, it was never as clear as this. I get it; I'm a whore. Sex then money. I stand on wobbly legs, finding the money sitting perfectly.

"There must be a thousand dollars here," I whisper, picking it up and thumbing the stacks. I don't know whether to be pleased or disgusted by the amount. Hell, I basically just sold my virginity to him.

I laugh—an uncontrollable, belly-cramping laugh. I laugh at the

fact that even though Landon slipped out, paying me for my pathetic way of life, I would do it all over again. The way my body, heart, and soul connected to him last night, the magnetism I had toward him, was so surreal. I shake my head. *He's right; I'll never forget last night, never forget him.*

"Asshole," I exclaim, slapping the cash back on the counter. I've been looking out for myself since day one, and I've been fine.

Besides, I should be used to this feeling after the last twenty-four hours. I've grown accustomed to its ache deep in my chest. I slip my black dress on and notice small streaks of blood between my thighs. "Shit," I whisper.

Screw it, I'll get a shower at home. I don't want to be in this fucking place any longer than I need to be. I sit on the leather couch and put my heels on, eyeing the money on the counter. I'd be stupid not to take it. Jayden and I need it desperately. It'll pay rent and put food on the table.

I shove the stacks of cash down the cups of my dress. *Fuck it, I earned it. Hell, I even bled for it.*

Guilt strikes my chest as the cool cash sweeps between my breasts. The demeanor of staying strong and keeping my chin up faltering by the second. I fear I'll never find my place in the world. I'll always be second class, and treated like dirt. I thought Landon and I had something, a connection of some sort. I'm afraid this is a wound that will turn into a dark scar, changing my view on my life.

I take the elevator to the main floor, and the lobby is huge. Brown and tan marbled floors make up the space, and a large glass dome ceiling looks over the entire lobby. I look down at myself and swallow nervously. *I'm so out of place here.*

Walking through the lobby, I hold my head down, my hair shielding my face. Glancing out of the corner of my eye, I can see the staff look at me with a wary eye. I find women grabbing their men a little tighter, as if they're threatened by me. I hurry my pace, trying to get away from the cynical glares. As soon as I reach the outside, I tilt my head back and inhale deeply. My chest heaves, taking in large gulps of fresh air.

I pull my shit together and start my walk of shame back home. Finally, after walking for what seems like forever, graffiti greets me at the last block, telling me I'm almost home. Strangely, I take odd comfort in the spray-painted buildings after the experience I just had. I know I belong here. That place Landon took me to was anything but inviting.

I turn the corner and find an ambulance and two cop cars parked close to my apartment. I watch as men shuffle in a green dumpster, pulling a woman with red hair out. She has nothing on but red heels and a short, black leather skirt. Her body is purplish with dark spots around her throat and legs, evidence that she's been dead for hours.

I gasp and cover my mouth at the sight of her. I've never seen a dead person before.

"I warned her," comes from behind me, making me jump and turn. A black woman with caramel-colored hair puffed out, stands behind me with her hands on her hips. She has on a skimpy gold dress that is *way* too short, with black ripped stockings up her thighs. Her makeup is heavy, and her red lips are bright.

"What?" I ask confused. The glitter on her chest blinding me, I hold my hand above my eyes to shield them.

"I warned her, you can't work these streets without a pimp," she explains, shaking her head. Her eyes trail from the scene of the dead woman to me, eyeing me from head to toe with an arched brow. "You should get a pimp."

"What?" I give a weak laugh. Her face doesn't show any humor, making my own fall. "I'm not—"

"Right, none of us are," she interrupts, plucking a cigarette from the black purse slung over her chest. "I'm just saying, you want to run these streets? You need protection, baby. You find yourself needing one, find Daddy Mick over at the Fever Hotel." She inhales a large drag from her cigarette, her eyes trailing my chest. I look down at what she's looking at and notice the cash trying to escape the top of my dress.

"Shit." I roll my eyes and push it back in place.

"Mmhhmm," she murmurs, her lips pursed. "I'm telling you, baby, it's safer." She walks away, puffing a cloud of cigarette smoke, her shiny heels clicking against the pavement as she sashays.

I glance back at the green dumpster, finding the crew closing up the girl in a black body bag. The sound of the zipper has goose bumps racing up my spine.

●●●

My body tenses as I walk down my street, images of Chasen and his buddies grabbing me ruthlessly triggering in my mind. *What a bunch of assholes.* The angry flashback slowly fades, leaving Landon and all his glory when he rescued me. A warm smile covers my face at the thought.

Looking at my apartment, I find our landlord Henry out smoking a cigarette, watching the cops load the dead woman's body in the ambulance. I stop. My first reaction is to run in the other direction, but then I remember I actually have money to catch us up on our rent. His eyes light up as I grab some cash from my chest.

"Don't worry. I got the money." I smile.

"Your girl already paid," he remarks, blowing out a puff of smoke.

"What?" I question in disbelief, but he just flicks his cigarette and walks inside, ignoring me.

What the hell? How did Jayden get money to pay our rent? I huff and hurry up the steps.

Seconds after I enter the apartment, Jayden shows up.

"Holy shit! You look like, well, shit," Jayden insults while walking in the door.

"Gee, thanks," I huff. I glance at myself in the cracked bathroom mirror and agree. *I do look like shit.* My makeup is smeared, and my hair looks like I was just fucked seven shades from Sunday. I kind of was. I sigh and throw Jayden's heels over in her area before heading to my side.

"How did you manage to pay our rent?" I ask, sitting down on the bed.

Jayden shrugs. "I have my ways," she remarks.

I growl, sick of that answer. She used it with the ID.

"What the fuck is that supposed to mean?"

She turns, her eyes angry. "I said don't worry about it. I don't need your judgment. I get things we need using what I have to my advantage. I survive," she mutters the last part, pointing at her sweaty chest with determination.

"You use what to your—" I pause as she throws her hands out to her sides, showcasing herself. *Her body.*

"You mean you sleep with men?" I frown and bite my inner cheek at the thought of her sleeping around to pay our rent. The feeling of guilt riddles up my spine. I should have taken better care of her , tried harder to get a job.

I open my glossy eyes and find a confident Jayden, waiting for my reply with her hands on her hips. I tilt my head to the side, curious how she's so sure of herself and the way she goes about it. I sold myself to Chasen. I just sold my virginity to Landon, and I feel so shameful I can't even look at myself.

I don't see my life getting any better than this. I have no job. I got a shitty education, and no man is committing himself to me. I'm white trash, and that's all I will have in my future. My life has never been smooth sailing. I'm programmed for only the worst things the world has to offer. It makes me question who the hell my mother was, and the karma she left in her trail. *I guess I can't ever say she never gave me anything.*

"Like I said, Charlie, I don't need your judgment," Jayden snaps, catching me from my thoughts. I sigh and shove my hands down my chest, pulling out the stacks of cash, revealing my own sins.

"What the fuck is that?" Jayden exclaims, rushing to my bed.

I shake my head, eyeing the money and laughing nervously. "I used what I have to my advantage." Jayden's eyes shoot to mine in knowing before she falls back on my bed in a fitful of laughter.

"It's not funny, Jayden," I respond seriously, slapping her leg to get her attention. "I feel..." I stop short, closing my eyes.

The bed dips when Jayden sits up, and her hand rubs my back. "Don't feel ashamed, Charlie," she comforts, her tone soothing.

"But I do. I feel disgusting. I—" I pause. "I feel cheap, and I feel used."

Jayden grabs my face harshly, making me look her in the eyes. "Charlie, we need money to survive. We have no food, and the landlord is itching to kick us out. We can't get jobs. We are *fucked.* We do what we need to so we can live. Don't feel ashamed of yourself for living," she justifies, her soft tone gone. "It gets easier, I promise."

I pull my head from her grip, looking at the new sheets I bought from the extra money Chasen gave me. The feeling of being worthless is ruthless, a pain riddling in my gut that's shameful. But all the things I have from it... clothes, a phone, food, even our rent is caught up.

"I can't lie. Having the money after something that seems so insignificant such as sex—"

"It's nice, right?" Jayden laughs. "I always find the hottest guys. It's like a challenge, ya know?" I raise a brow at her goals in life. "They usually pay the most, surprisingly."

"How long have you done this?" I ask, my eyebrows narrowed.

Jayden shrugs, picking the fray of her shorts. "Whenever I needed to," she responds, like she's talking about coloring her hair. I shake my head and look at the counter of food. It's disappearing quickly.

"Did you see that woman they were pulling out of the trash?" I question, changing the subject.

Jayden closes her eyes and runs her hand through her crazy hair. "I did," she replies grimly.

"She was a prostitute," I point out.

"Gah, I *hate* that word," Jayden growls, shaking her head.

I shrug. "It is what it is, Jayden; no need to sugarcoat it." I look up at her, my jaw clenched. "I'm a whore. A prostitute. I sleep with men and get paid for it," I whisper. Finally voicing the truth of what I am, what I'm destined for hurts, but not as bad as it should. I know I should try again at finding a job. But I know I won't, I can't. Jayden and I are on the run, and my resources are limited. Screwing men for money puts food on the table and keeps us off

the radar.

"I prefer 'escort'," Jayden huffs, leaning back on my bed.

"Some woman told me if I was going to work the streets, I needed protection. She told me I should go to a motel and ask for a guy name Mick," I inform her, fidgeting with the money on the bed. If Jayden is going to do this, I'd rather her not do it behind my back and get hurt in the process. I'd rather her be safe, that we were *both* safe. I'd never forgive myself if something happened to her. She's the only family I have.

"You mean a pimp?" Jayden shifts so she can face me, her forehead wrinkled in questioning.

"I mean, I guess that's what it is. I know I was almost raped by Chasen and his buddies last night. They were rough and angry with me. So having protection doesn't sound like such a bad idea," I whisper the last part.

"Fuck, Charlie, are you okay?" Jayden shoots up on the bed, her face wide with fear.

"Yeah, Landon saved me," I mutter, a smile creeping on my face from the memory.

"Landon? Sounds like a rich guy's name. Is that where that money came from?" She points at the stacks on the bed. "I knew Chasen had money, but this"—she jerks her chin at the pile—"would be more than Mommy and Daddy's allowance, for sure."

I nod, looking the money over.

"It was from Landon," I confirm.

"Damn, what the hell you do to earn all that?" She chuckles.

I stand, flexing my sore body. "I gave him my virginity," I respond seriously. I look over my shoulder, finding a wide-eyed Jayden, mouth parted.

"Holy shit," she mumbles, looking back at the money. "I didn't know you were a virgin. Are you going to see him again?"

I trail the pad of my forefinger over my bottom lip. Images of Landon in ecstasy come to mind, and my body aches for him once again.

"I doubt it," I whisper.

"You—" Jayden pauses, pointing a finger at me. I snap from memory lane, my eyes wide as I stare at Jayden's accusing finger.

"I know that look in your eye, and let me give you a very viable piece of information, if you are indeed going to sleep with men for money. This game, there's no room for feelings or emotion. Get that through your head now," she scolds, her tone serious.

I sigh and head toward the shower.

"I don't think I'll be seeing him again anyway, so it won't be a problem." I peer up from under my thick lashes, finding Jayden watching me intently. "The way our bodies connected, like we had known each other for so long... I can't explain that feeling."

"Charlie, don't do this to your—"

"It doesn't matter. He left me with a stack of cash, and some stupid fucking note and without as much as a goodbye. He built a wall of ruthless reality that nobody could bring down," I interrupt.

"And what reality is that?" Jayden tilts her head to the side.

"This is as good as it gets for me," I respond softly, glancing around our apartment. Lost in my own torment, I didn't even realize Jayden moved from her spot toward me until I feel both of her hands grasp mine in comfort. I look down at our joined palms then up at Jayden.

"We can go check this Mick guy out, and if you don't like it," she pauses and shifts on her feet, "we'll figure something out." She gives my hand a light squeeze. "It's up to us to climb our way to the top, Charlie, and thanks to our parents and the failed system of family services, it won't be in a respectful way."

I nod, knowing exactly what she means, but I want to wait until we have no other option. *Which won't be long.*

"Just let me think about it."

CHARLIE

Two Weeks Later

"Okay, you distract him with…" Jayden pauses, looking at my chest.

"My tits," I finish her sentence, laughing.

"Yeah, push them out your top some." She reaches forward and grabs my boobs, pushing them upward in my black ripped shirt hanging off my shoulder. "That did nothing." She bites her lips, still pressing on me. I roll my eyes and place my hands on my hips as she manhandles my small tits.

"I think I could have managed pushing my own boobs up." I laugh.

"Then do it," she huffs, taking her palms off me.

I shrug. "It won't work. I don't have the massive boobs you need to create cleavage."

"Okay, I'll do the distracting." Jayden pulls her white tank top down and presses her breasts upward. I'd rather do the stealing

anyway. I haven't seen how good Jayden is at stealing, and the last thing we need is to get caught.

"Damn, why don't you push them up a hint more, give him a nipple shot," I tease, flicking her tit.

"Ouch, ho!" Jayden hisses, grabbing her boob.

"This calls for desperate times. Rent's due next week along with utility bills, and we need food with what's left over. So I'll distract and you steal the booze," she instructs, making me laugh. Not being able to afford booze is not a desperate situation, but I could use a drink, that's for sure.

I nod, knowing the plan. It's not my first time stealing, after all. I've stolen food from markets, clothes for the winter, and I've also been caught before, so I know what *not* to do, as well.

Jayden walks in and heads right to the counter where the store clerk stands, looking at a magazine. I sneak toward the back of the store where a sign reads 'liquor'. I quietly open the door to the cooler and grab a twelve-pack of beer. My heart hammers against my chest with excitement, the idea I could get caught a high.

"Oh, my God, is that a real tattoo?" Jayden flirts, her voice echoing through the store.

I grab the beer and try to shove it down my shirt. After failing miserably, I head toward the exit quickly, turning my back toward Jayden and the short store clerk when I pass. I spot a package of pink snowball cakes and grab one on my way out.

I step across the street and wait for Jayden to leave the store. As soon as she walks out, she spots me leaning against the wall and runs toward me with a huge grin.

"Run! Go!" she squeals. I hold my hands against my chest to keep the beer from slipping out and sprint.

I laugh so hard I can barely keep up. I trip over my feet and nearly wipe out from giggling so hard. I can't remember the last time I laughed so hard it hurt.

I stop two blocks away to catch my breath.

"Did you get it?" Jayden huffs, out of breath. I glare at her mock-offense. Growing up in care, stealing is second-nature. You do it to live. Sometimes you steal for fun, but not often.

"Yes, I got it." I'm not sure how she missed it with them sticking halfway out of my top. I pull the beer out from under my shirt and hand it to her. "I got these, too." I toss over the cakes, and her eyes light up.

"Fuck yeah!" she praises. "Let's get drunk and plan our future, Charlie." Jayden turns, walking down our block.

"About the pimp?" I question, still out of breath.

"Yeah. I mean, if you want to." She looks at me, squinting from the sun.

"What do you think we should do?" I prod, finally catching my breath. I can actually say this is the one time I'm not sure what I want to do.

"I think we should do it. Making some money and not having to worry about paying rent and where our next meal comes from doesn't sound like the worst thing in the world. To be honest, I'm sick of mac and cheese, and ramen noodles." She laughs.

"I'm sick of it, too. Eating cheap can food and noodles is only tolerable for so long. I can't get a job, and giving sexual favors isn't the worst," I respond. If I could just get my heart to wrap around the idea of it, I would be okay. My soul is telling me I'm selling myself short, but my mind is telling me it's easy fucking money.

I sigh. *In the realm of things, it'll keep us safe. It'll keep Jayden safe.*

"Let's check it out. Let the motel and this Mick guy do the

selling, see what he has to offer," I finally agree.

"Sounds like a plan." She rips a beer can from the plastic, handing me the rest as she digs in her pocket.

"What are you doing?" I ask, confused.

"Shot-gunning it," she responds, pulling out a pocket knife.

"What the hell is that?"

"What, the knife?" She holds it palm up, revealing the small blade.

"That, and what the hell is shot-gunning it?" I clarify.

"I grabbed the knife from the counter when the clerk wasn't looking, and shot-gunning is when you stab the end of a beer can, take a few big gulps, then open the tab at the top," she instructs. *I guess she* can *steal.*

"And that does... what?" I laugh, not sure what the point is.

"Makes the liquid rush out so you can drink it faster. Get drunk quicker." She shrugs.

I snort in response and pull a beer can from the plastic. I watch Jayden stab the end of her can and suck from the cut, beer dribbling down her face as she hands the knife to me. I grip the can and repeat her actions. Instantly, beer sprays me in the face, making me squeal and Jayden laugh.

"Hurry, drink it!" Jayden hollers around her own beer. I quickly place the can to my lips and drink. Cold beer slips from my mouth and spills down my chest.

"Okay, now open the top." Jayden giggles, finishing her own. I use my other hand to search for the tab then open it. The action makes the liquid rush into my mouth so fast I can barely keep up.

I drink it all and squeeze the can like a man would. This is what I missed out on growing up. Just having fun, and being dumb with friends. This moment may seem stupid to some, maybe even childish, but it's a memory with Jayden I won't forget.

"Wow." I wipe my face with my arm. "Who taught you how to do that?"

Jayden shrugs. "I saw my dad and his buddies do it all the time." I nod, not sure what to say. Sounds like her dad partied a lot around her when she was a kid.

"Come on, ho, let's do another," Jayden suggests, pulling another beer free.

I can't help but smirk. "Let's go inside so we don't cause any unwanted attention first." I point toward our apartment.

"Sounds like a plan," Jayden sings, turning to walk up our steps.

•••

Jayden and I walk to the Fever Motel, located just a few blocks away from where we live. I stare at the run-down building from the sidewalk, and my face immediately twists with distaste. There looks to be about twenty rooms in total, ten upstairs and ten down. The paint is this god-awful blue with all the doors painted an off-white. Right in the center of the old roof is a sign reading Fever Motel.

"You should breathe, Charlie. Your face is turning purple," Jayden remarks, looking me over.

I exhale, releasing a breath I didn't even realize I was holding. I have this feeling in my gut, that last morsel of self-respect telling me I should turn and walk away. That I can keep trying to get a job, even though I know deep-down that won't ever happen.

"This place—"

"This place is going to keep us safe, remember? And it's going to make us money," Jayden interrupts, reminding me why this is so

important: protection.

"Right," I mumble, blowing out a steady breath.

"Charlie, we're just asking questions today. Getting information on how all this works. We are *not* committing to anything." Jayden sighs, tucking a hair behind my ear.

"You and I both know there's nothing better out there for us. At least here we'll be safe." I give a tight-lipped smile. I look back at the motel, and a shiver runs up my spine as the sign's lights flicker on.

I peer out from under my lashes, glancing at Jayden who's looking the place over with a worried expression.

"I'm not going to lie. I'm scared." I breathe heavily, although I've had time to cope with the idea of sleeping with men for money. Having the hunger pains in my stomach, and the fear of being kick-ed out onto the streets next month, it makes your mind adapt to the unfair tactics of survival. No matter how devious it is.

"I'm just as scared as you are," she admits. "But next month the rent is up, and then what? The guys I slept with before, they aren't repeat customers. They're going home for the summer and things are going to get difficult, even more than they are now. Not to mention more dangerous the more we mess around on these streets."

The glimpse of the dead girl flares behind my eyes. I nod and straighten my back. "Right. We can do this," I say with more confidence than I'm feeling.

"You showed up," sounds behind us, causing Jayden and I to jump.

The lady I saw the other day stands with her hands on her hips, a confident smile plastered across her face. Her dark skin is glistening with sweat, causing her white dress to go sheer, revealing her bare breasts and dark-colored thong beneath it.

"Name's Margo. I gotta say, I didn't think you would show," she remarks, digging in her black shiny purse.

"Why is that? Is there a reason why she shouldn't show up?" Jayden asks, looking at me warily from the corner of her eyes.

Margo places a cigarette in her mouth and lights it, blowing a cloud of smoke into the hot air before answering.

"Most girls are stupid. They think they know the streets because they can open their legs well. That doesn't mean you have a hint of an idea of what kind of men walk on these streets." She scratches her big hair and smiles, pointing at us with her cigarette. "But I can tell. Yeah, I can tell you girls are street-smart. Mick is gonna love you." She takes a drag of her cigarette, shifting on her ridiculous high heels.

"Why would—"

"Follow me," Margo interrupts Jayden who shakes her head in anger, crossing her arms before following Margo toward the shitty motel.

Walking through the door labeled Management, I'm greeted with the smell of lemon air freshener and stale cigar smoke. A white man sits behind a desk with his head down, messing with a cigar when we walk in. His head is shaved, a big diamond earring in one earlobe. Two men stand behind him with their arms crossed, both wearing black shirts with jeans, a big gold chain hanging from each of their necks. They're tall and built with short, light-colored hair, and they have tattoos painting their arms and neck. Basically, they look scary as fuck.

I expected a more stereotypical pimp. One who wears a purple suit and a top hat, maybe. A gold cane, with gold teeth. Not some guy who looks like an outlaw, like any passerby in Vegas.

"Margo!" the guy I presume is Mick chimes, dropping the cigar on the desk and leaning back in his ripped leather chair. His face is round, his eyebrows thick and dark. He's wearing a white suit with a black tie and looks menacing as hell. One brow stays arched, and his eyes hold a permanent glare as he stares at me. My pulse begins to throb in my temples with the unease.

"Who are your friends, baby?" he questions, nodding toward Jayden and me.

"Potential bitches," Margo remarks, plopping down on a couch in the corner. I scowl at her calling Jayden and me 'bitches'. *She doesn't even know us.*

"Hmm," he murmurs, rubbing his chin and giving us a once-over.

"I'm sorry, but I ain't no bitch," Jayden sneers, shaking her head.

"It ain't personal, baby. It's just easier than saying Margo, Jewel, Angel. It's how we do." He glances down with arrogance and shrugs.

"Umm," I interrupt. "Can't you just call them girls, women, or even employees?"

Mick looks up and nods slowly, his lip curling with a hint of a smirk.

"Looks like we got a smart one on our hands," he snarls.

"Yeah, but is she street-smart?" Margo pipes up, squinting as she looks me up and down.

"Seriously? I've lived—"

Mick holds his hand up, stopping me. "I get it, you have the most tragic back story ever." He glares at me then Jayden, rubbing his hand over his bald head.

"Join the club, baby," Margo mutters, shifting on the couch.

"You don't even know me!" I snap, my voice laced with venom.

"You're right, and I don't want to get to know you," Mick snaps, and I exhale an angry breath. It seems no matter what I say, it's not right.

"But, if I had to guess, you're here for an entirely different reason than she is," he clips, pointing to Jayden. I look beside me, my eyes catching hers.

"You're apprehensive about being here, and your friend isn't. At least, not as much as you are, anyway," Mick points out.

I swallow and try to stiffen my spine. I *am* worried, but I don't want to let on I'm more worried than Jayden. I want to be strong for her.

"That's where you're wrong. It was her idea to come here," Jayden speaks up, her hand grabbing mine in support as she looks at me with care. Her simple gesture in grabbing my hand and standing up for me shows she has my back no matter what. I love her for that.

"Is that right?" Mick sneers, giving a small chuckle. "Either way, I could use some new girls," he mutters, sitting up and interlocking his fingers, resting them on his desk. The way he says *new* makes me flinch. *He didn't say* more *girls, he said* new. *Are the other girls worn out? Did they leave? Are they dead?* It's unnerving.

"What's your names?"

"My name is Jay-"

"Stop!" he roars, causing me to jump.

"I don't want to know your real name, nor does any trick you're fucking. What is your street handle?" His tone leans on the side of irritated as he lifts his chin, waiting for our replies.

"Umm," Jayden stutters.

"Fancy. My name is Fancy," I go first, giving Jayden a second to come up with something.

"Hmm, Fancy. Don't think we've had a girl named Fancy before," Mick says, smiling.

"We haven't," Margo adds.

"And you?" Mick points at Jayden.

"Rarity," Jayden informs, her back straight with confidence as she answers.

"Don't think we've had one of those, either," Margo states, stuffing tissues under her arm pits. *How classy.*

"All right, this is what we'll do. Margo will show you the ropes." He points at Jayden. "She'll teach you how to work the corner, Rarity. And you, Fancy, will work the motel."

"How much do we get?" Jayden butts in.

He runs his tongue along his bottom lip, looking her over. "I get it all. In return, I will pay your rent, and make sure you have food in your fridge—"

"Ha!" I blurt, turning to leave.

"You gotta any better options?" Mick hollers, catching me in my step.

"You're telling me we use our bodies and don't get a dime?" I question, my tone hostile as I turn around furious. "Then I say. Fuck. You," I spit.

Done. I am so done with this whole thing.

"Then go. Work the streets alone without my protection. I'll send dead roses to your funeral-"

"They won't have a funeral. Ain't nobody know they here. Look at them," Margo adds, standing and waving her finger up and down as she points at us.

"Who the fuck do you think you are?" Jayden steps up to Margo, her fists clenched, ready to throw down. I follow her lead, ready to have Jayden's back. *This Margo chick is starting to get on my last*

106

nerve.

"That's my bottom bitch," Mick informs, serious.

"Your what?" I can't help but laugh.

"You know, bottom bitch. It means she's been around since day one, my most trustworthy bitch," Mick explains, smiling big at Margo.

"I'd back off," one of the men standing behind Mick seethes, his chest puffed out. I kind of forgot they were even here; they're so still and quiet.

I close my eyes, conflicted with what to do.

"Look, how about for the first week, I'll give you a percentage depending on what you make. That's the best I can do. You don't like it, then bounce. But I either get both of you or neither," Mick offers, and I can't help but scoff. Accepting his offer will back us into a corner. We won't have any money to leave if we ever wanted to, because he'll have it all.

"Don't be stupid," Margo whispers, catching mine and Jayden's attention.

"I'll take care of you girls, so you won't have to worry about your next meal. You won't have to worry about how to pay for a doctor when you're sick. You're mine," Mick pleads his case. His hands steeple as he trails his eyes over us. He knows where we're weak, knows what we need, and he's using it to the point we would be stupid to decline his offer. The way he watches my face, my body after every offer he puts on the table, after every word he says, he's looking for a way to hook us, to hook *me.*

"We'll figure it out," Jayden mutters, grabbing my hand. I look from our joined hands to her gray eyes. She's been hooked. I can't resist this offer. What will I do if Jayden or I get sick, or hurt? We can't afford a hospital.

Our worries of surviving are over if we accept.

"Like you didn't use me? You took that money without any problem."

"You've already whored yourself out. Why fight who you are?"

Chasen's words echo in my head. This is what I do. I have sex with men, then take their money. There's no better path for me. I can't bail on Jayden. She needs me. We need each other.

"Fine," I mumble softly.

"Excellent. You start now. Margo, dirty these girls up," Mick instructs, not taking his eyes off his cigar as he twirls it between his fingers.

"You got it, baby," Margo coos, opening the office door.

"Oh, and ladies," Mick stops us. Jayden and I turn, waiting for him to continue. "You try and stiff me on my money, you won't like the consequences." His nostrils flare with rage, his eyebrows narrowed with promise. I swallow hard and nod.

"Okay," Jayden mutters, her voice cracking.

CHARLIE

Following Margo, I notice the blue paint is chipped along the motel, and the concrete beneath our feet is cracked. Looking across the way, I see half-naked girls – prostitutes – waiting outside their doors, smoking a cigarette and eyeing Jayden and me.

"This is us." Margo points to an off-white door with the number 1 on it.

Inside the room, there's a bed with nothing but white sheets and a shitty air conditioner under the window blowing warm air into the room that smells of stale cigarettes. A black fridge, dresser, and chair are the only pieces of furniture apart from the bed.

"Seems Daddy Mick just *loves* you, huh?" Margo props her hands on her hips and glares at Jayden.

"I, uh," Jayden stutters.

"Strip," Margo instructs, kicking her heels off. "I need to see what I have to work with," she clarifies, heading toward the closet.

"Do you always dress Mick's new girls?" Jayden sasses, taking her top off.

"I do whatever Daddy Mick asks of me, as you should, too. He's saving you, ya know?" She turns her head, looking over her shoulder, her tone snarky.

"How so?" Jayden laughs.

"No man who knows you're with Mick will touch you out of anger. You won't go hungry ever again. You need air in your apartment? Mick will get it. You need clothes? Mick will take you shopping. He is your savior," she explains, throwing out a slew of dresses. She makes Mick sound like a god rather than a pimp.

I give a tight-lipped smile and glance around. Jeez, it's as if I just walked into a dress shop with all the clothes, shoes, and makeup displayed everywhere.

I spot a bright red dress on the bed and smirk. "Hand me that red dress," I instruct Jayden, my fist clenching with anxiety. She grabs the dress and hands it to me while smiling. She's happy. She feels safe, knowing our worries of surviving are over, and that makes me happy.

"Oh, you'll need these." Margo turns and opens a dresser drawer, pulling out something and tossing it on the bed.

"Fishnets? Isn't that a little cliché?" I giggle, looking at Jayden who's laughing, too.

"Embrace ya' stereotypes, baby. These men, they want that taboo feeling of being with a prostitute. The back of cars, dirty motel rooms, that's what sells around here," Margo advises, tossing Jayden a pair of stockings.

"Let's do it then." Jayden nods, undoing the tangled stockings.

"Rules," Margo starts, sitting on the bed while Jayden and I dress. "If your trick is fat, you compliment him on his hair. If he took the time to brush his teeth before seeing you, you tell him how sexy he is. If a man reeks of body odor, you ignore it. You don't ever say anything about it. If a man has greasy hair or dresses lousy, you never say anything. If they say they love you, you tell them you love them back," Margo rambles, talking as if she's reading from a handbook.

"Why?" Jayden shrugs.

"Because we're the trick's escape from the nagging wife, the bitchy boss, and every other judgmental person in their life. It's why they keep coming back. You get repeat customers, you get praise from Mick." Margo looks at Jayden with narrowed brows as she explains. I can tell Margo is head over heels for Mick. He is the sun to her world. "It's all about acting, really. Make the trick feel like a king."

"So, what do we do if they smell to the point we can't—"

"Pretend he smells of roses, hold your breath, and suffer through it," Margo states matter-of-factly.

I snort, then laugh. I can't help it.

"That funny?" Margo asks with laughter of her own.

"A little. Especially when I think of Jayden stuck under some smelly guy," I respond. Margo rolls her eyes at my humor. *What a bitch.*

"You'll always wear a Jimmie," she continues, her tone on the edge of irritated.

"A what?" I question, shifting in my dress. This thing is way too short. If I bend over, my ass will show. It dips between my breasts, and there's a cut-out right around my belly button. Lots of skin shows, and I can't help but feel self-conscious. I guess I don't have to worry about the dress giving me a wedgie, considering I don't think it has enough material to reach the crack of my ass.

"A Jimmie, you know, a condom. Always use one, and make sure it's from *your* stash. I've seen some desperate men out there looking for a reason out of marriage." Margo shakes her head, digging in her purse.

"What do you mean?" Jayden asks, running her hands down her gray dress. It covers her breasts and her crotch with the entire middle and back open.

"Men will poke holes, or say they don't have one," Margo responds, lighting a cigarette.

"Jesus," I mutter, pulling on a stocking, my toes getting caught in the holes.

"No, baby, Jesus isn't with you. Not in this game." Margo puffs on her cigarette, looking at me to disagree.

I sigh and sit on the bed to put on some fuck-me heels.

"What do we do if a guy doesn't pay? I ask.

Margo lifts a brow. "I suggest you don't let that happen. Hit the fucker over the head with a lamp if need be." I flinch from her harsh tone. "You follow those rules, you'll be fine, babe," Margo comforts, rubbing my back.

"Why did Mick split us up?" Jayden asks, sitting next to me.

"Probably because he knows we're trouble together," I tease.

"Does it matter? What – you two seeing each other? Because if so, Daddy Mick will charge double for that kind of show." Margo throws her head back and laughs. Jayden glances my way, her lip curled in disgust.

"No, we aren't gay," I spit. "I don't like being away from her is all," I continue, my forehead wrinkling with concern.

Margo puffs on her cigarette, squinting with the rolling smoke clouding her face.

"Daddy Mick can tell your girl needs to be broken in slowly."

She points to me, and I roll my eyes and look at the gray curtains in my line of sight.

"I suggest you get your shit together quickly," Margo snaps.

"Fuck you," I sneer, standing up. Jayden stands with me, her fists rolled tightly.

"Honey, you better sit your little ass down." Margo doesn't even flinch at my harsh tone. "Coming in here acting like you're too good, that your pussy is made of gold or some shit." She licks her bottom lip and levels us with a death glare.

"You don't know shit about either of us, so shut your mouth, bitch." I step up to the bed, Margo standing on the other side.

"I suggest you get your emotions under control, because your mommy and daddy aren't here for you to cry to. This is the real world," Margo insults, crossing her arms. My nostrils flare and my face burns with rage.

"Like you have room to talk. You're just being a bitch because you're jealous of—"

"Jealous of what? You?" She shakes her head and laughs softly.

"Maybe not me, but you're jealous that Mick took to us so quickly. What – did he give us special treatment that you didn't get?" I cock my head to the side and watch Margo's eyes go wide. I hit her soft spot. "Yeah, thought so. Why don't you get *your* emotions under control?"

Margo's upper lip curls, and she slams her half-smoked cigarette in the glass ashtray.

"You better watch it." Jayden points at Margo with a stare that has me a little nervous.

Margo looks at a small alarm clock on the night stand.

"It's late. It's time."

"What does that have to do with anything?" Jayden asks with a

shrug.

"The later it is, the more subject to sin men are," I state. I glance up to see a wide-eyed Jayden and a Margo smiling wolfishly.

"Exactly." Margo nods approvingly. Standing to leave, she grabs my hand, pulling me back.

"My best advice to you, baby? Build a shell, protect your feelings from getting involved. It'll save you in the long run. Then you can get a hold of what's real and what isn't."

I nod, my heart suddenly pounding against my chest nervously. I can't keep up with her 'bad whore, good whore' tactics.

"Drugs help," she mutters, grabbing my hand and pushing something into my palm before walking away. I slowly undo my fist and find a very small baggy with a white powdery substance in it. Coke?

• • •

"You look good dirty, I must say," Mick chimes, rubbing his chin while sizing us up in our new attire.

"Thanks," I mutter, looking down at my red dress and gray heels. It's a miracle I can even walk in the damn things.

"So!" Mick claps his hands. "Rarity and Margo will hit the streets, learn the ropes, and you, Fancy, will head to room 2."

I look at Jayden, hating leaving her.

"It'll be fine. You'll be fine," she mutters, nodding.

"She's in good hands, don't worry," Mick states, reclining in his chair and kicking his feet up on the desk.

I watch Margo and Jayden walk out of the office, leaving me to Mick and his men. I feel alone.

"Sex is four hundred dollars. If the trick wants anything oral, it's one-fifty. Anything else, I'll handle beforehand. You collect the money before delivery, and get it to me after the deed is done. Understand?" He lifts a thick eyebrow, waiting for my response. I take my gaze from the door Margo and Jayden went through and peer from under my lashes at Mick.

"Yeah," I mutter.

"When you get a customer, I'll send them your way. Till then, kick back, watch TV, do your nails. I don't really give a shit," Mick instructs. I nod and turn to leave.

"Oh, and don't worry. I'll have Terris stand outside your room for protection," Mick adds, making me look over my shoulder at him.

"Who's Terris?" I question, shaking my head in confusion.

Mick snaps his fingers, and one of the guards behind him steps forward.

"You'll learn you're safe with me, girl." He shrugs, a big smile across his face.

•••

Room 2 is no different than room 1. The bed has nothing but white sheets and a few pillows. A black fridge with a small TV sitting on top of it and a dresser and chair are all the furniture. The only thing different in here is there's a bowl of condoms on the night stand.

I finger the little baggy of cocaine, my mind racing back and forth with whether I should snort it or not. I've never done drugs before. I'm sure it would help me get past the nerves forming in the pit of my stomach, but I don't think I want to be so far gone I don't know what I'm doing. Having sex with strange men, I think I

should have my wits about me. I stand on shaky legs and toss it in the trash bin.

I lie on the bed, looking up at the ceiling for what seems like forever.

"My best advice to you? Build a shell, protect your feelings from getting involved. It'll save you in the long run, at least until you get a hold of what's real and what isn't."

"You get repeat customers, you get praise from Mick."

"It's all about acting, really. Make the trick feel like a king."

Margo's words replay in my mind, haunting my subconscious. *I have to pull this off. I have to make the trick want me for a second time, and a third. I have to make them believe they're everything the world thinks they aren't.*

A firm knock sounds at the door, making my heart beat with such force I feel light-headed. I inhale deeply, preparing myself for what kind of monster walks through that door.

"Com- come in," I stutter nervously. The door clicks and opens slowly, and a man with curly brown hair, maybe in his late twenties, steps in. His jaw is sharp, forehead large. His brown eyes are friendly with a sense of sincerity as he looks me over. He's dressed in a black suit, but nothing like the kind Landon wore. This one looks cheap. The buttons look plastic, and there's string fraying from one of the seams.

"Wow," he mutters, shutting the door behind him. I clear my throat and stand, looking over at the TV and seeing the music video to "Wicked Games" by The Weekend.

"You were *not* what I was expecting," he mumbles, loosening his red tie.

"What *were* you expecting?" I laugh nervously, brushing a stray of hair behind my ear.

"Not something as gorgeous as you." He chuckles, looking toward the wall, his cheeks turning a shade of red.

"I'm St—" he pauses, closing his eyes. "I'm Smith," he continues. It's fake, but whatever. It's not like Fancy is *my* real name.

"I'm Fancy, and you don't look so bad yourself. In fact, you don't look like you need to pay for sex, so why are you here?" I ask bluntly, tilting my head to the side. I thought for sure I'd have some large guy who sits around playing video games in here asking for me to spread my legs. Definitely not the likes of Smith, who looks like a law student, or real estate agent, maybe a car salesman even.

He smirks, walking toward me, his stride confident as he tears his tie completely off and throws it on the bed. The breath races from my lungs. *Shit, this is happening. This is really happening. I'm about to have sex for money.* It's different than before; it's on purpose this time. There's no sugar-coating my devious acts. He wants me for one thing and one thing only: sex.

"Are you supposed to ask me that?" he questions, his voice taking on a deep tone.

"Ask you what?"

"Why I'm here," he repeats, little wrinkles forming on his forehead.

I shake my head, my hands fidgeting with each other. "Probably not." I laugh nervously.

"I like that. I like that you talk to me like a normal person. That you don't tell me what I want to hear." He tucks his hand behind my head, tilting my head upward, and looks me up and down hungrily. My fingers and toes tingle, and my lips part.

"I'm here because my fiancée took the notion of me asking her to marry me to the point we shouldn't have sex until our wedding

night. I'm going on a four-month dry spell, and have eight more months to go," he explains, his tone dry. His jaw clenches as he surveys me like a piece of meat, and I like it. My body responds to the way he eyes me like I'm the only one he sees, like I'm the subject of sex.

"You'll never make it eight months," I whisper, my voice laced with lust. My body warms, surfing with the craving to release its tension of the night. "So, what can I do for you, Mr. Smith?" I ask, running my tongue along my bottom lip, enticing him.

He runs his thumb over my lip, soaking up the trail of wetness my tongue left behind, and leans in to kiss me — but I dodge him. My eyes widen at my sudden reaction, but there's something about being kissed that makes my current haze of desire dissipate. My mind races to Landon and the way my body came alive when he kissed me. I didn't realize how alone in life I had truly been until he kissed me that night. It doesn't matter, though. Whatever I felt from that kiss, Landon apparently felt none of it. I need to protect myself.

I arch my body, loll my head back, and push Smith's head into the crook of my neck. He takes to me quickly with kisses along my skin, the fire of want surfacing between my thighs slowly. My skin burns with the admiration Smith's hands have for my body.

A growl escapes his throat as he pulls back eagerly, tearing his suit jacket off. I fist him by his white dress shirt and throw him on the bed roughly, just as excited. He lands with a bounce, a smirk across his face.

"Fuck yes," he breathes heavily, unbuttoning his pants. My blood rushes through my veins so fast I go deaf; the only thing I can hear is my rampant heartbeat. I straddle his legs, pressing my knees on each side of his hips as my dress crawls up my thighs, revealing I'm not wearing any panties.

I push on his chest, laying him down on his back fully before I unzip his pants and shove my hand down his boxers, pulling his dick free. It's not as thick as Landon's, and it's not as long, either. I close my eyes and shake my head, trying to shake anything Landon from my mind.

"Anytime you get turned on, any partner you have sex with in the future...you'll always think of me."

Landon's voice haunts me, causing me to grit my teeth and close my eyes.

Stop thinking of Landon.

He's not the man I thought he was. He wasn't a savior. He used me, taught me that every man is the same. Chasen, Landon, this guy Smith. All for sex. Well, it's my time to use them back. In doing so, I'm going to ride Smith's cock so hard Landon is a tumbleweed in my mind's eye. I'm determined to get Landon out my mind and forget him.

"This what you want, sexy?" I open my eyes and stare at him seductively, my voice heavy with lust.

"Yes, fuck yes," he grits, sitting up on his elbows.

I pump Smith's cock, getting him ready, and his mouth falls open with pleasure. The power I have over this man is a poison to my soul. *I have the control. I am what they want. I hold the power between my legs.*

"You like that?" I tease, looking at his state of bliss. He doesn't answer, just nods.

"After a long day at work, you need attention," I coo. My heart palpates with how quickly I'm taking to the role of a prostitute. Maybe this is what I was born to do. Seduce men, be worshipped by the opposite sex. Romance and love at first sight isn't real. It's

not practical and it's not what pays the bills. *Bills. Shit, this guy hasn't paid yet.*

"Yes, I do," he mumbles, thrusting his hips up.

"So, before I go further, you know the price?" I stop touching his hard length, waiting for him to pay. The last thing I need is for this guy not to pay and I get on Mick's bad side.

"Yes. Yeah, I do," he answers frantically. He pushes his hips upward, lifting us, and pulls his wallet from his back pocket. Taking out four hundred dollars, he throws it on the mattress beside us.

"Don't stop. Don't tease me," he whispers, his eyes begging me to continue. I smile sweetly and lean over him, grabbing a condom from the wicker basket that sits on the nightstand. I bite my lip, tear the package with my fingers and pull the condom out. I look at Smith's dick, then back at the condom. I'm not one hundred percent how one works.

"Let me," Smith breathes heavily, his voice muffled with raw hunger. He takes the rubber from my hands and sheaths his cock with it. "Fuck me, Fancy," he demands, slapping my ass.

I take a big breath. *Here it goes, no turning back.* I lift up on my knees and hover my heat right over his cock. I plant my hands on his chest and lower myself slowly onto him. My heart drums against my chest violently as I fully take him inside of me. I still; it stings from only having sex once before.

"Holy fuck, you're tight," he grunts, thrusting his hips up. I try not to wince and attempt a small smile. I push myself up and down, looking for that ecstasy I found with Landon. When he claimed my body, that fullness he brought filled my insecurities, my emptiness. That sensation of being alone and abandoned vanished with nothing except falling into pleasure. I growl, frustrated that I'm still thinking of Landon, and thrust harder on Smith, literally trying to fuck Landon out of my mind.

"Yes. Yes," Smith huffs, grabbing onto my hips. I close my eyes, focusing on my own selfish need to come.

"You're so good at this," I pant. *No, he's not. He's not even close.*

"So big!" I holler. He's small in comparison to what I've seen.

Just when I think I feel a hint of warmth spread through my limbs, the start of something pleasurable, a whimper escapes my lips. I fist his shirt hard and pump myself up and down quicker, chasing that feeling of satisfaction, but Smith stiffens beneath me. He grunts and trembles as he comes. *Already?* His legs kick beneath me, and a squealing noise leaves his gaping mouth as he finishes. I pull myself off him and roll over, collecting the money while blowing out a breath of frustration. I mask my irritation and turn toward him.

"Thanks, Smith." I flutter my eyelashes at him. "We should do it again sometime," I suggest sweetly, pulling my dress down. But on the inside, I feel anything but sweet. I feel anger and resentment.

"Yeah," he pants violently.

He stands and peels the condom off his length, tossing it in the waste basket.

"See you around, Fancy," he says, shoving himself back into his pants.

I fall on the bed, my head pounding with what I just did. Adrenaline flees my system, leaving realization in its wake. *I fucked a man for four hundred dollars.* My eyes sting with the welling of tears at the thought. I liked it, though. The way his hands explored my body, the way he looked at me. Trying to fuck Landon's voice out of my head wasn't so bad, either. In fact, I found some sanctuary in it. It wasn't until I was so disappointedly let down from

not reaching my own release that my conscience reminded me that I just knowingly stamped myself as a whore. I shake my head and wipe at a tear escaping the corner of my eye.

"Get a fucking grip," I chastise myself, heading to the bathroom to clean up. Going back into the main room, I don't hear the music playing on the TV. I frown in confusion.

"You're a natural," Mick announces, sitting on the bed, his legs crossed as he puffs on a cigar. His white suit sticks out like a sore thumb amongst the crappy motel room.

"Excuse me?" I ask.

He points to the smoke alarm above the bed and grins.

"This room is on video. I send girls I'm not sure can deliver in here in the beginning, see how they handle their first fuck."

"You videotaped me?!" I shriek, my hands ball into fists with anger. *I just went from prostitute to porn star in the matter of minutes.* My legs shake with rage, and shame bubbles in my chest.

"I didn't record anything, baby, so calm down. I just watched. I needed to know if you had what it takes, and I must say, you surprised me very much." He laughs, expelling cigar smoke into the room.

Having his approval, I relax my stressed stance for some reason and cross my arms. The delight of such praise from Mick is a high I didn't expect.

"So, can I join Jayden then?" I question, and shrug my shoulders.

"No, you cannot join, not just yet. But you *can* take the rest of the night off, and from now on, you'll be in room 3." He stands, his index finger and thumb cradling the dark cigar.

"And you better start calling Jayden by her street name." He puffs out a bunch of smoke.

I roll my eyes and huff at my slip-up.

"Does your apartment have air, Fancy?" He raises a brow, waiting for my response.

I narrow my eyes. "No."

"It will now." He cups my cheek and looks into my eyes with admiration.

"I can tell you had it rough, girl, but this is your family now. This is your home."

I blink rapidly at the care he displays. I'm not sure what to make of it. This stranger, this man I know nothing about, has more care for my wellbeing than people I've known for years. There's something unsettling about that.

"Mick has you now, baby girl." He places his cigar between his teeth and pats my cheek. "I'll get the address to your place from Rarity." He turns to leave, smoke following him. "Go home and clean up. You did good tonight."

After Mick leaves, the smell of cigar prominent in the room, I expel the breath I was holding when he touched me. I can't help the satisfaction forming in my chest from pleasing him, shocking him. I don't think I've ever done anything right in my life. I shake my head, confused why I care so much.

Eleven

LANDON

"Where's Claudia?" I question my brother Roman as I look over the charts of the girls' earnings. Claudia hasn't had any clients for days now. It's unacceptable.

"I told you, she went missing a few days ago, bro. None of the girls can reach her," he explains, sprawling out along the wing-backed chair in front of my desk, a tumbler of scotch in hand. His dark hair is messy and uncombed, his gray shirt wrinkled and un-tucked from his jeans. Roman never was one to be organized, and it hasn't changed with getting older, either. Being the youngest, he gets away with it. But even at the age of twenty-five, I still have our father breathing over my shoulder at my every move.

"So, we know nothing. One of our girls up and disappears and nobody knows anything?" I scorn, tugging on my blue tie in frustration. Turning this place around is becoming a hopeless battle.

"I didn't say that," Roman remarks, tilting his head to the side arrogantly.

"Would you tell me what's going on already?" I roar.

"Veronica said she thought she saw her down by that shitty little café you hang out at from time to time. So, I'm guessing if she was around that side of town, she probably went to Mick."

Veronica is our step-sister, a bitchy twenty-year-old. I can't stand her. She'd do anything to have a position at this estate. It's pathetic most of the time.

"DAMN IT!" I slam my fist on the desk. Mick has been taking our girls from under our nose for over a decade now. He's not the only sleazy pimp who targets our girls. Since I've been appointed head of the estate, I've done what I can to stop it, but it's not enough apparently. I need to make a bold statement, something to show the wannabe pimps and our girls that things are changing.

"Someone's slacking," Roman sneers, making me grit my teeth. I know this game better than most. Read the girl, find her weakness and use it against her. You have to make her feel like she can't live without you. I can reach all aspects of a damaged woman — greedy women wanting money, girls hiding out from authorities, or the ones who need the comfort from another. There's no woman whose emotions I can't play against her. But I can't reach Claudia because she has a drug addiction, and that's not something I tolerate here at the Blackwell Estate. My father may have let it slide when he was in power, but I won't have it. A woman with an addiction is dangerous and weak.

"Or has that girl you met at the café tainted your pimp hand?" Roman laughs. I glare at him from under my lashes, annoyed with his flippant tone.

"I don't know what you're talking about. You've clearly had too much to drink," I sneer, my jaw clenched.

"Right." Roman chuckles.

"Father had me followed," I state rather than question. I rest my elbows on my desk and steeple my hands in irritation. It's just like my father to have me followed. He can't seem to keep his nose in his own affairs.

"What did you expect? You were gone every day for hours. Of course he had one of our men figure out where you were going, only to find you at that café. Learning you took a girl to a hotel room was just a bonus," Roman chuckles. I narrow my eyes at him, warning him he's about to step over the line.

He takes a sip of his scotch, his brows furrowed. "If I didn't know any better, I'd think that woman has gotten under your skin, and now you're screwing up." He ticks his tongue against his teeth and shakes his head. I curl my lip. Charlie was different, I give her that. But saying she has me off my game is a laughable concept.

"That girl is not a problem, I assure you," I convince Roman, sitting back in my chair.

CHARLIE

Black wings flap violently in the night's sky. Glancing up, the moon casts a glow upon the wings as they weave back and forth. Crying. I hear disgruntled cries from what sounds like a little kid. I try to move toward the sound, but I'm cemented in place. I look down at my feet, finding them buried in muck. I shift and shove at them to move, but they won't budge. I look up, noticing the wings have moved closer. They're flapping faster, like they're angry. The cries are getting louder and more frantic, and yet I still can't fucking move. The wings suddenly wrap around me and squeeze me so tight I'm nearly suffocating. I try to scream for help, but nothing comes out. No sound, not even a whisper. The black, ominous feathers start to crush me, breaking my bones like toothpicks. My skin begins to turn black, blending with the wings as one.

"Charlie, you awake?"

I jump from my nightmare, my body covered in sweat. "I am now," I mumble into my pillow, my heart pounding against my chest. I peel an eye open and find it's still dark outside before closing my eye again.

"How did your first night go?" Jayden whispers. I think of Smith and the pleased face of Mick.

"It was okay," I groan, flipping over on the bed.

"Mick said he was getting us air conditioning because of how well you delivered," she continues, her tone soft.

"Mmm," I mumble.

"I didn't do as well as he hoped, so he put me in the motel tomorrow," Jayden whispers. I pull my head up from my pillow, my vision blurry from sleep.

"Seriously?" That can't be. Jayden has had way more experience than me. Well, at least I thought she did.

"After Margo gave me the low-down on how to spot cops, I went to work. I worked two cars, both with some fine-ass men from the college. But then there was a car that pulled up to our corner that had two men with evil looks on their faces. Their lips were curled with a sense of anger, and their teeth were stained yellow. I could smell their body odor just from standing on the outside of the car. So, I refused service. I stepped back and said 'no thanks'. Margo snatched me by the arm and was pissed. She

waltzed me back to Mick and told him I wasn't what she thought."

"Shit, Jayden, I'm sorry," I whisper. "We should be able to say who we work and who we don't. That's bullshit," I state, my voice heavy with sleep. "Besides, I think Margo is just pissed that Mick liked us so much. Maybe he isn't usually so taken with girls. Maybe he's really an asshole or something," I suggest, trying to make sense of the whole thing.

"Yeah, well, I'll prove them wrong tomorrow," Jayden sniffles, turning over on her bed. I arch an eyebrow, shocked. Mick has found her weakness and is playing it against her. Jayden is a very confident girl; she can have any guy she wants, and she'll make Mick a bunch of money. I know that, and I'm sure Mick knows it. That's why he's doing this to her. *He's working her mind. He's smarter than I thought.*

"Don't believe his shit, Jayden. You're falling right into his trap of psycho bullshit. You have to stay strong, don't show him your insecurities," I inform, my tone coming off stern and direct.

I see her head bob up and down in the dark, nodding in agreement.

"Okay. You're right. I just—"

"I understand. He snakes his way in, finds what you need. He did it to me with complimenting me. We can't fall for it. At least you'll be close to me, being back at the motel," I grumble, closing my eyes.

•••

I stack the condoms one by one while I wait for my next trick. Jayden's so hell-bent on proving Mick she's worthy today, she even did some yoga stretches before we left. I wouldn't be a friend if I didn't warn her about the camera in room 2, so I told her. She kissed me for telling her. I should've been surprised that she wasn't upset about being watched while having sex, but Jayden is a free spirit and wasn't alarmed at all.

A small knock sounds at the door, making me hurry and throw my stack of condoms in the bowl.

A man with long blond hair and dark scruff on his cheeks walks in, wearing a distressed black shirt and ripped jeans with dirty work boots. His skin is a golden tan, and his large hands have white paint on them. No, it looks too abrasive for paint — concrete, maybe? *I bet he's a construction worker. He's sexy as hell.*

"Hey, I'm Tim," he introduces, his tone deep and rough. He runs his hand through his hair and smirks. My mouth parts as his voice climbs up my legs like an aphrodisiac, my body heating instantly from just the look of him.

"Fancy," I greet, standing on purple heels.

"Goddamn, you're sexy. Where has Mick been hiding you?" He shakes his head, swiping his thumb across his chin. He's a regular of Mick's, I see.

"You're pretty sexy yourself," I purr, sliding my hand down his sweaty shirt. He's rugged and rough around the edges, but he pulls it off.

He fists my dress roughly. The strength in his hold should scare me, but it has me swooning instead. My body ignites with the alpha pouring from him. He releases me and grabs me by the ass with his large, callused hands. I feel so small against him, and my sex instantly wets. He's like a caveman, from the vulgar grabbing of my body, to his muscled frame, and the grunts that escape his mouth.

"What can I do for you, Tim?" I groan, rocking myself against his belt.

"Fuck. I want to bend you over and fuck you," he growls deeply. My body races with the craving to tease him, to have that control he so desperately wants.

"Four- four hundred," I stammer, so aroused I can't think clearly.

He drops me, causing me to stumble on my heels, and pulls out four hundred dollars in fifties, tossing them onto the bed. I lean over, grab a condom, and hand it to him. He lifts his chin with arrogance as he undoes his belt and jeans, shoving them down to his boots. I drop my gaze from his fierce blue eyes down to his cock, finding it to be a decent size. Bigger than Smith's, that's for sure.

"Bend over," Tim demands. I furrow my brows at his aggressive tone, but do what I'm told. I turn around and plant my hands on the bed. He lifts my dress to my hips and pulls my panties to my knees.

He slaps my ass hard, the burn racing up my skin. Before I can respond to his roughness, I'm impaled by him. The hard intrusion makes me whimper with pain but shiver with excitement. It's painful, yet feels so good.

He growls and pounds into me hard, his death grip on my hips bruising my skin. My core throbs as he tears into me, and I want to tell him to ease up, but I don't at the same time. I want the pain. I want to be punished. I'm angry with myself, angry with the cards life dealt me. Just fucking angry.

He grabs the back of my neck and shoves my face into the bed hard, the sheets nearly suffocating me with my harsh breathing. My legs ache, and my body hurts from the abuse. I can't take much more.

My fingers begin to claw at the fabric as my lungs burn to

breathe, the crappy motel sheets chafing my cheeks as I'm thrust upon them. He pulls my head up by the back of my neck and thrashes my face hard into the mattress, causing my nose to bash into a bed spring. My nose burns, and my eyes water.

Tim growls like a beast, finally reaching his climax. I don't move, don't look up, waiting for him to leave. My legs tremble, and my hands shake with terror. He zips his pants and slams the door on his way out, not saying a word to me as I lie here, bent over the bed. A tear cascades down my cheek. *I'm so fucked-up.* "Ma'am?" Terris, one of the guards, barrels through the door, his tone frantic.

"I heard crying. Are you okay?" he questions frantically.

"I'm fine!" I cry, my tone more angry than I intended. I stand up on shaky legs and grab the bed to steady myself.

"Fuck, Fancy," Terris mutters. I look down, finding the skin around my hips already turning a shade of purple from the grip Tim had on my hips. I purse my lips and shove my dress down to cover myself when a drop of blood splashes onto it. I frown and touch my nose with my fingertips, curious where the blood is coming from. I bring my hand back, finding the culprit. *The bed spring must've busted my nose.*

"Fuck," I whisper, staring at the blood.

"Get that fucker!" Terris yells, running off.

I stumble to the bathroom, my hands gliding against the wall, guiding me while my eyes flood with tears. My face doesn't really hurt, not as much as my pride.

When I finally reach the bathroom, I slump against the wall and fall to my ass.

"Fancy!" Mick yells, rushing into my room.

I don't move. I just sit here against the bathroom wall, my eyes fixed on the dirty sink in front of me. I can feel it, the grit, the dark,

all of which make up rock-bottom. Here I am, sitting at rock-bottom, my mind, body, and soul destroyed. I would think I would've hit rock-bottom a long time ago, but here it is... all by one trick. Showing me my place in the world. I don't have power. I have no control. I don't have shit. I'm not safe, and nobody can save me.

"Look at me, Fancy," Mick instructs, pushing my chin to look at him. My gaze slides from the wall to his round face, his thick eyebrows furrowed with concern as his bald head shines from the light above.

"That guy will never come near you again, and he *will* pay for this," Mick threatens, his other hand sliding against my cheek. He shifts, grabs some toilet paper, and dabs at my nose.

"Don't bother, I asked for it," I mutter, pulling my chin from his grip.

He scowls. "Did you? Did you verbally ask for it?" Mick questions. I don't answer, just stare at the sink. "Answer me, Fancy!" Mick roars.

I jump slightly and level him an angry glare. "No!"

"Then you didn't ask for it," Mick remarks, standing. "He'll be handled. As for you, no guy is going to pay for a chick with black eyes and a busted nose. No sex this week. Oral only, and that's if we're lucky," Mick instructs, leaving me to sit on the nasty motel floor with tissue shoved up my nostrils.

•••

As the week went by, so did what was left of my conscience. Every day, I woke up from a night filled with nightmares of wings and walked my sorry ass to Mick's motel. I'm numb, my emotions gone. My thoughts are gone.   I'm… gone. I can feel my heart beating, can taste the air entering my mouth. The two important things I need to live, yet I don't feel alive.

I gave head to two men, and one a hand job. Surprisingly, they were all good-looking. But still, with every rip of the foil to a Jimmie, as Margo calls them, a little piece of my heart goes a shade darker. Although, Jayden and I have a fully stocked fridge, and air conditioning. The day after that john gave me a bloody nose, Jayden and I went home to find a new couch with a TV sitting on a box crate. Mick has kept his word; he's taking care of us.

Jayden finally got praise from him after he watched her performance with a trick in room 2. His words were along the lines of Jayden looked like she belonged in a porno. Doesn't surprise me, though. Smith returned for round two. He wanted sex but Mick told him no, so he offered six hundred dollars instead of the usual four. Money speaks wonders in this business, because Mick accepted his offer. Mine and Smith's round two was an experience I won't soon forget.

"God, you're sexy. Better-looking than my fiancée even," Smith groaned as I rode him.

"Yeah?" I laughed, holding myself up with my hands on his chest. I'm the other woman. Deep down, I felt a little sorry for his fiancée. But I had to admit, it gave me a rush that he thought I was sexier than the girl he planned to spend the rest of his life with.

"Oh, yeah. In fact, I can't get you out of my head, Fancy," he panted, cupping my cheek.

"Well, aren't you sweet," I flirted, sweat building up my chest. It was actually a little creepy. I lolled my head back and moaned loudly as a flicker of ecstasy built in my abdomen, my sound of bliss Smith's undoing as he came. He stiffened and pulled my chest to his face,

riding his release and depriving me of mine.

"Fuck, I love you, Fancy," he groaned. I stilled, my eyes wide. Margo said the rule was I had to say it back.

"I—" I choked. "I love you, too," I whispered, my voice strained. My vision blurred, like all the blood in my system fled, leaving me lifeless. I just told a stranger I loved them...

A knock at the door breaks me from memory lane. I don't get up, though; I just sit here with my legs crossed. My skimpy purple dress climbs my thighs, revealing my fishnet stockings.

A fat guy walks in, causing me to swallow hard and my eyes to widen. He has red curly hair and overalls that fail at hiding his large gut. The warm air from outside sweeps past him into the room, and I draw back and gag. He smells like body odor. Imagine an entire football team throwing their sweaty jock straps into a pile after a football game to simmer in the summer sun. That's exactly what this guy smells like.

"Hello, I'm Dave," he greets, his double chin jiggling as he talks. I swallow and nod. I can't talk, because that means more air — and therefore body odor — entering my lungs.

"What—" I choke. "What can I do for you, Dave?" I ask, trying to hold my breath.

"Do you suck cock?" he asks, a big yellow-toothed smile wide on his face.

When I said I reached rock-bottom before, I lied. *This* is rock-bottom.

Before I answer him, he's undoing his overalls, letting them fall to his sneakers which are not tied but velcroed.

"One hundred and fifty," I inform him, holding my wrist to my nose for the smell of my perfume. Margo told me that even if men stink, you have to do it. There's no backing down from a trick.

Think of roses, suffer through it.

Dave shuffles his legs to the bed and sits down, out of breath. He starts fisting his cock, and my throat retches. I can't do this. There's no pretending with this guy. I'm not strong enough.

"Come on, baby," he encourages. I look at him from the corner of my eye and try to pull every ounce of willpower I have. I slowly kneel in front of him and hold my breath. I spread his legs using his knees, and then my lungs demand air. I inhale, and the rancid smell does it for me. My gag reflex hurdles puke upward. I turn, finding the door to the motel room, and quickly open it. I crawl forward and expel my dinner on the sidewalk.

"You took one of mine, so I'm taking one of yours!" I hear beside me as I heave for fresh air. I turn to look at who's talking, but before I can get my head turned all the way, vomit races up my throat again.

"No, wait! Claudia came to *me*, man. Take her ass back. She's in room 7," Mick begs.

"I could fucking kill you, Mick. You stepped over a line! You took one of mine, so I'm taking one of yours!" roars beside me, like a song stuck on repeat. The familiar voice is threatening, and an odd knot forms in the pit of my stomach from its presence.

"Fine," Mick mumbles. I turn my head to look at Mick and the familiar voice, but my vision is blurry with tears from throwing up.

"She'll do," the voice clips angrily. Before I can make out who the voice belongs to, the blurry image rushes toward me. Searing pain races through my scalp suddenly, making me scream as I'm pulled to my feet. My nails dig into the hand that's laced into my hair from behind.

"Charlie!" Jayden screams, rushing out of a motel room.

"Jayden!" I cry, tripping over my heels as I'm yanked back-

wards. Jayden races toward me but Mick catches her, halting her movement. Jayden pulls from Mick, trying to get to me.

"Don't!" Mick yells at her, picking Jayden up off the ground.

"You said you would protect us!" she screams, pounding against Mick's chest.

"I can't this time. It's out of my hands, Jayden!" Mick roars, grabbing Jayden's wrists to calm her.

Before I can react to what's happening, see who has a hold of me, I'm thrown into a car. I sit up and look around, finding myself in a... limo? There are black leather seats all around, and little twinkle lights illuminating the space around me.

"Drive to the estate," the familiar voice demands. I take my gaze from the driver in the front to the man who had ahold of my hair just moments ago.

My eyes widen, and my heart stammers against my chest.

"Landon?" I whisper in disbelief, butterflies swarming in my chest.

Landon's green eyes shine, and his full lips part as he inhales. I can tell he's just as surprised to see me as I am him. But as quickly as his startled expression came, it disappears. He straightens, fixes his tie and his eyes harden.

"Charlie," he greets formally, his tone holding an edge to it. He squares his shoulders, his body taking up most of the seat.

"Landon, what is—" I stop myself, confused. I shift in my seat to get closer to Landon, and his head whips from looking out the window toward me. I notice his jaw clench, and his hands fist angrily.

"Jesus, I barely recognize you, Charlie," he sneers, running a hand through his hair. I wince from his harsh tone.

"Landon," I respond meekly, my chin trembling. All I want is to crawl in his lap and have him hold me, comfort me after the Hell

136

I've been through lately. But the way he's staring at me, I can tell that's not going to happen.

"Don't." Landon shakes his head and starts muttering under his breath. "Whatever happened between us, Charlie, it never happened." He looks up, his eyes piercing mine. "You are an employee of the Blackwell Estate now," he scoffs.

I close my eyes and shake my head in confusion.

"What?"

A smirk curls Landon's lips as he fiddles with the cuffs of his sleeve. "Actually, an employee has the option to leave after their contract has expired." He smirks and tilts his head to the side. "*You are owned by the Blackwell Estate now.*"

My nostrils flare to allow the harsh breathing to escape, and my heart races in my chest. *Owned? He can't be serious.*

"You can't keep me, I'll—"

"What – run away? Call the cops?" Landon shifts in his seat and taps his fingers on his knee. "You don't want to say that to me, Charlie. I can, and will, lock you in a room, never to escape again, and we both know nobody will come looking for you." His tone is malicious. "And the cops will just bring you back to me, considering most of them are in my pocket anyway." He shrugs.

I close my gaping mouth. I can't go to the cops even if I wanted to with Jayden and I fleeing foster care the way we did. I scowl at him and turn my head toward the window. I believe him, for some reason. I believe he would lock me away in some room, never to see the light of day. The way he reeks of money and the look in his eyes hold that dark promise. It's the darkness I knew he was capable of when I met him. It dwells in his voice and burrows in his gorgeous eyes. He's capable of being a monster, just as he is a gentle lover.

Relinquish

"What is the Blackwell Estate?" I ask gravely, watching bright lights go by my window.

"You mean what is *your* position at the Blackwell Estate?" Landon counters.

"Sure."

"You will be an escort," Landon replies with a breath.

I close my eyes and let the tears fall from my eyes.

I'll be a whore. Go figure.

CHARLIE

We drive far from the city lights and eventually find ourselves in front of an iron security gate. After the driver punches in a few buttons on a black box outside the gates, we move forward. We wind up a long driveway with little torches placed along the way. We don't need them, however; the place that holds my fate is clear as day, even at this time of night. It's huge and spotlights shine upon it from every angle.

The limo stops and Landon steps out without a word. My heart takes flight in panic as I shift in my seat nervously. My door is yanked open and Landon holds his hand out, offering to help me out of the car. The smell of his fresh scent swims past me and I inhale deeply.

"What? You don't want to grab me by my hair?" I smart, getting out without taking his hand. He sighs, undoing the button on his suit jacket. As soon as Landon shuts the door to the car, it drives off, leaving me a gaping mess staring at the mansion. It's made out

of large stone, brick for brick, grooves and crevices painting every inch of the foundation. It's so distinguished with character I can't look away.

"You like it?" Landon questions, his tone a shade softer than before.

"It's- It's incredible," I stammer, not sure how to describe it.

"Welcome to the Blackwell Estate, Charlie. Let's go draw up some paperwork," Landon suggests, pressing on the small of my back. I tear my eyes from the glowing windows placed sporadically along the building and turn toward Landon. *That's right, I almost forgot; I'm his* owned *whore now.* I jerk myself from him, anger fueling my senses.

Walking inside the estate, it's just as breathtaking. The floor is made up of white marble, and a grand staircase sits right in the middle, rising to another floor.

"This way." Landon walks past me, leading the way. Following him, I find a door that leads into a dining room filled with a large, oak dining table. Passing that room, Landon leads me past a black piano and an overwhelmingly large fish tank until finally, he opens a door behind the staircase.

"Take a seat, Charlie," Landon commands, walking in behind me. I look around the oval-shaped room, ignoring his demand. A mahogany desk with a black leather chair sits in front of a wall of windows, with two black winged-back chairs placed before the desk. Looking away, my eyes find a black Persian rug placed elegantly in the middle of the room, and a large red couch along the back wall. There's a wet bar in the corner, stacked with glasses and bottles filled with amber liquid. I peer up, finding a huge crystal chandelier illuminating the room, setting off little rainbows of light amongst my skin. This is so different than the motel, than anything I've ever seen. I'm stunned, as I've never been around such riches in all my life.

"Charlie," Landon clips, grabbing my attention. "Sit down," he repeats, pointing to one of the chairs in front of his desk. I scowl at him, take my heels off and head toward the chair.

"You're not a guy who hears the word 'no' very often, are you?" I ask, quirking an eyebrow at him.

Landon chuckles and shakes his head. "No, I'm not. Why do you ask?" he replies, a playboy smile fitting his face.

I shrug and look around the place again. "By the looks of this place, and the arrogant authority in your voice, I'm just guessing."

Landon drapes his suit jacket over the back of his chair and rolls his sleeves to his elbows. His chair is stunning, black with gold trimming, and exhibits power. My eyes trail up his toned arms, and my body defies my anger. My panties dampen with the thought of him grabbing me and throwing me on this desk. His body is like a hostile storm, taking charge of wherever he is, leaving a wake of masculinity and power. It's hard not to be affected by him.

"What happened to you?" Landon mutters, shifting his chair to sit in it. I pull my eyes from his arms, and glance down at my hands. *What happened to me? What a laughable concept. I should tell him to fuck off, that it's none of his business.*

I peer out from under my lashes and glare at him. *While I've been trying to live, keep myself alive, he's been living like a king?*

"Life happened. Life happened to me, Landon," I grit, my hands squeezing my shoes. I want to throw them at him, fucking impale him with the heel.

Landon shakes his head and opens a drawer, pulling out some papers.

"It doesn't matter. It's nothing my team can't handle," he mutters coldly, slamming the drawer shut.

"Team?" I question, tilting my head to the side.

"You look like trash, but my team will make you appear like a respectable woman," he clarifies, plucking a pen from a cup holder. My mouth gapes open, offended.

"Yeah, well, the tricks don't seem to complain," I sneer, crossing my arms defensively. I curl my fists on themselves, the twitch in them wanting to pummel his face with the amount of disrespect he has toward me.

Landon closes his eyes as if my words physically slapped him.

"Charlie, around here, we do not refer to our clients as 'tricks'. They have names, and you will use them or refer to them as 'client', understood?" Landon lifts his brows, waiting for me to respond. I roll my eyes and look up at the chandelier.

"Understood?" Landon roars, slamming his fists into the desk and making me jump.

"Yes," I mumble, my eyes leaping from the pretty lights to his serious face. The hairs on my arms raise with alarm, scared at the monster before me. His face is red and twisted, his fists clenched like he's just as angry with me as I am with him. He's not the Landon who swept me off my feet at the hotel, and he's definitely not the man I've fantasized about in the back of my mind for weeks now.

"You ask what happened to *me*, but what happened to *you*?" I ask, squinting as I take in the man I thought I knew. The man that was caring and sweet at the hotel.

"You assume you know me, Charlie, but we fucked. That was it." I flinch at his brashness. "You know nothing about me, and you won't," he snaps, his voice grave and cutting me. I was right. There was nothing there that night; it was all me falling for a fantasy. "Tomorrow, my team will clean you up, and we'll get you tested." Landon looks at me with a cynical eye as he mutters the last part, and I scoff.

"I used Jimmies, so I don't have anything," I inform him, shifting in my seat, annoyed at the conversation. Then my eyes perk, remembering Landon and I didn't use protection.

"You're the only one I was stupid with. We didn't use anything, remember?" I tilt my head to the side and purse my lips. We were so lost in the moment, so ready to just have each other, we didn't even think about it.

His brows slice forward, etching his face with an eerie look. He clenches his jaw and looks away from me.

"After the team cleans you up, we'll start training-"

"Training?" I sneer, my lip curled in disgust. "Mick already trained me. I know what I'm doing."

"Considering you talk like you're from the streets, and we only offer high-end pussy to our clients, yes, you need training. We don't refer to condoms around here as 'Jimmies'. Let that be lesson one," Landon responds, his tone condescending. "Training will tell us where to place you, and how much you're worth."

I grit my teeth and shake my head in anger. *Worth? He should just put a tag in my ear and brand me like a damn cow.*

"Was my virginity worth the thousand dollars you left me?" I raise a brow and inhale an angry breath. Landon's mouth parts, his eyes slicing inward with a death glare.

"Brother, have you handled the Claudia situation?"

I slowly tear my eyes from Landon's and turn in my chair, finding a guy with dark, messy hair closing the door behind him. He's wearing black dress pants and an untucked white dress shirt.

"Now isn't a good time, Roman." Landon levels the man with a hard stare.

Roman's eyes find mine, and he stops in his tracks.

"Oh, I didn't realize you had company." He smirks, running a hand along the back of his neck.

"Well, you're here, so you might as well meet our newest girl, Charlie." Landon blows out a frustrated breath.

"My, you are a pretty thing," Roman chuckles, heading toward me.

"Don't," Landon clips toward Roman who rolls his eyes, holding his hand out for me to shake.

"I'm Roman, the fun one. You already met my uptight brother who runs the place," Roman jokes, making me laugh. Landon's eyes find mine, fire spreading behind his emerald eyes as I giggle at his expense. I should stop, but I can't. I haven't done this in so long I almost forgot what it feels like.

"You have a beautiful laugh," Roman flirts. My cheeks blush as I shake his hand.

"That's enough Roman. She gets it, you're horny," Landon patronizes. Roman's eyes find Landon and glare, his forehead wrinkling as he squints with anger.

"Right, well, I'll see you around, Charlie." Roman smirks before lifting his chin at Landon and leaving.

"You can stop blushing, Charlie. You won't be sleeping with him," Landon bashes, causing my moment of glee to vanish.

"As you have many rules to learn, Blackwell brothers at the estate have one rule to live by." Landon places his hands on his desk and leans forward, the muscles in his arms stretching the material of his dress shirt. My lips part, and that delicious ache returns in my core as I watch the fabric fit around the muscles snugly.

"No having sex with our escorts. Period. No sleeping with clients, nor anybody associated with our escorts or clients," Landon explains. My eyes whip from his arms to his eyes.

"So, who *do* you sleep with then?"

"I go out and find a—" He stops and shakes his head.

"Find a nobody," I finish his sentence. He sighs loudly and looks down at his desk, but he doesn't deny it. *How cliché am I to fall intimately for the guy who took my virginity?* I shake my head, my thumb rubbing along my bottom lip. *I'm pathetic.*

Landon looks at the large clock on the wall.

"It's getting late. Let's get this paperwork worked out so I can get you into your room," Landon remarks, shuffling papers around on his desk.

"My room?" I ask.

"Yes, your room. What aren't you understanding about that?" Landon tilts his head to the side, his jaw clenched as he takes in my reaction.

"Can't I go home?" I question nervously. The severity of my situation begins to rise. "Jayden will wonder where I am, or what happened to me," I ramble. Landon laughs wickedly, the sound causing my body to quiver in fear.

After he contains himself, he glowers at me. An evil smirk marks his face perfectly, causing anger to race through my limbs.

"No. You cannot go home. I told you. I own you."

"I don't even know what that means. You just show up, grab me by the hair, and throw me into your limo saying you own me, and you expect me to just fall in line?" I throw my hands around wildly to emphasize my point, panic filling my body at the thought I'll never see my crummy apartment or Jayden again.

"You don't need to know anything, Charlie. You are a part of the Blackwell Estate, and that's all the information you need." Landon steeples his hands once again and sets back in his chair, that fucking know-all smirk smug on his face.

"You're dumber than I thought if you think I'm going to accept that as an answer. That is *not* going to happen." I slowly stand, my nose flaring with rage. The way I'm feeling, the anger flowing through me, I'm a loaded gun ready to fire. I'm unpredictable, dangerous, and ready to claw Landon's eyes out if I have to. "I want answers," I seethe.

Landon inhales a large breath and sits forward, resting his elbows on the desk and interlocking his fingers.

"Mick took one of my girls. I could have killed him, could have had my men teach him a lesson, but he wouldn't learn anything. Everyone who thinks they're anybody will send someone to hurt the competition physically, and if you kill them, someone else will just take their place. So, an eye for an eye. He took my girl, so I took his." Landon sits back in his chair again, sliding his hands behind his neck.

I exhale a steady breath, trying to calm myself.

"Now, can we get this paperwork finished?" he growls.

"What is this paperwork even?" I scowl.

"Gives me some detailed information on your health and background," Landon explains.

Mick didn't have me do any of that. Looking at this place compared to Mick's, though, they're worlds apart.

I take my gaze from the room to Landon, my eyebrows perking up in confidence and my spine stiffening. "No, we can't. I'm not signing shit, because I didn't agree to become an escort of the Blackwell Estate." I fold my arms and cross my legs stubbornly.

"You just got your first no." I smirk arrogantly. "Now, take me home," I demand.

Landon rubs his chin, his squinting causing wrinkles to form at the corner of his eyes. But he doesn't look angry. In fact, he looks... *amused*?

"Do you have any idea what you're passing up? No girl has ever said 'no' to the position. Women beg to be a part of–"

"Then why did one of your girls go to Mick?" I tilt my head sideways.

"I don't tolerate drug addicts in my estate. I heard she was using, and I tried to put her in rehab. I thought she was doing well, but she must have started again. I told her if she kept it up, she wasn't welcome here, and I guess instead of talking to me about it, she just left." He exhales a heavy breath and rubs the scruff on his chin. "Still, most women wouldn't give up such an opportunity."

"Well, I'm not most women," I state.

Landon lowers his head and grins. "No. No, you're not." He gazes up, his emerald eyes finding mine and making me suck in a sudden breath. Landon shakes his head, and his soft eyes turn stormy.

"With that, I will just have the staff lock you in a room then." Landon grabs the phone off his desk, and the arrogant smirk that was across my face disappears into pure panic.

"Lock me in a room? What? You can't do that," I ramble, my sudden confidence gone.

"Oh, I can and I will. Nobody will even know you're gone," Landon sneers, slamming buttons on the receiver to make a call.

"Jayden," I stammer. "Jayden will know I'm missing." My eyes go wide when Landon twists his face like she doesn't count, making me furious.

"Stop! Listen to me," I plead, trying to get his attention, but he doesn't even look at me. He's too busy with the phone, anxious to lock me away.

"Jean, can you—"

I lean over and swipe the phone off his desk and onto the floor. Landon's face takes on a surprised look before finding my eyes and glaring.

"Fine, I'll sign the papers. Just- just let me go home. I want to go back and see Jayden, say goodbye," I plead, pressing the palm of my hand to my head, trying to think past my manic state.

Landon sighs, rubbing at his tired eyes.

"Please," I beg, tears pricking at my eyes. My anger, my fury, and dangerous state have dissipated to pure desperation. Landon's head whips up from my trembling voice, his face taking on a look of sympathy.

"I'm just supposed to trust that you won't try and run?" Landon questions, his tone lighter than he's been speaking to me the whole night. I shrug, not sure what to say to that. He shouldn't trust me, but I need him to.

He runs his hands through his hair and nods. A loud sigh leaves my mouth, relieved I will get to go home, even if it's for the last time.

"I'll send Osborn with you. He'll be watching you throughout the night, and if you so much as try anything..." Landon lowers his head and glowers, the muscles in his jaw ticking. "That person who means so much to you—Jayden, was it—will suffer the consequences," Landon threatens, making me swallow hard. "You *will* return bright and early tomorrow, arriving ready to start your position as an escort," he continues.

"I will." I nod quickly, sealing my fate as a sex slave for who knows how long. I thought getting a pimp was bad, but this? This is so much worse. I can feel it in my gut.

"Charlie, make sure and say your goodbyes, because tomorrow you're mine fully. Kiss your old life, your friends, family, Mick, all farewell."

I close my eyes, trying to hold the tears pricking at my eyes at bay. When I finally get a grip on myself, I find Landon picking up the phone from the floor.

"Osborn, I have a job for you tonight. I need you to take Charlie back to her place, and see to it that she does not go anywhere else. She is to return back to the estate at sunrise," Landon demands before hanging up.

His demented green eyes find mine, eyes I used to find gorgeous yet all I see in them now is a monster. Landon clearly isn't the guy I thought he was. Well, guess what? He doesn't know who the hell he's fucking with. I won't make my staying here easy on him.

"Enjoy your few hours of freedom, Charlie."

Thirteen

LANDON

I slump in my chair, tearing my tie from my neck. I'm angry. So angry, I could throw this fucking desk out the window. I can't make up or down of this situation. When I saw her in the back of the limo, my chest constricted and my dick twitched to have her. Regret plowed through me like a sledgehammer for leaving her at that hotel. But I quickly reminded myself *why* I left. *I lose control around Charlie, and I need to stay focused.* She's a problem, a very big problem. She gets under my skin, causes me to question why I'm even running this estate.

It's my legacy to sit in this chair and hustle women, but it's a promise that has kept me here. A promise that I would restore the Blackwell name, but Charlie has me questioning all of it.

She told me no. She fucking told me no. Nobody *tells* me no. No woman turns down a position at the Blackwell Estate. It irritates me, yet makes my cock hard at the same time. She told me she was that boy's whore when I met her, but I just thought she was being hard on herself. After the way the night unfolded, I was sure of it. However, after the last hour, I don't know what to fucking think.

"She gone?" Roman peeks his head around the door, looking around. I nod, rubbing my thumb and forefinger over my chin.

"Forgive me if I'm wrong, but that girl looks a lot like—"

"Don't!" I interrupt, my fists clenching with anger. I know what he's going to say. Father had me tailed, so I'm sure there were photos taken of Charlie at the hotel.

Roman sighs and slumps down in one of the chairs in front of my desk.

"I get it, man."

"No, you don't. That woman, that girl..." I point at the door and look at Roman, my forehead sweating from anger and confusion.

"Landon, you're the only guy I know, Blackwell or not, who has never had a woman at some point bring him to his knees. Blackwell training be damned," Roman explains, shaking his head.

We were trained growing up to resist temptation. After all, we sell women who use their bodies as paychecks, to gain what they want and need out of life. It's up to us to resist it, to run a business.

Growing up in the Blackwell Estate, Roman and I were preached to daily about how sex clouds the mind, that lust is a drug and becomes addictive. It was repeated over and over by those who trained the Blackwells, dating back decades. I took it as an oath, and Roman took it as a challenge. We were taught how to control our urges, see women as objects rather than humans.

Roman's always diving into forbidden pussy. He knows the rules yet still sneaks around with the escorts. That's why the women have no respect for him. He's just another client to them, using Roman like another man with a wallet.

I'm not saying I don't have sex; I sleep with women all the time,

but I don't break rules. I don't have sex with our escorts. I don't have sex with any of our clients, and I don't conspire with anyone who may know any of our clients or escorts. That's the biggest rule for a Blackwell. But I'd be a damned liar if I said Charlie didn't stick out amongst every female who spread their legs for me, making the laws of the estate a blur.

"Are you going to be able to handle her?" Roman questions, looking at me with concern. I swallow and close my eyes. *I have to be able to handle her. In the end, though, Charlie will hate me.*

"She's just another escort," I remind him, and myself.

CHARLIE

"Oh, my God! Charlie, I was so worried!" Jayden flings herself into me as soon as I walk through the door, nearly knocking me over.

I smile and hold her close, the smell of cocoa wafting from her hair a solace. She squeezes me hard, making my ribs scream with pain, but I don't care. To feel loved, to know someone would miss me if I disappeared is unfamiliar.

"I'm fine, I'm fine," I whisper into her shoulder.

"I thought I'd never see you again," Jayden cries into my hair. "What happened?" Jayden pulls herself back using my shoulders, her gray eyes filled with unshed tears.

"Landon happened," I grumble, pulling from her fully and throwing my shoes by the bed.

"I'll be right outside this door, Charlie," Osborn states, reminding me he followed me up here. I look over my shoulder at him.

Osborn is a muscular man who looks like he just swallowed a
year's worth of steroids. His shoulders are broad and muscled to
the point he doesn't look like he has a neck. He's in a black suit
with black sunglasses placed snuggly on his face, even though it's
night.

"Who the fuck is this?" Jayden shrieks, not noticing Osborn
followed me in before now. I grab her arm, stopping her in her
pursuit of anger.

"He's the watchdog," I sneer. Osborn doesn't even flinch, just
shuts the door behind him as he leaves.

"What?" Jayden questions, wiping her cheeks with her hands.

"Landon, the man who gave me that thousand dollars—"

"What about him?" Jayden interrupts.

"I guess he runs some escort business. I work for him now –
actually, I'm *owned* by him. It looks like Mick got himself in some
kind of situation, because I no longer work for Mick," I clarify,
peeling my dress off my sweaty body, leaving me in my bra and
panties.

"You can't be serious. He can't *own* you." Jayden shakes her
head in confusion, her forehead wrinkling in panic.

"He's very powerful, and has made it clear what happens if I try
to defy him." I take my gaze from Jayden, debating if I should tell
her that Landon threatened her life. I bite my lip and decide
against it. She doesn't need anything else added to her plate of
terror; losing each other is going to be enough.

"He's not to be messed with, Jayden."

"When you say *owned*, do you mean, like, you won't be living
here anymore?" Jayden asks, her voice taking a tone of sorrow. I
look at her, my expression clearly telling her everything she needs
to know.

"No. He can't do that. We can run. We can call the police." Jayden tears up, her hands grabbing at me frantically.

"No, we can't, Jayden. We just... can't," I stumble on my words. I can't dive into telling her how obviously powerful Landon is. This is unbearably painful for me, to know this is the last time I may see Jayden. All I want to do is slump to the floor and cry with her, but I can't. I won't give Landon that power. I'll savor the time I have with Jayden and be strong for the both of us.

"You're all I have," Jayden whispers, making my eyes snap to hers. I grab her into a hug, needing that feeling of comfort.

"You're all I have, too," I respond. "I'll work something out. Get you in there as an escort, see if I can come home on the weekends, or find a way out of there — something," I mumble into her curly hair, her fingers digging into my back as she cries.

I start to pull away. "It's late. Let's get some sleep," I suggest, but Jayden doesn't let go. I reach over and turn the light off then walk us over to my bed. I pull the sheet back and pull myself from Jayden's grip. Too stunned to move on her own, I unzip her red dress, letting it fall to the floor. I climb into the bed and hold the sheet up, encouraging Jayden to crawl in beside me. She kicks her heels off and crawls in, her back to my front, and we snuggle close to each other. Her body shakes as she sobs, the heat radiating off her causing me to sweat, but I don't pull away. I don't even kick a leg out from under the sheet.

"We've been through so much together. You're the only person who understands me and doesn't hold judgement." Her voice cracks with emotion. "Charlie, you can't leave me. Promise me you'll come back," she sobs.

I take a deep breath, not sure if I'll be able to deliver on that or not, so I lie.

"I promise."

•••

A loud knock at the door has Jayden falling out of the bed and me pulling the sheets up over my head.

"What?" Jayden yells, opening the front door. I smirk. I know she's in her bra and undies. She has no shame. *At least she didn't sleep next to me naked, though.*

"It's time," Osborn remarks, his voice deep.

"Yeah, okay," Jayden clips, slamming the door, probably in his face.

I sigh and throw the blankets back.

"We could take him, you know," Jayden mutters, pulling the sheet from her bed to cover herself. I laugh. The two of us trying to wrestle Osborn, tie him up so we can run, is an image to be seen just in my head.

"I don't see that playing out too well." I half-laugh, shaking my head as I slip on a sports bra. "Besides, Landon would come for me, and I know he'd find us," I tell her, grabbing some ripped jeans and a dark blue shirt that has the sleeves cut off, revealing my white sports bra. I hate leaving Jayden, but at least I don't feel as apprehensive about being a part of the Blackwell Estate. If Landon is anything like I thought he was, maybe I can leave on the weekends and have Jayden come see me or something.

"Fuck him," Jayden snaps, making me laugh. A knock sounds at the door, reminding us that Osborn is waiting.

"I *will* be back, Jayden. I *will* get in touch with you," I whisper. Jayden pulls me close and inhales, like she is programming me to memory. She turns quickly and chuckles nervously, wiping the

tears from her cheeks, and sitting on her bed. I tilt my head and give her a tight-lipped smile.

"I gotta go." I lean over the bed and kiss her forehead, muttering, "Be safe."

"You, too," she whispers.

I look around our dump of an apartment, not really caring to take anything with me. Eventually, I open the door to find Osborn.

"Let's go," he grunts, pushing his sunglasses on the bridge of his nose.

The ride to the estate is quiet, the driver sitting at the front of the limo only looking back to check on me a few times. Osborn sits beside me, his large size taking up most of the seat.

We pull up to the estate, and Landon is standing on the steps in a crisp, expensive suit. The limo comes to a stop, and he opens my door.

"Charlie," he greets. His body is like a storm — powerful, strong, and fearless. I swallow hard, that familiar ache in my chest resurfacing.

"Landon," I reply dryly. His eyes rake me from top to bottom, leaving a blazing trail of lust behind them. I can't help the way my legs clench to stifle the intolerable throb escalating between them, but it doesn't override the wave of anger I have toward him, either.

Landon leans in, causing me to stiffen.

"Stop clenching," he whispers, a smirk crossing his face. My mouth hangs open with shock, but I shut it as quickly as it flew open.

"I can't help it, your driver is hot," I smart, walking past him.

I hear Landon laugh like a school boy, his footsteps sounding behind me as I let myself into the mansion-like house.

Landon grabs my upper arm, swinging me around with haste, and plows me against the large wooden door. His fresh scent seizes the air from my lungs. His face lowers mere inches from mine, his green eyes turning a shade darker, causing a bundle of nerves to twist in my stomach.

"That mouth will start wars between us. I'm not sure if I should wash it out with soap or fuck it," Landon seethes. All the oxygen in my chest races out, leaving me speechless. Landon smirks, proud of himself.

I inhale a large breath, gather my courage, lean my head toward his, and smile. "Give me your best shot." He doesn't scare me; I'd like to see his worst, in fact.

Landon takes a deep breath and licks his bottom lip. "I'm not sure if you could—"

"Is this the new girl?" We both look over, and Landon quickly releases his hold on me. I have to bite my lip to stop from smiling. I affect him, and that alone is empowering.

"Veronica," Landon enunciates slowly. The woman has long, golden-blonde hair that comes to rest on one shoulder. She is tall and thin, wearing a long, light pink dress that trails behind her. Her makeup is done lightly, but her red-stained lips stand out amongst her porcelain skin.

"The team will have their hands full with this one, that's for sure," Veronica sneers, her lip curled in disgust as she eyes me. I wince, shocked a complete stranger would be such a bitch. *But then again, look at Landon.*

"She's not too bad," Landon defends, a smirk crossing his face, his forest eyes holding a tone of friendliness. I scowl at both of them, angry they're talking as if I'm not even standing in the room.

"I'm sure *you* would think so," she clips. "They're waiting

upstairs for you." She nods toward me before turning, picking her dress up, and walking back up the stairs.

"Please, don't turn me into a Barbie," I plead to Landon. He chuckles and runs his thumb over his chin.

"Would you like breakfast, Charlie?" he questions, lowering his hand and placing it on my lower back. His hand is large and takes up the small of my back. My memory takes me back to waking up in that hotel room by myself — no breakfast, no man, just a stack of cash. My body hums from his touch, but my mind barks out uncontrollable anger from the flashback. My logic winning this battle, I grasp Landon's arm and tear it away from my body.

"How about we save the crap. You're not a nice guy, and I'm not a nice girl. I don't have a clue why you're being nice to me, but stop. Oh, and it would be pointless to have breakfast and pretend to have small talk, when we both know I'm here to be your employee, your toy for money—"

"Charlie, you *want* me to be nice to you. Because by the end of all this, you will hate me more than you do right now," Landon interrupts, his face masked with anger as his jaw clenches.

"Just show me to the team," I mutter, unaffected by his threat.

Landon steps back and runs his hands through his hair, his chest lifting as he inhales deeply as if he's trying to control his anger.

"This way." He points ahead of me, walking up the stairs. I let out the breath I was holding and follow him.

Landon takes me to a room which looks like a mini-salon and massage parlor mixed into one. A large mirror is outlined in bulbs, with every kind of hair product sitting on a table beside it and a black swivel chair in front of it. At the back of the room, there is a large open window with a small padded table placed in front of it, possibly a massage table.

"You must be Charlie." My head snaps to look behind me, finding a man and a lady walking in behind us. The lady has black hair bunched on top of her head and she's tall. Her face is in the shape of a kissing fish, or like she just ate something too sour. Her lips are dark purple, matching her purple dress which hugs her neck and falls to her calves. The man has dark-colored, spiked hair, the front of it splashed a bright red, and he's much shorter. His black-rimmed glasses are too small for his face. My eyes trail down his small frame, noticing he's wearing a pink shirt and dark blue jeans with green shoes. I quirk a brow at his choice of clothes. They're very flashy.

"She doesn't want to be a Barbie," Landon mocks, a small smirk across his face. I purse my lips at him and roll my eyes. "Find me when you're finished," he demands, walking off with his hands in his pockets.

"What should we do with her hair? A bob maybe?" she suggests, tugging on a strand of my wavy hair.

"Oh, Michelle, don't you dare touch her hair with scissors. We haven't had the opportunity to work with such beauty before," the man scolds, his eyes wide and mouth gaped open as he looks at my hair with awe. I'm stuck frozen while they argue over cutting my hair, scared they'll hack it all off.

"Oh, Gabe, don't be so dramatic." Michelle rolls her eyes.

"Sit," Gabe demands, pointing to the chair. I swallow hard, fighting my nerves, and sit in the chair. *Jeez, is everyone around here so bossy?*

For the next three hours, I am picked, prodded, waxed, and peeled. My entire body either burns or itches from all the beauty procedures I've endured. That massage table turned out to be a

thing of nightmares. It's where you lie to have hot wax torture. The only break I had was when a doctor came and took a blood sample then examined my private parts. Getting poked by a needle was the least painful of everything, strangely. I feel violated from head to toe right now.

"So, I'll start the makeup if you want to go buy the wardrobe," Michelle states, handing Gabe the chart with my body measurements on it.

"I'm on it. Oh, you should do a smoky eye shadow, but nothing heavy." Gabe lights up, looking me over with excitement.

"I'm sorry, are you shopping or doing makeup?" Michelle props her hand on her hip and tilts her head to the side. Gabe rolls his eyes, throwing a hand at Michelle dismissively as he walks out of the room.

I feel like a doll being morphed into the perfect candidate for some lonely man. Even with all the glamour this place has to offer, I feel alone.

"You all right?" Michelle asks, her forehead wrinkling with worry lines.

I shrug and sit in the makeup chair. I haven't said much the entire time, except to call her or Gabe a bitch when they yanked a strip of wax off my private parts. They've pretty much been doing all the talking while fighting over me like a piece of meat.

"It isn't so bad, you'll see." She smiles, grabbing some makeup from her black bag.

"You mean you've—"

"No, I wasn't an escort, but I've seen girls who were nervous at first, then a month later were in nothing but pure delight." She pauses in her step and smiles wide. "You'll see." She nods excitedly.

I give a kind smile in return, but I'm not nervous. I'm not sure *what* I am, but nervousness isn't one of the feelings I'm experiencing.

"I've seen women with some of the biggest celebrities around here getting their picture taken, going from nobody to somebody, all because of working here." Michelle's face widens as she rambles in excitement. "Do you know Ring Ryno?" she asks, opening some of the eye shadow containers.

"The actor?"

"Yes, him. He's one of the Blackwell clients, and he got one of the girls an acting job on the side of working here. She has a beautiful house and looks very happy, if you ask me." Michelle shrugs.

I look down at my hands and bite my cheek. *Is that supposed to make me feel better?* I didn't ask for fame, and I don't care for high profiles to swoon over. I just wanted to pay my rent, not feel so lonely, and be free. Have some control over my life. But in the end, I'm owned again. Only this time, it's not by the state. I'm owned by Landon Blackwell.

"Do you mind if I use the bathroom before we start makeup?" I question, turning in my chair to look at her. I need a moment alone, some fresh air maybe. I keep taking deep breaths, but I don't feel as if I'm getting any oxygen into my lungs.

"No, go right ahead. It's right across the stairs." Michelle smiles, setting the makeup down. I tighten the robe they gave me to wear after the hot lava of wax treatment and head toward the bathroom.

"I'm just on my way to get some apparel, Mr. Blackwell," echoes throughout the large house. I stop and peer over the banister, finding Landon stopping Gabe by the front door.

"How is she doing?" Landon questions, his hands in his pockets.

His tone is laced with care, like he might actually be worried about me. I frown, not sure what to make of it.

"Beautiful. She looks amazing," Gabe replies proudly.

"Hmm. I'm sure," Landon remarks, running a hand over the nape of his neck. He looks almost nervous, and it's kind of cute.

"I was thinking about getting a blue dress, or white, or maybe a short red dress with her dark hair—"

"Black." Landon blurts, looking down at the floor.

"I beg your pardon?" Gabe questions, his voice taking a tone of surprise.

"Get a black dress." Landon looks up at Gabe and shrugs. "Every woman should have a little black dress, isn't that how the saying goes?" Landon hesitates, as if he didn't mean to add his input.

"Uh, yeah. I will. I'll find a black dress." Gabe sounds almost confused, shocked that Landon offered any input on clothes.

Landon gives a firm nod before heading toward the stairs. I flinch and hide behind a pillar next to the banister, hoping he doesn't see me. After the front door closes, I risk a look and find Landon and Gabe gone. Landon must have gone to his office.

I let out a heavy breath and scamper off toward the bathroom, not entirely sure what I just witnessed. Is Landon treating me like crap because I'm his escort? He's trying to make me hate him, make it easier for him to walk away. Am I happy that it's not personal, or angry he's trying so hard?

CHARLIE

"Which one do you like better, Charlie? Black or red?" Gabe asks, holding up the two dresses. I take my gaze from the mirror, looking over the makeup Michelle just finished, to glance at the dresses.

My mouth hangs open when I see the black one. I stand from the chair and caress the material between my fingertips. The fabric is soft and new, no wear, stains or tears. It'll cup my shoulders perfectly, and it looks like the sleeves go to my elbows. It has a large V-neck that will reach well below my breasts, making me swallow hard. My eyes follow the material down, knowing it will rest on my ankles or lower.

"Landon himself asked for this color," Gabe announces, tossing the red toward the chair. I don't even know what the red dress looks like, and I don't care, either.

"He did?" Michelle questions, shocked.

"This one," I whisper, taking the black dress from its hanger.

"Here, take these, too." Gabe hands me a black thong and some black, strappy heels. I look at the heels, which are beautiful and weren't stolen. My eyes fill with tears at the things in my hands. I've never had something so nice before, and by the looks of these, so expensive.

"Are you okay, hun?" Gabe mutters, rubbing my back for comfort. I nod, smile, and drop my robe to try them on.

After I dress and pull my hair from my neck, I turn to look in the mirror.

My eyes widen as I take in a sudden breath. I look... stunning. My hair is curly, shiny, and smells of strawberries. My makeup is subtle, with some light blush, lip gloss and smoky eye shadow. The dress is snug, showing my curves to perfection. *I don't look like a Barbie. I look like Barbie's hot vixen cousin.*

I look over at Michelle and Gabe, giving each other high-fives.

"I'll find Landon for my next instructions," I state, leaving them behind in a giggling mess.

I head down the stairs, my hand trailing along the banister before turning toward Landon's office. My heart is beating a mile a minute, and my breathing comes in short spurts. I know I look good, and the bad girl in me wants to show it off, but my mind reminds me how Landon is a monster. He's made me his puppet, and he's the puppet master. I'm nothing but a figure to him in his pocket book. Just standing here outside his door, I can feel his strong energy from the other side, his smell making me second-guess whether or not he *is* a bad guy.

I don't even knock, just open the door and enter.

"What is it?" Landon questions, his head tilted down as he scribbles across something on his desk. I don't respond, just cat-walk to his desk and stand there, waiting for my next order.

Landon huffs and glances up, doing a double-take. His eyes go wide and his mouth parts.

"Charlie," he rasps.

"I'm…" I trail off, taken aback by his look of raw hunger. "I'm here for my next assignment," I manage to spit out.

Landon pushes from his desk and stalks toward me, his eyes on fire and devouring every inch of my body.

"That dress, it's perfect," he groans, looking me up and down shamelessly. My body heats, heart pounding dangerously as my stomach knots and panties dampen.

"Well, you know, every woman needs a little black dress," I remark nervously, looking at him from the corner of my eye.

He smirks knowingly. "That they do."

He steps behind me, his large hands resting on my shoulders, and my senses are consumed by the smell of him. He smells like fresh air and spice, causing me to close my eyes and inhale deeply. He brushes his nose up the side of my neck, the feeling of him touching me so intimate it smothers any morsel of resentment I have. I want to be mad, be a pain in the ass, but I'm sick. I'm fucked-up and just want to feel something, feel someone and not be isolated with the inevitable loneliness. If I've learned anything over the last few weeks, it's that only Landon has seemed to stifle that ache in my chest.

"What do you think you're doing?" I question, my words muffled from arousal. He doesn't respond, just caresses his lips along the sensitive skin of my neck seductively, causing my head to loll to the side. A rush of desire races through my chest, and my breathing picks up.

"We can't, remember? You're my pimp, and I'm you're escort. Rules," I whimper, reminding him of his words from last night.

He growls, the sound of his teeth grating. "Don't ever call me that," he rasps into my ear. The heat of his breath causes me to moan. He turns me around and picks me up, his fingers digging into my dress-cladded thighs.

"What if you're not my escort right now? No rules," he breathes heavily, placing me down on his desk.

"Like, pretending?" I question, digging my heels into his ass, pushing him closer.

"Exactly," he whispers, brushing my hair from my face. "Just two normal people."

"How do normal couples meet? What do ordinary people do when they're together?" I murmur, not having the first clue how a normal couple does things.

Landon slides his hands up each of my thighs, pushing my dress up quickly, revealing my smooth legs and thighs.

"We met on a golf course. I asked you out on a date," he mutters, his words drawn out and heavy with his harsh breathing as I undo his pants.

"I don't sleep with a guy until date number three," I inform him, my hands fisting his hard cock and pulling it free. My mouth parts when I see it. I forgot how big, how thick it is. He hisses through his teeth as I slide my fingers along his shaft.

"Two, because you couldn't resist me when I bought you some stupid necklace my shitty-paying job paid for," he grunts. His hand dips below my dress and pulls my thong to the side, swiping a finger between my wetness, causing me to buck against his hand with an uncontrollable urge.

"You're soaking," he sighs heavily. I am. My body doesn't respond to other guys like it does for Landon. He does something to me. Maybe it's because he's a prick. Maybe...

I spread my legs wide and grab him by the tie, pulling him toward me.

"Take me, Landon," I beg, my mouth parted to allow my harsh breathing to escape. I can't help my weakness for this man. He's a vast ocean of sex and sin, and I'm just along for the ride. His tide is unavoidable.

He darts his hand behind his back and pulls his wallet out. His fingers tug at a condom and he rips it open with his teeth, placing it along his impressive length.

My eyes flicker from his cock to his green eyes, my body warming with excitement. He smirks in arrogance, slides my thong to the side again, and grabs me by the ass cheeks with the other hand, plowing his hard cock into my heat. My body arches, my hands choking his tie as he growls out with intolerable need.

"Yes," I whisper, pleasure blossoming in the pit of my belly. All the air in my lungs vanishes with the breathtaking feeling of him deep inside me. This is what I needed, *who* I needed. When he's inside me, he puts all the shattered pieces of my life back together. I can't figure out for the life of me why I'm so drawn to him, but at this moment, I don't give a fuck.

He thrusts into me again, a guttural moan leaving his lips as he picks up the pace. I close my eyes and allow the sensation of something other than pain, more than rock-bottom taking hold of my senses.

"Kiss me," I moan seductively. I pull on his tie, bringing his lips to mine. As soon as they find purchase, my world explodes with feeling. His tongue seeks mine with greed, and I accept with a craving so hungry it will never be satisfied. Not with Landon.

I nibble on his bottom lip when he tries to pull away, bringing him back for one last taste. His palms graze the inside of my thigh,

causing me to hiss with satisfaction. They sweep upward, his thumb finding my clit. He gives it a hard swirl, and that's it for me. My eyes snap shut as I'm thrown into oblivion. My body thrusts uncontrollably and I spasm beneath him. My foot kicks the phone off the desk. I whimper, the pleasure borderline painful. He takes his hand from between my legs and grabs me by the ass cheeks hard, pounding into me as he roars with his release.

I pant for air, him still inside me as we both come down from our high, the sounds of our harsh breathing filling the silent room. He pulls his cock from me, causing shivers to race up my back.

He glances at me and swipes his thumb along his bottom lip.

I push my dress down and hop off his desk, the room strained with our silence.

A knock sounds at the door that has Landon shoving himself back into his pants quickly.

"Have you seen— Oh, there you are." Veronica glares at me. "I was looking for you," she remarks, crossing her arms.

"Here I am," I reply, brushing my hair down.

"Yes, yes, you are," she murmurs, arching a brow at me. "You clean up well." She smiles, but her snarky-ass tone contradicts the expression.

"I take it the paperwork is filled out?" She looks around me, searching for Landon.

"I'll take care of it, Veronica," Landon clips, sitting in his chair. I bite my cheek, remembering that damn paperwork. I don't want to fill it out, considering it's the last nail trapping my freedom in a coffin.

"Yes, I'm sure you will," she sneers, turning to leave.

"We're done for the day. We'll pick up with the paperwork tomorrow." Landon doesn't even look up at me, just resumes the paperwork on his desk. I bite my lip, my chest feeling the pinch of his cold tone. He'd do anything to get me out of here right now, which stings. I close my eyes and think about Jayden.

"Is there any way I can go home on the weekend, or see Jayden?" I question, peering up from under my lashes at Landon.

Landon flicks his gaze to mine, his jaw clenched.

"I'll have Osborn give her a cell phone paid for by the company, so if she wishes to come by anytime, or speak to you, she can." He picks up the phone on his desk, breaking eye contact. It's not entirely what I was hoping for, but it'll have to do. I nod, accepting his offer.

"Can you get Charlie a room in the east wing, please? Yes, the east." He hangs up and turns back to me.

"That will be all, Charlie. A housekeeper will meet you at the stairs to show you to your room. Try and get some sleep; you have a big day tomorrow." My lip curls with disgust. Disgust with myself. He acts like he cares, that he wants me undeniably so when he's fucking me. But as soon as he pulls his dick from me, I feel like an expensive ho.

I spin toward the door and hold my head high.

"You might want to take that condom off," I sneer as I'm leaving.

I head toward the stairs, where I find Veronica standing at the bottom step, her arms crossed.

"Charlie," Veronica greets. It sounds as if she's speaking of some disease that kills innocent people rather than my name.

"Let me give you a piece of advice. Stay away from Landon. You think you're the only whore he's showed any interest in? Do yourself and me a favor and keep your legs closed. I don't want to have to find another slut to replace you when Landon can't stand

to look at you." She arches an eyebrow and pops her hip out.

"Whatever you think is going on—"

"Don't try and lie to me. I know what I walked in on, and his father would kill him if he found out. If I find you two together again, I'll make sure not even Mick will take you back when I throw your ass out onto the streets." She narrows her eyes in anger as I bite my bottom lip, rage flowing through me like a steady poison. *I'm so sick of being told what to do, and how to do it.* Just as I open my mouth to tell Veronica what I think of her, she stomps past me, her heels clicking against the floor as she heads off into another room.

"Charlie?" I turn around, finding a short, black-haired woman in a maid outfit.

"Yes," I mutter.

"I'm Jean. This way, please." She smiles and walks up the stairs slowly. "And don't worry about Veronica. Nobody likes her," the housekeeper huffs as she climbs another stair.

"Is she Landon's ex-girlfriend or something?" I ask. The way Veronica got so possessive over him, I can only guess there's some kind of connection between the two.

"No. Landon's father, Miller, got remarried to Tara, and Veronica is Tara's daughter from another marriage," she explains, finally reaching the top step.

"So they are—"

"Brother and sister," she smiles, heading east. My head nearly explodes with the information. *Does Veronica want in Landon's pants?* But then again, look at Landon. If he were *my* stepbrother, I'd still be just as attracted to him.

"Here you are. There's a phone in your room if you need anything. Or you can ask Landon." She points to a door all the way down the hall.

"Landon stays in the east wing, too?" I ask, looking at the door. It sits all the way at the end, by itself. There isn't a door near it except mine.

"Yes. I'm surprised he has you down here and not in the west wing where all of the girls stay." She shrugs and turns to leave.

My eyes flutter with the information as I inhale deeply. *Why did Landon want me so close? Is this a game to him? My feelings, my emotions, my life?*

"Do the other girls live here, too?" I question, still looking at his door.

"They come and go," she informs me. I tear my eyes from Landon's door finally and find a bright-eyed Jean looking back at me.

"Goodnight, Charlie." Jean smiles.

"Night," I whisper, my eyes trailing back to Landon's door. I wonder what his room looks like. *Is it just a room, or does it look like a house? Is he a slob, or very clean?*

I shake my head and open the door to my room.

A large canopy bed sits in the middle, white and black sheer fabric hanging off it elegantly, and a huge, white comforter is placed perfectly on the bed. I gaze along the grayish walls, finding expensive paintings of half-naked people and a floor-to-ceiling window covering the entire back wall. A dresser and armoire are made out of the same dark color wood as the bed. *This room is overwhelming, so many nice things.*

Removing my dress, I kick off my heels and climb into the plush bed. I pull the covers over my head, hiding myself from the world, from myself. I take advantage of the expensive thread count surrounding me and cuddle close with the fine fabric. I'm so

Relinquish

confused. I thought I could fight my attraction toward Landon, but I can't shake the pull I have toward him. If I'm being honest, though, a piece of myself wants to be here with Landon. The moments he looks at me like I'm his world, and the way his fingers pull toward me when he's near... it's all surreal.

But the way he acts as if I'm his stars one moment and then the dirt on his shoe all in a blink of an eye, I know I shouldn't feel anything but resentment toward him. *What is wrong with me?*

LANDON

I toss the condom in the trash and zip my pants. My heart drums against my chest and my forehead sweats. *I just fucked her.* I close my eyes and pinch the bridge of my nose. The way she looked in that black dress, though, it was like watching a black panther prowl into my chambers. Something possessive and dominant escaped me without me even acknowledging it.

I blow out an irritated breath and lift from my seat, the smell of her and sex prominent in the air. I grab a tumbler and pour some scotch. Lifting the glass to my lips, my fingers brush against my nose, giving away the sweet smell of her pussy. I grit my teeth and throw the glass against the wall in a sea of rage. *She hasn't been here five minutes and I've already managed to fuck this up. I need to stick to the plan, to the mission at hand and gain some damn control.* I've never been so affected by a woman in my life; it bewilders me and pisses me off all at the same time. I need to get a hold of myself and remember what Charlie's place is here at the estate. I close my eyes, knowing that's going to be a hurdle. One

172

I'm not sure I can leap.

"Sir?" I turn quickly, finding Jean red-faced and eyes wide. "Is everything okay? Do you want me to clean that up?" She points to the wall with pieces of glass and scotch dripping down it.

"No, Jean. I'll get it, dear," I reply softly, my ball of rage slowly lifting from the nervous state she's in. She's been here since I was a boy. I respect her, especially because if I ever disrespected her growing up, my mother would slap me upside the head. She nods and ducks out of the office.

I stride over to my seat and sit, rubbing my temples to cure the ache that resides in my head. I could compare the pain to dehydration, and the only thing to quench my thirst is Charlie.

"Charlie, you are going to destroy me," I mumble, staring at my desk which showcases two perfectly round butt cheek prints from where Charlie was sitting.

CHARLIE

"Time to wake up!" Jean hollers, dragging me from my deep sleep.

I pull the sea of blankets from my face, finding Jean yanking open the curtains to let in the blinding sun.

I groan and roll over.

"Wake up. Wake up!" she yells, grabbing the blanket and pulling it off my warm body. A cold breeze rushes up my legs, causing goose bumps. I curl into myself for warmth and scowl at Jean.

"Breakfast." She points to the end table next to the bed. I follow her finger to a stack of pancakes and OJ. The smell of hot, buttery

pancakes lights the wick to my appetite and my stomach growls.

"When you're finished, you're to meet Landon in his office. Here are some more of the clothes Gabe bought you, as well." She points to a bunch of bags next to the bathroom door. My eyes widen at the shopping bags with designer names printed on the sides. I didn't know they bought me a whole new wardrobe.

"Thank you, Jean," I mutter, rolling over for the plate of food.

After I eat and shower, I start pulling clothes from bags. I find some black slacks and a white blouse and put them on along with some gray heels before leaving my room.

I look down the hall at Landon's door and sigh heavily. I have to be strong today, build my wall of defense or Landon will cause me to self-destruct from the inside out. I close my eyes. *Why? Why does he affect me so much?* I barely know him, yet my heart and body throb for him like a lifeline. Like I'm a sinking ship, and he's the only one to save me from anchoring myself into the depths of no return.

I head toward the stairs, finding an older man and Veronica standing at the bottom talking. The man has pepper-colored hair and is wearing black dress pants and a white button-up shirt.

I take a step on the stairs, and it catches their attention.

"This is the new girl," Veronica informs sweetly, her tone surprising me. But then again, I'm guessing the man is her stepdad, so she's probably kissing his ass for something she wants. I cock my head to the side, not really sure what it is she does here to begin with.

The man squints, and his mouth slightly opens as he takes me in. "Is it now?" he questions, his voice cracking with age. A shiver races up my spine from his tone of voice, and my heart picks up its pace, causing my head to spin. I freeze at my body's reaction.

Taking a large breath, trying to calm myself, I head down the stairs, mustering a smile at both of them.

"I'm Charlie." I hold my hand out to shake his.

"Charlie, I'm Miller." He accepts my hand and shakes it, his eyes still taking me in. My palm goes ice cold when he touches it, but I'm not sure if my reaction is from his touch or his voice.

My temples throb, making my vision sway. I feel like a little kid meeting the monster beneath her bed for the first time. I can't breathe, can't focus. I take a deep breath, not sure why I'm reacting the way I am. I blink, trying to clear my thoughts before finding Miller looking right at me. His face is lined with wrinkles, and he has bags under his eyes. I tilt my head to the side, lost in the light-green orbs. His voice... it sounds familiar.

"There you are." I slowly take my eyes from Miller to find Landon scowling at me, his hands in his suit pockets. He looks good, as usual. His dark hair is combed back, his toned body trying to rip through the material of his suit. Just by walking into the room, his body demands a powerful presence.

"This is the new girl, huh?" Miller asks, finally breaking his gaze with me for Landon.

"It is." Landon nods.

"Miller, baby!" I look up the stairs and find a woman with dirty-blonde hair rushing down the steps. She's wearing a white nightie and an untied champagne-colored robe.

She flies past me and wraps herself around Miller, the smell of her perfume causing me to gasp for air. She looks to be in her mid-thirties, and Miller looks to be in his sixties. The age gap is large and has me thinking she's a gold digger. *Not that I'm one to talk about being with men for money.*

"You said you would be right back," she pouts, trailing a

manicured finger along his jawline. He looks down at the woman and gives a wrinkled smirk.

"I was just meeting our new girl. Tara, this is Charlie" He squints and cocks his head to the side, hitting me with that conflicted stare again.

"Oh, hello. I'm Tara," she greets, her voice high-pitched.

"Hi." I smile. My back breaks out in a nervous sweat, feeling Miller staring at me. I don't need to see that he's looking at me. I can just feel it.

"We have paperwork to do, Charlie," Landon clips. I sigh in relief, actually thankful for that damn paperwork for once.

"Yes, well, I won't keep you." Miller gives a tight-lipped smile before heading past me with Tara close to his side. He glances over his shoulder, a look of confusion on his face as he and Tara make their way upward.

"Want to go for a swim, lover?" Tara asks him, bringing his attention back to her. She trails her hand along his neck and down the back of his shirt, revealing a few inches of skin. Tattooed skin.

"Charlie?" I hesitantly break my stare from Miller as he and Tara round the stairs to Landon who is looking at me with furrowed brows.

"I'm coming," I mumble, looking back up the stairs to where Miller just left. Lost as to why my body races with dread when our eyes met.

CHARLIE

"Please sit." Landon directs his hand toward the chair in front of his desk.

I comply, crossing my legs and sighing loudly. *I'm so ready to get this over with.*

"Rules are as follows," Landon remarks, tapping his fingers on the desk, his other hand in his pocket. "You are to come to me every day for your agenda of clients." Landon adjusts his tie and sits in his chair. "You will not receive any payment; that's something I take care of beforehand. You are to make sure your clients wear protection at all times, and our doctor will be placing you on birth control when your test results have come back," Landon rambles, as if he's reading a list of rules off a piece of paper.

I nod, but all I'm really focusing on is the gorgeous green tree he has outside his window. *Fresh air. I feel like I haven't been outside in forever.*

"If you are to escort a client to a function, you are to keep quiet

unless spoken to. You are not the center of attention; the client is. Understood?" Landon's voice is serious and stern, making me turn my gaze from the tree to him.

"Yeah," I mutter, blinking rapidly to clear my thoughts of fresh air. He lowers his head and raises a brow at me, and I shrug and look away. I'm not sure what he wants from me. Hearing how you are to behave like an object and not a human, it's breaking. But to show that emotion, he'll just play off it, use my weakness as his power.

"Money. What you make will determine what you receive. But since you live here now, I don't see money being a problem for you anymore. You'll have anything you ever need."

I roll my eyes and stare off.

"In that case, I'd like to send what I make to Jayden." I cross my arms and sit back in my seat. Landon's face takes on a softness, his lips parting with a look of shock. It's like he's surprised I would just give my money to Jayden. But if I have everything I need here, why make Jayden work in a dirty motel room for money, when I can just give her my earnings? I don't need it.

He shakes his head, as if he's clearing his thoughts, and slides a packet of papers across the desk to me. I arch a brow at him and lean forward to collect them and a pen.

"This is just some information for our records," Landon explains. I look over the papers and notice it asks for name, health history, medications, and if I'm a drug abuser. I fill out the paperwork, starting with the question of any previous STDs or pregnancies, and if I have any family around the area. My eyes widen a little when I come to the question asking me for my number of sexual partners.

"Um, why do you need to know how many men I've slept with?"

My eyes flicker from the paper to Landon.

"To know how experienced you are," he answers, rubbing his scruffy chin with his fingers.

"You've slept with me twice, what do *you* think?" I tilt my head to the side and squint in questioning. I notice the corner of Landon's lip twitch, trying to keep from smiling.

"I think– It doesn't matter what I think." Landon stumbles on his words, causing me to laugh silently.

I sigh and resume filling it out.

"How many?" Landon mutters softly.

"How many what?" I respond, lost answering the next set of intrusive questions.

"How many men have you slept with?" he asks, his tone deep. I take my eyes from the paperwork and find Landon looking at me closely. His hard stare pins me, causing my heart to beat rapidly. I close my eyes and bite my bottom lip.

"Three. I've slept with three men," I murmur. I risk a glance at Landon; his strong jaw is clenched and his face takes on a shade of red. He stands and runs his hand through his hair, staring out the window behind his desk.

"Just finish the paperwork," he rasps. I swallow the lump in my throat and finish the last question before sliding it back on his desk.

"Terrific," Landon remarks. He turns and sits, his face unreadable as he takes the paperwork.

"This is a contract, saying what is expected of you as an escort and how long your term at the Blackwell Estate is for. It lists a minimum of two years, and at the end of the two years, we re-evaluate the time you have spent with us and decide if you should be let go, or if renegotiating another two years is in everyone's

best interest." I get the impression there's a but at the end of all this by his sly smile.

"But?" I encourage.

"But that is for someone who wasn't traded, or owned by the Blackwell Estate, so it would be pointless to sign it." He shreds the contract and tosses it to the side. I take in a sudden breath as I stare at the torn document. It's nothing but ink and paper, but it held the fate of me possibly being free at some point. Him tearing it, telling me there is no out, wasn't necessary. He did it to remind me of where I stand with him: powerless.

My soul was ripped from my chest just like he ripped the paper. *Is he being a prick because he's really a prick, or is it because he's jealous I slept with other men?* Maybe this has to do with why he became so cold after we had sex yesterday? I close my eyes, trying to fight the emotions racing up my spine.

"Are we done?" I ask before standing, my pulse drumming so hard in my temples my vision blurs.

"I'm sorry?" Landon leans back in his chair, looking at me with that smug-looking smirk.

"Are we done? I would like a client already. I would like to go to work now, make a living!" I shout, losing control of my anger. I need to feel. I need to feel wanted, cared for, anything but the gut-wrenching hurt I'm dealt when I'm around Landon, when he treats me like dirt.

"Hardly," he replies drily. I scoff and turn around, trying to get ahold of myself. *How can he be so warm, so alive when he's inside of me, but turn cold the very next moment?*

"Are you going to talk to me about last night?" I mutter, turning back around and slamming my hands on the desk. My hair falls over my face in my rage.

"Why would I?" Landon sits up straight in his chair and steeples his hands.

"*Why would you*? Why *wouldn't* you?" I sneer, my face twisted with annoyance.

"Because nothing happened," he states, striking my heart with a vengeance.

I clench my teeth, close my eyes and seethe, "I'm pretty sure—"

"It won't happen again!" Landon roars, making me jump. He straightens his tie, gathering his composure.

"You are far from being ready for any of our clients with that loose mouth of yours, and I still need to get the test results back from our doctor. God knows what you've fucked." Landon's face scrunches with disgust. My nostrils flare with rage, pissed we're back to him treating me like some common whore.

"That didn't stop you from screwing me yesterday, did it?" I jeer, glowering at him.

Landon stands, placing his hands on his desk as he leans over. The powerful, 'take charge' vibe radiates off his confident stance.

"You—"

The door to the office is thrown open, and Veronica walks in. "Mr. Harron is ready!" she cheers, clapping her hands excitedly, a stupid train of a red dress falling behind her.

"Great. Take her!" Landon sits in his chair and throws his hands at me to dismiss me.

•••

I groan while looking down at the bowl of salad, the forks and spoons of all sizes setting around the placemat. A tall man wearing a butler-looking outfit paces in front of the table. His black hair is

balding, causing the lights from above to glow off his scalp. His hands are tucked behind his back as he sticks his large nose into the air. He looks like a snob for short, and the way he keeps staring at me with disdain, I can tell he doesn't think highly of me.

"It's all about size, Charlie," Harron starts. I nearly snort with that statement. "The smaller of the two forks is for the salad. The larger, the dinner fork," he instructs. I nod, grab the fork and dive into the luscious-looking greens.

He turns and groans, pinching the bridge of his nose.

"Close your mouth when you chew. You sound like a cow," he mutters, rolling his eyes.

I close my mouth, wiping away dressing that trickled down my chin. My face turns into a permanent frown from his harsh tone.

"Sorr—"

"No elbows!" He points to my elbows sitting on the table, his brows narrowed in anger.

"Okay, chill out," I murmur, taking my elbows from the table. *This guy is starting to piss me off.*

"Don't speak with your mouth open. You disgust me." He tilts his head to the side, eyeing me as if I have grown two heads. My eyes go wide, shocked at his amount of hatred toward me. There's no reason for him to speak so ill of me. I close my mouth and swallow my food, staring at him while my anger fuels my fury.

"Where did the Blackwells pick you up from? I mean—"

"That is *it*!" I stand and throw the stupid napkin, which I had to re-adjust perfectly in my lap thirty times before I got it just right, into the salad.

"Screw you! I'm done!" I shout, walking out of the dining room. I will *not* sit here and be talked down to. I won't feel any less of a human than I already do. Landon is one thing; he holds my fate here. But this pompous ass can go to Hell.

"You get back here, right now. I have never had anyone leave one of my training sessions!" Harron grabs my upper arm, halting me just outside the door. His face is flustered and red, and his nose is making a whistling sound from his heavy breathing.

"Well, it's happening now," I seethe, trying to pull his fingers from my arm.

"You are trying to make a fool of me in front of the Blackwells and I won't allow it," Harron threatens, tightening his grip on my arm.

"You're hurting my arm," I grit between my teeth, my voice wavering from the pain.

"Do you think you're special? I have news for you. You're nothing," he sneers, lifting his nose into the air.

"You have about two seconds to let go of my arm," I threaten right back, fisting my other hand.

He laughs, holding a tone of mockery. "You despicable whore," Harron insults. "I'm the man here, honey. What could you possibly do?"

Just as I'm about to swing my fist, a flash races past me and a loud smack echoes through the hall. Harron instantly falls to the ground with a loud thud. I glance from a passed-out Harron up to a red-faced Landon, holding his fist and glowering at Harron. My eyes grow heavy with realization that Landon just came to my defense.

Landon turns and raises his brows. "Are you okay? Did he hurt you?" Landon looks me over, squinting with worry.

"I- yeah, I'm okay," I stutter, trying to get a hold over what exactly just happened.

"He shouldn't have ever talked to you like that, Charlie." Landon

shakes his head, looking down at Harron. I arch my brows and laugh. *Is he serious? The way* Harron *talked to me?*

"Him? Have you heard the way *you* talk to me?" Landon's eyes trail to mine, his brows slanting downward and causing two small wrinkles to form between them. He opens his mouth to say something but quickly closes it and turns. He rubs the back of his neck, his head tilted down as if he's thinking.

He whips his head around and looks at me with such intensity it has me shifting on my feet.

"I- You don't understand. I—" Landon begins but is cutoff.

"Landon, what is this?" Miller questions, looking over the banister. We both look up at Miller who is quickly making his way down the stairs to inspect the scene. My body instantly grows cold again. I cross my arms, an act of protecting myself.

"Harron is fired. He is unethical and put his hands on Charlie," Landon informs his father, his tone serious. He looks more collected, as well, not so frazzled.

Miller finds his way to us, looking Harron over before his light green eyes find mine, causing the shrill of panic to bloom in the pit of my stomach. I quickly look away, breaking eye contact. *I don't know what it is about this guy, but my body goes into a state of alarm every time I'm around him.*

"I see. Are you all right?" Miller questions.

"Fine," I mutter.

"Did you do something to anger him?" Miller proceeds. I look at him, my mouth parted in shock. Landon's head snaps to his father so quickly I think it may twist off.

"Excuse me?" Landon sneers, glaring at his father.

"I'm just pointing out that Harron has been around for years without incident."

"I'm in charge, not you! Not anymore. I said he's fired, end of discussion!" Landon bellows, pointing his finger in Miller's face. Miller takes in a deep breath and glares at me with accusing eyes before walking away.

I shrink against the wall from his intensity.

"Very well," he grumbles, making his way back up the stairs.

•••

Looking out the window of my room, I notice a large cage off to the west. I chew on my cheek, wondering what's in it. My curiosity getting the best of me, I leave my room and head toward it. At the bottom of the stairs, on the opposite side of Landon's office, I find big double doors leading off the back of the house, and exit. The smell of fresh air makes me stop to inhale its crisp scent. A smile creeps on my face as I make my way toward the cage.

Getting closer, I notice the cage is actually an exhibit, like you would see at the zoo. There are gilded bars where I stand, but further back it goes into a concrete housing where whatever animal is in here can escape from the open. Looking around the exhibit, I notice lots of trees and thick ropes, a couple of tire swings, and a hammock hanging. I furrow my brows, not sure what was, or is, in here.

Movement catches my eye near the back, and my mouth parts.

"Is that a—"

"Gorilla." I look over and see Landon standing next to me. I didn't hear him walk over here I was so lost in the exhibit. My eyes catch his hand, noticing his knuckles are bleeding.

"You should wrap that up." I lift my chin toward his injured hand. Landon glances down and flexes it.

"It's fine," he mutters. I smirk, his bad-boy attitude a complete turn-on.

"That's Jaheem. He doesn't like anyone," Landon explains, pointing toward the primate. Landon looks like a child right now as he watches Jaheem stretch and yawn. My eyes dart to where Jaheem came from, and I find another gorilla walking out.

"That's Ebele. She's a lush for a treat." Landon laughs and I echo it, watching the two apes wake up lazily.

The two apes hold hands and walk toward us.

"Awww," I coo.

I lift up on my toes, excitement building as they come to us. I catch Landon looking at me from the corner of my eye. When I turn, I find him smiling, an unreadable expression on his face, but one that makes my heart pound harder.

The apes stand in front of the bars, just inches from us. I'm shocked at how close they are. Their fur is the blackest of black, matching their eyes. Jaheem is muscled and toned, with a little bit of silver coloring around his ears. Ebele is rounder and chunky, with silver along her neck.

"Hey, Ebele," Landon greets, putting his arms through the bars to touch her. Ebele gets excited, her mouth parted while she shifts from foot to foot as Landon holds her hand. My heart just explodes. To see Landon show such care and love toward an animal, I know there's more to his story. This right here, and the man he was in the hotel that night, *that* is the real Landon.

I smile and look over at Jaheem, who is staring at me intently, tilting his head back and forth as he looks at me curiously. I don't break eye contact but just smile at him, letting him know I'm friendly. He thrusts his fists into the ground and closes the gap between him and the bars. His quick movement and size has me flinch backwards as he grasps the bars and brings his face to them. I look at Landon, confused if I should pet him or not. Landon's face is scrunched in confusion, as well, little wrinkles forming on his forehead.

"I've never seen him do that before. He won't come to anyone." Landon shakes his head like he can't believe it. I take a deep breath and slowly raise my hand to touch Jaheem. My heart beats wildly against my chest as I move closer. I close my eyes and push my hand forward, caressing the soft fur. I open my eyes and find Jaheem has closed his, enjoying my touch.

"Holy shit," Landon mutters. I give an uncontrollable laugh and deepen my petting.

"Hey, buddy, I'm a little offended," Landon jokes, walking up beside me. Jaheem opens his eyes and peers up at Landon before taking off toward Ebele.

"I come out here several times a day, see them to bed, give them treats and toys, and his ass never comes to me. I always have to leave his things for him to collect when I'm gone," Landon explains, watching Jaheem preen Ebele.

"They're magnificent," I admire. I grip the bars, watching Jaheem show love and care to Ebele. They look truly in love with the way Ebele looks up at Jaheem as he picks at her fur. They are letting out little noises back and forth, talking to each other, lost in their own world. I furrow my brows, looking at their surroundings.

"They should be free," I mutter. I look at Landon for his reaction, and notice him sigh and run his hands through his hair.

"I agree. I'm working on it." He exhales. "My grandfather got them from a circus years back. My grandmother didn't like the way they were being treated, so he just bought them off the guy.

As much as I don't want to see them go, they deserve to be free. I've been looking for the right home for a couple years now," Landon admits, putting his hands in his pockets. "I want them to have something big and deserving. Not something where someone throws some slop their way twice a day." He shrugs and looks at me.

I nod in agreement and look back at the gorillas. "They have programs where they can teach them how to survive on their own, don't they?" I ask.

Landon nods. "Yes, they do, and I've called a few people. I'm waiting for a call back is all."

I smile.

Jaheem is leaning over and pressing his lips to Ebele, who is smiling and communicating with him. I can't help but laugh. I catch Landon staring at me from the corner of my eye. I bite my bottom lip and turn, finding him still staring at me. A look of endearment crosses his face as his upper lip curls into a smirk.

"What?" I ask, trying to get a handle on my giggling.

"You. That laugh, it's..." He pauses, swipes his tongue across his lips, and looks back at the gorillas. "It's something else." My cheeks heat, as does the rest of my body. My heart, once cold and questionably dead, is warming and growing with need. The worst part is it's because of Landon, who has the potential to rip it from my chest and make it to where I'm dead to anyone following his footsteps.

Looking back at Jaheem and Ebele, he has her cradled in his lap, still trying to kiss her. They look so lost in one another, and I'm jealous. I want that.

"They seem to have it all figured it out," I mutter weakly.

"What?" Landon grabs the bars, his hands brushing against

mine and causing a tingle to spread to my toes. I don't move my hand, just leave it next to his and take my gaze toward him. He looks at me as if he might feel the same pull I do.

"Love."

Landon's face softens, his eyes holding a fire behind them as he stares at me. I watch his Adam's apple bob as he swallows and turns his head back to the primates, his profile hardening and jaw clenching.

"There is no such thing as love. Not here," he rasps. "Love is an amateur term to diagnose one's affection for another. In reality, we're all animals, and that so-called love is just us wanting to reproduce. To fuck. Love has nothing to do with it."

I sigh heavily. At one time, I would've said Landon was right, but I'm not so sure anymore. There's a difference between the throbbing between your legs and the longing in your chest.

"I refuse to believe that," I whisper.

Landon's head whips in my direction and he smirks. "Oh, yeah? Are you one of those 'love fixes everything' kind of girls?" he jokes.

I laugh. "No, quite the opposite actually. I'm just talking about those old couples who sit on the porch and hold hands throughout the day. Or a husband who sits by his wife's grave day after day after losing her from some terrible incident. They don't need to fuck. They care about each other. They love each other."

Landon worries his bottom lip between his teeth as he sucks in a breath. His eyes narrow in a way I've never seen before. Almost like he's confused, yet intrigued.

"Well, I've never seen it."

LANDON

I pour myself another scotch and sit in my chair. I'm... confused, but that word doesn't even come close to what I'm feeling. Tormented, depraved, outraged. I feel insane from all the mixed emotions cocooning themselves in my head and chest.

"Do you know what Father and Veronica were just talking about?" Roman flies through my office door, his hair disheveled and, of course, his shirt is untucked.

"No, what?" I ask, uninterested, but I know he's going to tell me anyway. Might as well amuse him.

"You and Charlie. Father says you're taking interest in this escort and he doesn't like it. Veronica said it was all Charlie, that she's some whore seeking love. I- I—" Roman stutters, pacing my floors frantically. Roman is afraid of our father. Miller was a very powerful man at one time, well-respected around Vegas. I once was scared, too, but then I grew up and realized my father is just some old man. He's served his term and is dead-weight now.

"Let them believe whatever they want. Harron shouldn't have touched Charlie. I was doing my job," I defend, downing the rest of my drink. There are cameras in a few places of the estate, one being the dining room with all the fine china we have in there. I saw how he was talking to her, and it was pissing me off. But when the hall cameras showed Harron grabbing onto her like that, I lost all control.

"You fucking punched him, Landon. Are you kidding me right now?"

I swirl my drink, lost in the amber color.

"Are you listening to me?" Roman slams his hands on my desk, grabbing my attention and angering me. I set my drink down and clench my jaw.

"You tell Father that I was doing my job, which is protecting the escorts. The women come first. If it weren't for them, this place wouldn't be here," I seethe, my teeth gritted. When my father was sitting in this chair, the simple principle of making the women come first was never in his line of sight. I aim to redeem that.

Roman chuckles, the sound of his laugh a mockery to my anger.

"Have you given her any clients?" Roman crosses his arms and stares at me.

"She's in training." I exhale an irritated breath.

"You should be working her a list of potential clients." Roman runs his hand through his hair and chuckles.

"She's not ready," I reply.

"She *looks* ready, Landon," Roman insists, nodding for emphasis.

"I've seen girls come through here for years, Roman. They all have this dead look to them, their eyes don't shine, and their smiles don't quite reach their eyes. They'll do anything you ask of

them, and don't react in any way to the manner you speak to them."

"But?" Roman interrupts. I take my eyes from my empty scotch glass and look at Roman.

"But when I look at Charlie, *really* look at her, she's not quite dead inside."

"You better get her there, and quick. I destroyed the files of the men Father had follow you. Nobody will be able to place Charlie. But Landon, I can only do so much before you blow your own fucking house down." Roman shakes his head and leaves, slamming the door behind him.

I let out a large breath and turn in my chair, looking out at the landscaping. It could be said that I hate my father. I didn't always hate him, though. Leaving my mother to die alone was the turning point in our father/son relationship. He was shitty to my mother for years before that, but nothing compared to him deserting her when she needed him the most. She was diagnosed with aggressive cancer five years ago, and because he couldn't bear her chemo, to watch her body die a little day by day, he sent her to California. Put her in a house with some doctors to die alone. I visited every weekend, but it was only Roman and I who ever went to see her.

Two weeks after my mother's funeral, my father moved Tara in with her slutty daughter Veronica. He met Tara at a fundraiser for cancer, funny enough. Disgust builds in my chest thinking about how he banked off my mother's illness, when in reality he was wishing she'd just die already. My mother passed away not long after her diagnosis.

I haven't left this estate because of a promise I gave my mother, and Charlie stands in the way of that promise. It's conflicting. I want Charlie, but I can't break my only promise to my mother. I need to get Charlie clients, and it's going to kill what's left of me to do so.

CHARLIE

I slip out of bed and tiptoe toward my door. It's late and everyone should be asleep by now, giving me the perfect opportunity to find some answers. I open my door and slowly close it, hoping not to make any noise. I look up and down the hall before I resume my mission toward Landon's office. I'm not sure what I'm looking for, but I need something. Every expensive painting, every closed door, it all leads to secrets. I can feel it.

I scamper down the stairs and head to Landon's office. I don't notice any lights on under the door so I open it, finding it empty. Running to his desk, I start opening drawers, my palms sweating nervously. I find paperwork on other escorts and their earnings. My eyes turn as wide as saucers seeing some woman named Clarity made ten thousand just last week, and that isn't even the highest number I've come across on the chart. I close it and open the next drawer, finding a gun. I gasp and stare at it. My legs begin to tremble, and my mouth parts. *Why does he have a gun?* I've never seen a gun before. I slowly close it and open the last drawer, containing receipts, menus for takeout, and a map.

I loll my head back and sigh. *What was I thinking? That Landon would just hide all of the estate's dirty secrets right here in his unlocked desk?* I slam the drawer shut angrily, wincing at the noise it causes. My back begins to sweat with nerves, scared the loud bang caused unwanted attention. I run out of the office, up the stairs and back to my room, my heart racing faster and faster with every step. As soon as I make it into my room, I shut the door and slide against the back of it till my bottom hits the floor, my body heaving for air.

I got nothing. I clench my hands in my hair. Landon having a gun goes to show this place is not as top-notch as he makes it seem.

•••

"Time to wake up, Charlie." A blossoming warmth ignites in my chest as the deep voice wakes me. I roll over, a small smile across my face as I open my eyes and find Landon hovering over me with a smirk. My face falls, and I groan in irritation.

"I got you a client for tonight. You need to train today."

"A client?" I ask, sitting up.

"I have someone who needs a female appearance tonight at a gala. Therefore, you will need to learn to dance." Landon sits at the end of the bed, adjusting his blue tie. He looks so big sitting at the foot of the bed, it makes me feel small. The smell of him is so alluring, I'm forced to clench my legs. Luckily, they're under the blanket so he can't see them and call me out on it.

"So, I'm arm candy?" I twist my face in question.

"Yes. No sex. Now, find a beautiful dress and meet me in the ballroom." Landon stands with a panty-dropping smile. I sag in relief, glad I'm not sleeping with anyone for money. A small, naïve piece inside me is hoping Landon is taking his time training me on purpose. I know that same small piece is what's going to get me hurt in the end, too.

"Wait, meet *you*?" I ask in shock.

"Considering my last trainer had his nose broken, yes, you will be training with me." Landon turns and rests both hands behind his neck, a devious grin across his face as he leaves.

My God, he's going to be the end of me.

•••

I slide a white dress down my frame, the bottom of it skirting around my ankles with a small, brown braided belt secured around my waist. I flip open some boxes, find a pair of heels that match the color of the belt, and slip them on. The smell of new shoes is amazing. I never knew shoes even *had* a brand new smell. I head toward the door when the phone rings, making me jump and grab my chest in panic.

"Shit," I mutter, taking the phone from the night stand and answering it.

"Hello?"

"Hey!" Jayden greets.

"Hey, how are you?" I question, a smile on my face. It feels so good to hear her voice. It's only been a few days, but I miss her.

"I'm doing good." Jayden's voice cracks with emotion.

"How's everything going?" I ask, sitting down on the bed.

"Good, I guess. You?"

I sigh, looking at the door, thinking of Landon and my place at the estate.

"I'm trying to settle in," I mutter. I *am* trying, but it can be difficult. My emotions for Landon interfere with the reality of my situation.

"I woke to some men in suits delivering me a beautiful short

green dress and an invite to the Blackwell Estate for a party to-night. It was from Landon," Jayden informs. My mouth parts in surprise at the information. *The gala! It's here, and I get to see Jayden.* It's acts like this that tell me he's not the bad guy he wants everyone to think he is.

"I'm asking Mick for the night off. I just hope he lets me," Jayden mutters.

"Oh, you *have* to come, I haven't seen you in forever," I beg, my face scrunched while I plead.

Jayden giggles. "I'll see what I can do," she promises.

"Yes! I can't wait," I cheer, nearly bouncing on the mattress.

"Besides, a dress this gorgeous needs to be worn at least once," Jayden whispers.

"How is everything at Mick's?"

"Eh, I'm still working the motel, but it's all right. I was up all night, so I'm tired as hell." She yawns into the phone for emphasis.

"I'll let you go then. It was good to hear from you, though." I smile but hate to hang up.

"See you tonight, babe," Jayden mumbles.

"See you tonight. Go get some sleep," I laugh, hanging up.

I make my way toward the staircase and find Jean the housekeeper dusting some paintings along the wall.

"Um, Jean?" I murmur.

"Charlie! You look beautiful, darling," Jean lights up when she sees me, making me grin.

"Thank you, Jean. Can you direct me to the ballroom?" I ask. I have no idea where it is, and I know if I go looking for it, I'll get lost for sure.

"Of course." She steps down from her ladder and heads down the stairs, taking her time with each step.

"I have so much to do before the big party," Jean pants, watching her step. "Everyone will be here. It's so exciting."

I give a smile as she rambles about. As she hits the last step, she exhales a big breath.

"This way, miss," Jean directs, turning right. She waddles over to a double wooden door and turns.

"Here you are," she pants before walking off toward the stairs. *That poor lady is going to have a stroke with those steps.* I look back at the doors and take a deep breath, preparing myself for what mood Landon will be in. Will he be the arrogant master of the estate today, or will his mask be lifted and the caring, passionate Landon be present?

I lightly press on the doors and they both swing open, revealing a large, empty ballroom. The floor is tiled with blue marble, and there are windows and French doors along the walls, allowing sunlight in. My eyes shoot upward to stare at the largest chandelier I've seen at the estate yet, its sparkles bouncing off the blue and white floor.

"There you are." I tear my gaze from the crystal lights and find Landon strutting toward me, his dark hair shifting as he walks with confidence. Those forest eyes pin me where I stand, causing me to suck in a tight breath. I look down at myself, feeling a little insecure from the hunger in his eyes.

"I love that dress on you. Wear it tonight," Landon requests, now standing in front of me. I blink rapidly, my train of thought fleeing. The dark scruff on his cheeks is thicker than before, like he forgot to shave. My fingers twitch with the urge to run them over his jaw.

"Now, do you have any experience with dancing?" Landon reaches out, brushing a stray hair behind my ear. I swallow hard.

Looks like we're the caring Landon today.

"No," I respond, shaking my head.

"Take your shoes off." Landon juts his chin toward my feet.

I look down at my heels, a little confused, and back up at him, finding him walking toward a stereo built into the wall.

"Take them off," Landon repeats, his tone serious. He's not even looking at me; he just knows I'm not listening. I roll my eyes and do as he says, kicking them off as Landon messes with a stereo.

I pad along the floor as I make my way to the middle of the ballroom. He pulls his suit jacket off and tosses it on the floor, leaving him in just his dress shirt, which he's rolling up the cuffs on.

"I'll teach you the basic box step. You can use it pretty much anywhere." I just nod, because I have no idea what he is talking about. The speakers crack, and Joe Strummer and The Mescaleros sing "Mondo Bongo".

Landon lowers his head, his eyes peering up under his lashes, and holds his arm out crooking his finger for me to come to him.

"Come here, Charlie," he demands, his voice husky. My eyes go heavy with desire, and my feet move on their own accord, walking toward him.

"Step forward on your left foot." Landon steps forward, and I follow. "Then step to the side with your right foot." I watch him and imitate his move. "Now, bring your feet together," Landon instructs. "Good, now step back on your right, and then to the side using your left foot." I do as I'm told and look at Landon for confirmation that I did it correctly. "Just like that. Now, bring your feet together and repeat the steps. You just did a box step." Landon smirks, doing the dance all in one move. I smile and practice the steps.

198

"Who taught you how to dance?" I ask. Landon's eyes furrow, and his cheeks clench with tension.

"My mother," he mutters. By the look on his face, I can tell something bad happened to her, so I don't question where she is.

"Now, place your arm on my shoulder and cup my hand," Landon coaches, grabbing me by the hips and bringing me to him. My palm tingles, being held by his so strongly, my cheeks heating from just the simple touch. "This time, try the box step using your tiptoes and let me lead," Landon tells me, taking the leading step.

"My tiptoes?" I look down at my feet.

"Yes, it will prepare you for actually dancing in high heels." Landon chuckles.

"Oh." I giggle and my cheeks flush.

"Look at me. Keep your chin up," Landon requests. I take my gaze from his shoes to his eyes, and my heart skips a beat. The way his eyes shine and look right through me captivates me. Lost in our own world, not daring to look away, I wonder what it would be like if Landon and I met at a different time. If things would be easier for us, or more difficult. If he could fully love me, and I him.

"What about you? Where is your mom?" Landon asks, dancing me along the ballroom floor. I nearly trip over my feet at his question, causing me to look down.

"Eyes up." I lift my eyes and exhale a large breath.

"I'm not sure where my mother is," I answer honestly. Landon slows his lead, causing us to stop dancing. He slides his hand behind my head and pulls gently on my hair, making me look upward.

"You really don't have anybody, do you?" he mumbles, little wrinkles etching his handsome face. I slide my tongue over my bottom lip, the feel of his hand in my hair clouding the reminder of

my abandonment.

Landon sighs, his teeth worrying his bottom lip as he looks at me with longing. That scar right above his lip stands out along his tanned skin. In one swift motion, he slams his lips onto mine, his hand tangling itself deeper into my hair.

His tongue caresses my bottom lip before sweeping between them. My senses are lost, and the music is drawn out. I reach one hand behind his neck, the other caressing the scruff on his cheeks. The whiskers rubbing along the pads of my fingers feel divine. I want Landon like this every day.

He slowly pulls his lips away, allowing me to catch my breath as he trails his nose down my jawline. His hands slide from my hair down my chest, greedily grabbing my clothed breasts before continuing their journey to my hips.

"If you were mine, you would never feel alone again, Charlie," he whispers against the skin of my neck, giving it a slight nip. His fingers bunch the material of my dress in his palm, hiking it up my thighs. He grabs behind my knees and lifts one leg, wrapping it around his waist and leaving my bare hip exposed. I watch his Adam's apple bob as he swallows heavily, looking between our bodies.

"Pretend?" I pant, knowing this is where we pretend to be normal, act as if we're not obligated to hate each other. That we're ordinary people who want to be together. He slides his palm over my thigh, the feeling of his hand so close to my pussy causing my core to throb.

He nods, his breath heavy as his hand travels between my legs, a finger trailing up my inner thigh. My body breaks out in a sea of goose bumps as a shiver spreads through my limbs.

I moan, arching myself into him, so desperately ready for him to take me. His fingers find my panties, my pussy throbbing so hard I can feel it pulsing through my lower half. He pulls the fabric to the side and deftly slides a finger through my wetness. I buck against him, so wound up I can't contain my reaction. An uncontrollable moan leaves my lips from his touch.

"I could watch you come undone by my touch every day, Charlie," he growls, resting his forehead against mine, his finger giving another quick swipe against my heat.

"Yes, please. Don't let go," I whimper, not wanting him to stop. I never want him to leave my side, the fear of losing his warmth an isolation I can't bear anymore.

The doors to the ballroom creak, causing Landon to pull from me quickly. My world spinning with lust, I nearly fall on my face from his sudden departure.

"Landon, Father is waiting for our scheduled meeting." I glance over and see Roman leaning against the doorframe, his hands in his pockets and a wolfish grin across his face. His shirt is untucked and his hair is messed up like the last time I saw him. He's the opposite of Landon, that's for sure.

"Yeah, I'll be there," Landon bellows, his voice sounding on the edge of angry.

"Right," Roman remarks, eyeing me and then Landon before leaving.

"You need to keep tension in your arms." Landon reaches behind my back and pushes my posture upright with force. "Keep it locked," he demands, his tone taking more of an edge. I sigh. *Here comes the mask to Landon's emotions. The reminder of my reality. I'm just the whore.* I feel like I'm nothing to him, and that makes my heart combust with rage.

"Keep practicing," Landon mumbles, walking away. A whimper

falls from my lips as that worthlessness creeps back into my limbs.

"Landon!" I yell, stopping him just before he reaches the doors. He turns his head, looking at me from the corner of his eyes.

"I-" I stammer. "Don't go."

Landon looks at the doors, then slowly turns.

"It's not real, Charlie. It can only last for a few minutes before the reality of what we are, who we are, and what we stand for in this world comes into focus."

I let out a sob, his words taking a direct hit to my heart. I've felt alone in my life; not having a family or friends caused that. But I never feel more alone than I do after Landon pins his mask of darkness over his emotions and leaves me in a heaping mess of hopelessness.

I close my eyes and sigh. "I'm done," I whisper, looking down at the floor. The words leaving my lips cause my stomach to sink.

"What?" Landon growls.

I whip my gaze from the floor to him and glare.

"I'm. Done." I grit, anger fueling my temper. "Find another one of your whores to play make-believe with."

Landon's face goes pale and falls lax with my words.

"I can't do this anymore. You know, you once told me I deserved so much better. Remember? The night it was just us in the hotel?" I straighten my spine and lift my chin. "You're right, Landon. I *do* deserve better. I deserve better than you."

Landon's face turns red, his brows clenching inward as he stomps toward me. My heart panics with a racing beat.

The double doors swing open and Roman returns.

"Landon, everyone is still waiting," Roman informs in annoyance. Landon doesn't stop his strides toward me, and my knees tremble with the need to buckle in fear from the furious look on his face.

He grabs my forearm, pulling me toward him with haste, not caring that Roman is watching.

"What did you just say to me?" he seethes.

"You heard me," I hiss, my words holding more courage than I actually have at the moment.

"You. Belong. To. Me," Landon grits, his fingers digging into my flesh. My eyes go wide and my mouth parts. I'm not a toy. I'm a human, and I have feelings and wants in life, regardless of what some pimp may think.

"My body might belong to you, but my heart never will," I whimper, my tone giving away my cracking emotions.

"Landon!" Roman hollers.

Landon looks over his shoulder. "I said I'll be there!" Landon barks. Roman throws his hands up in surrender and backs out of the room.

Landon looks at me, his face slowly turning into a sly smile. "You don't actually believe that, do you? That your heart doesn't belong to me?"

My eyes widen as my mouth parts, self-doubt filling my chest. *Does my heart belong to Landon? Do I care about him, about us? Is this love that I'm feeling or just lust?* I mask my emotions, glare back at him and scoff, making him dig his fingers into my arm harder.

Landon flings my arm back at me and strides toward the doors, picking his jacket up off the floor as he does so.

"Why?" I scream, causing Landon to stop just before pushing the doors open. "Why do you act like you care about me? That you want to run away with me in our own world one second, but in a blink of an eye you act as if you can't look at me? That you hate

Relinquish

me?" I sob, tears filling my eyes.

Landon shakes his head, not even looking at me.

"You wouldn't understand," he mumbles under his breath. With all the emotions swirling through me, I almost didn't hear it.

As soon as Landon leaves and the double doors close, I clench my fists and scream. Angry because Landon just made me realize I *do* care about him, about us. And he only cares about himself.

The ache in my chest creeps through my body, making a violent sob escape my lips. I'm alone. I was before, I am now, and I will be tomorrow. I used to think I could take the little bits of care Landon gave me before, but now that I've had a taste of what it feels like to be in the warmth of his arms, I can't take those scraps anymore. I can't bear the cold feeling I get when I'm not with him. I need all of him, or nothing at all.

Seventeen

LANDON

"Landon, where is the new girl's paperwork?" my father asks, shifting through some papers sitting in front of him. A couple of times a week, we meet to discuss business, usually in a room that adjoins my office. It's simple with just a large table and chairs. I sit here, tapping my fingers along the top of the table, lost in thought as my father rambles on.

Nobody tells me no, and no woman walks away from me – especially Charlie. I close my eyes, the darkness behind my lids vibrating with Charlie. Her long, brown hair and small frame. Her attitude is feisty, but her shaky hands give away she's petrified.

Charlie is different. She's not like any woman I've come across before. The taste of her is sweet, her smell an aphrodisiac. My cold exterior with her is failing miserably. I lose myself around her. I can't keep my mind set on what I need to do, and what's expected of me. All I can think about is... Charlie. I clench my eyes hard and inhale a deep breath. It makes me feel sick that I would even think it, but Charlie is worth breaking my commitment to my mother.

"Landon!"

I promised her I would bring back the family name. I told her I would see to it that the Blackwell name become one of respect and power again. That I would make this estate rise from the shame my father placed upon it. But how can I do that if I break the first step in making this place strong again? I took Charlie to make a statement to the thugs of Vegas, that the Blackwells were back. That—

"Landon!"

I open my eyes, finding my father, Roman, and Veronica staring at me, my father and Veronica in annoyance and Roman with concern.

"I'll get it to you," I mutter, sitting up in my chair.

"Where did you say you picked her up from again?" my father questions, tilting his head to the side and narrowing his eyes.

"Mick. She was one of Mick's girls," I inform him, exhaling a tired breath. I've told them this before. Them asking me over and over again, and them not calling her by her first name even though I've told them it before, it's them telling me they don't approve. Which means I'm probably doing something right.

"I'm not so sure of this one. She's..." Veronica trails off, flipping her hair over her shoulder. I straighten my tie and smirk. Veronica doesn't like her because she smells competition. Call it what you will, but Veronica and I have played a game of back and forth behind our parents' back since my father and Tara got together.

I don't care about Veronica, not at all. In fact, I haven't even slept with her. I just like to watch her become so desperate for what lies in my pants. The woman is pathetic. I've seen escorts with more self-respect.

"Nobody really cares what you think, Veronica. In fact, why in the hell are you even in here?" I tilt my head to the side, eyeing her. She gasps, her eyes wide as she looks at my father in shock.

"Landon!" my father scolds.

"Do I need to remind you, Father, that *I* am in charge now? Not you, and surely not Veronica. You signed everything over to me, remember? And Charlie is mine, and she'll be our finest girl yet." I smile wolfishly at them, making Veronica scoff.

"Get me the paperwork. In charge or not, this is a family business and *we* are family," Father insists.

"You'll get it when I get it to you, Miller." Venom laces my every word. I'm not sure why he's taking interest. He's never cared before.

"Don't you use my first name. I am your father, and you will call me as so!" he roars, slamming his poor excuse of a fist on the table. I detest calling him my flesh and blood, but it's easier than listening to him ramble on about how family sticks together. It's bullshit. *Where was he when my mother was dying?*

"Yeah, sure. Are we done here?" I push my chair out and stand, fastening the button of my jacket.

My father gives me a cynical eye and quietly nods.

CHARLIE

Heading toward the kitchen, after changing out of my dress and into something more comfortable, I find Tara leaving the dining room with a tray of food.

"Oh, are you hungry?" she asks, her tone friendly. I smile and

nod. Her blonde, silky hair reaches her breasts, and she's wearing a short robe, revealing the tops of her thighs down to her bare feet.

"Yeah, I'm just heading to the kitchen to get something," I reply, running my hand along the dining room table.

"They just kicked me out. They're getting ready for the party tonight. You can come to my room and watch a movie, help me finish off these chicken strips," Tara offers with a friendly smile. "There's no way I can finish them all." She giggles and scrunches her shoulders up.

"Nobody wants to run off to your room and be buddy-buddy, Tara," a tall, black-haired woman insults, walking out of the kitchen. Tara swallows and looks the other way, her expression sheepish.

"And you are?" I ask, glaring at the woman. She has long hair with a gold band wrapped around her head, with a long, flowered golden dress to match. Her eyes are wide and colored green, her lips blood-red to match her nails.

"I'm Tabatha, the number one escort of the estate," she sneers, popping her hip out proudly and crossing her arms.

I scoff. *This woman seriously has her priorities messed up.*

"Tara, I would love to hang out," I state, my eyes never leaving Tabatha's. She snorts and smacks her lips together in a 'go figure' manner.

"Veronica was right," Tabatha smarts.

I furrow my brows in confusion. "About what?"

Tabatha gives a tight-lipped smile, and walks past Tara and me. "Nothing. Enjoy your loser party," she remarks. "Don't forget to throw up afterwards, Tara," Tabatha mocks.

After she leaves, I look over and find Tara looking down at her tray of food sadly.

"Does Miller know she talks to you like that?" I scoff. Tara frowns. "No, I can take care of myself," she snaps.

"I didn't mean-"

"You don't have to join me. I'm sure you can get some cookies or something."

"No, let's go," I insist. I am very intrigued by Tara.

She looks up, her face bright and cheery. "Really?" she whispers. I nod and grab a chicken strip from the tray.

"Follow me," she instructs. "With the party tonight, the girls are going to be wandering around the estate. They aren't *all* that bitchy, though," she continues.

I follow her up the stairs, and instead of going toward the left or right wings of the house, we go straight, passing a bunch of windows that display the setting sun. She presses her back against a door, juggling the food tray, and pushes it open.

"This is where Miller and I stay. Make yourself comfy," Tara remarks, setting the tray on the bed. I look around, noticing fancy clothes all over the floor and an unmade bed with gray blankets and sheets. The floor is made up of white carpet, and the wall in front of the bed is nothing but shelves of books and movies. A large TV displays a movie tucked between the bookcases, but I can't tell what's playing.

"I'm going to use the restroom and change," she tells me, prancing off toward a closed door. My eyes catch another doorway next to the bathroom that's open. I glance in, finding a desk and more books and files along the wall behind it. My breath takes a sudden absence. *This is Miller's office. If I'm going to find anything, I bet it's in that desk or in one of those files.*

I look back at the bathroom door and notice it's still closed and Tara is singing. I quickly head into the office and pull open some

drawers of the desk. My heart races that Miller might catch me rummaging through his desk. I find a few empty bottles of booze in the first drawer. I sigh, pulling open another. My eyes dart toward the door nervously before shuffling through the remains. I find some paperwork from other escorts and their earnings, but it's not what I'm looking for. *Shit*! I throw it back in its place, ready to give up, when my eyes catch a divider in the back of the drawer.

I purse my lips in curiosity and slide the drawer out more, finding some folders with dust on them. I open one, dust falling on my lap, and find some older photos of women, like they're at a party or something. My eyes trail across Landon in one of the pictures, just as serious in the photo as he is now. I close the tan folder and thumb through the other files that lay under it until I find bright red lettering printed on one. I pull it out and my head spins, my stomach falls, and I feel like I may vomit. It says Evans across it. *Evans, like my last name? What could Miller have on me?*

"Charlie?" My heart beats quickly, and I shove the folder in the back of my shorts, pulling my shirt down over it – or trying to, at least. My shirt's too small, not covering much.

"There you are." She smiles, walking into the office.

"I love this desk, and the view is amazing," I respond, my voice cracking nervously as I point at the windows. My hands are trembling and my heart is sputtering. I never was any good at keeping secrets.

"Yeah, Miller loves it." She puts her hands on her hips and leans against the doorframe. "I know what you're thinking."

I cock my head to the side, confused.

"You think I'm some gold digger, and that I'm only with Miller for his money and power."

"I—" I'm not sure what to say, because that very thought *has* crossed my mind.

"You'd be wrong. Just like the rest of the people at this estate. I love Miller." She smiles, and her eyes fill with tears. The reaction confuses me. "I hate this estate. When he talks about it, or gets involved with it, it makes him a monster. He's not a monster, though. He's so sweet and he's..." She stops and wipes her face.

"He's different with me. One day... one day, I *will* get him away from this fucking place." She levels me with a serious look. "I'll do *anything* to make sure that happens."

I swallow hard, not sure what to say. The only vibe I get with Miller is evil. But as far as Miller being a monster when it comes to the estate, I'd say his son Landon is just like him.

"You wanna eat? It's probably getting cold." She jerks her thumb over her shoulder. This woman is so left and right with her emotions, I can't keep up.

"Actually, Tara, I'm getting kind of tired. I think I'm going to go lie down before the gala," I lie, standing up from the desk. I watch my steps, trying to make sure the folder doesn't fall out of my shorts.

"Oh, yeah? Are you okay?" she questions with concern. I head toward her and nod, keeping my back out of her line of sight.

"Oh, yeah, I'm fine. Just a lot of stress from preparing for my first client," I half-laugh. Tara gives a wide smile and pats my shoulder.

"You'll do great, I know it. I have a knack for things like that." She scrunches her nose. Walking back into the bedroom, I head toward the door to leave.

"I'll see you tonight, Tara." I close the door behind me and let out the breath I was holding. My back is soaked with a nervous sweat, and my legs feel like jelly with the amount of adrenaline

coursing through them. I hurry down the hall, ready to get in my room and see what's in this file when Miller, Veronica, and a beautiful redhead turn the corner. I panic, my vision blurring from the amount of blood pumping through my body at such a high speed. I pull the file from my shorts and toss it into a plant next to a window, scared Miller might notice the file from my short shirt or something.

I walk quickly, trying to get far from the plant when Miller notices me.

"Charlie?" He furrows his brows.

"Miller," I croak.

"What are you doing down here?" he continues.

"I was just having lunch with Tara," I reply, trying to muster a smile.

"Oh," he mutters, looking me over. His eyes narrow into slits as he drills a hole into me. I look away, breaking the uncomfortable eye contact.

"Well, I gotta go," I squeak, walking past them quickly. I look over my shoulder, finding Veronica and Miller still watching me, and closely.

Shit, they're on to me.

CHARLIE

"Charlie?" shrieks from the phone intercom, the voice nearly bursting my eardrum.

"Yeah, Jean?" I reply.

"Landon asked me to call you and inform you that your date will arrive within the hour."

I roll my eyes. "Thank you, Jean." I resume my pacing of the bedroom floor.

"I have to get those files," I mutter to myself. "But how?"

My door opens, stopping me in my mission to distress the carpet.

Jayden walks in and shuts the door behind her. Her short green dress, sequined with pearls, fits her figure flawlessly, and her crazy hair's still just as wild as I remember. It's kinky, curled, and sticking out everywhere.

"Jayden!" I yell, flinging myself into her. She wraps her arms around me and squeezes me tightly.

"Man, I missed you," she whispers into my neck.

"I've missed you, too," I return.

She pulls from me and looks around my room. "This place, Charlie. It's—"

"Intense, I know," I interrupt, shaking my head.

"You hit the jackpot." She laughs, sitting on my bed.

I smile. It *is* great, but I'd rather not be owned by the Blackwells.

"You need to get me a job here," she continues, chuckling.

"You look good," I change the subject.

She looks down at herself before glancing up at me.

"This dress is stupid-nice. I've never had anything like it before. I was scared to wear it at first, but now I may never take it off," she remarks, her tone serious.

"I know all too well what that's like," I murmur, glancing over at the black dress Landon specifically asked for, hanging on the doorknob to the bathroom.

"So, how long do you have to stay here?" Jayden asks, fiddling with her dress.

"I'm not sure." I sigh, sitting on the bed next to her.

"And Landon? How are you and him?" She peers up at me, her gray eyes pinning me. I take in a sudden breath, looking away.

"I'm not sure. I feel that he wants to be with me sometimes, but then he blinks and I'm back to being the whore." I shake my head, the feeling of him walking away stinging like it just happened.

"Do you want to be with him?" she questions, leaning her head to the side. Her kinky curls shift to the side, and her eyes smile as she waits for my reply.

I take in a sudden breath. "I- I don't know," I stammer. "I do, but not if I have to pretend the whole time," I confess.

"Pretend?" Jayden questions, her face twisting in confusion.

"It's something that—"

The phone rings, catching our attention. I sigh and lean over Jayden to answer it.

"Yeah?" I answer.

"It's 'yes', not 'yeah'," Landon scorns.

I roll my eyes and huff into the line. "Did you need something?"

"Your client is here. Send Jayden down," Landon demands before hanging up. I growl and slam the phone down.

"That him?" Jayden asks, jutting her chin toward the phone.

"Yeah, it was. He wants you downstairs. My client is here," I inform, fidgeting with my fingers.

Jayden nods and stands. She walks to the door and stops, looking over her shoulder at me.

"Charlie, you're a good person. You may not come from a lot, but that doesn't make you any less special. But this?" She point to the walls, ceiling, everything that makes up the Blackwell Estate. "These people are not good people. Don't let them ruin you." She turns the doorknob and exits, leaving me in an emotional state. I know her heart is in a good place, but I don't care. My heart won't listen. It wants what it wants, and it wants Landon. My heart aches as soon as his name drifts through my mind.

I care about Landon, but I'm not so sure he cares about me. Jayden, *she* cares about me. I need to keep focused on my client tonight and think about how to get out of here. Away from Landon, and back to Jayden.

I throw the white dress Landon ordered me to wear to the side and look for something else. Defying Landon feels great. I grab a sequined dress with silver jewels around the bust which slowly fades into blue. It's strapless and will reveal a lot of my back, but

it's beautiful and will show Landon I couldn't care less about pleasing him. It's a step into the right direction of being done with him.

I put it on and grab some silver heels from a shoe box. Tilting my head upside-down, I ruffle my hair, giving it some volume before running to the bathroom and applying some bluish eye shadow and red lipstick.

I head toward the stairs, the noise of the crowd below informing me everyone is here. My heart picks up its beat, and my palms begin to sweat. I'm not sure how well I'll do around a big crowd.

Rounding the banister, I find the floor littered with people dressed from tuxes to the most colorful of dresses. I swallow hard and look down at my dress, suddenly insecure.

"This is Charlie, your escort for the evening," Landon introduces. I force my legs to move, taking me down the steps. I look up from watching my feet, making sure I don't trip over my dress, and find Landon. He's standing beside a gorgeous man with dirty-blond hair, buzzed on the sides, longer on top, and swept to the side. He has high cheekbones, thin lips, and cheeks full of blond stubble. He's tall, built, and looks hot in his black tux and blue tie.

"I'm Hudson. Hudson Mathew. And my, my, am I lucky tonight or what?" he compliments, his voice scratchy but so sexy.

I blush and shift on my feet nervously. When someone compliments me, I don't know how to react or what to say.

"Thank you," I respond, tucking a loose hair behind my ear. Landon sighs loudly, catching my attention. Squinting, his hands in his pockets, he looks displeased. I look down at myself, curious if I have done something wrong, when I realize I didn't wear the dress he wanted. I look back up and smirk at him, a blaze of excitement at my rogue behavior coursing through me.

"Shall we, Hudson?" I ask, still staring at Landon with a look of satisfaction.

"Yes, of course," Hudson responds, hooking his arm into the crook of my own.

Walking into the ballroom, I can't help but gasp. There are a bunch of little tables with the most gorgeous décor setting on them. Some kind of white candle holders contain three candlesticks with white and light orange-colored roses wrapped around it. Looking up, there are a paper flowers matching the color of the roses on the table; there must be hundreds of them. Not to mention the millions of twinkle lights surrounding the tables, dance floor, and doors leading to an outside patio I hadn't noticed before.

How was all this put together in a matter of hours?

"Are you hungry?" Hudson asks, gesturing toward a table.

"Yes, thank you." We head over to a table, and Hudson pulls a chair out for me to sit before sitting himself. I can't help but smile at his manners.

"Landon said you were breathtaking." Hudson grins and runs his hand through his hair, shaking his head.

"Landon said that?" My mouth forms into a big smile thinking about Landon calling me 'breathtaking'.

Hudson smirks and gives a small nod. "He did." He chuckles.

I wince at my thoughts. *No Landon. Who cares what he thinks? He isn't thinking of you.*

I place my hand on Hudson's arm, trying to get him to loosen up. I look around the room, curious if Landon is watching. Just as I turn my head back toward Hudson, my eyes find Landon. He's looking right at me, his brows pinched together like he's angry. His

black hair, which was swept back, is now disheveled, like he's been running his hands through it countless times. He looks over his shoulder suddenly and I frown in confusion at first, but then I see Tabatha wrap herself around his side.

I take a deep breath, trying to control my jealousy, and look back at Hudson. He takes a sip of his water and looks at me.

"You have this raw beauty about you that you just don't see in girls anymore," Hudson compliments, his words making me swoon. Not enough, though, because I find myself looking back over at Landon and Tabatha. Her hands are on his chest and down around his backside. With that, I grab Hudson by the lapels of his jacket and smash my red lips to his. It's not intimate, and there's no spark, but it's needed to taunt Landon. With the way he's been playing with me, it's only fair that I get to mess with his head right back.

Hudson's eyes widen, and he resists briefly before giving in and returning the kiss. I open my eyes, looking over at where Landon was standing, finding it empty. I pull away from Hudson and look around, but I don't see Landon anywhere. I sigh and run my hands through my hair in irritation.

After eating salmon and drinking wine, the DJ puts on Joe Strummer and The Mescaleros singing "Mondo Bongo." My lips part and my fingers grip the tablecloth with unease. *The song Landon and I danced to.* Images of my lustful state and his heavy stare flash behind my eyes.

"Do you want to dance?" Hudson asks, pulling me from my thoughts. My stomach falls, and my eyes widen. Landon showed me how to dance, but I'm not sure if I can pull it off. Especially if my mind keeps taking me back to the way Landon's skilled fingers explored me while this song played.

"Sure," I respond weakly. Hudson grabs my hand, his palm not near as big as Landon's, and pulls me to the dance floor. I exhale a shaky breath and straighten my back, perfecting my frame. I raise my arms to place on Hudson's shoulder and arm, getting into stance. Hudson cups my hand, his palm warm and slightly larger than mine, and his other hand tucks underneath my other arm and around my back. He smiles at me and takes the lead, my feet following on instinct. I keep my chin held high, my frame locked as Hudson whisks us across the dance floor. His body isn't as toned or muscled as Landon. In fact, Hudson's sloppy compared to him.

Hudson dips his head toward me, the smell of soap strong. "You're really good at this," he whispers. I turn my head and give a tight-lipped smile. "Who taught you to dance like this, baby?" Hudson continues. I have to bite my cheek at his term of endearment, as it sounds ridiculous coming from his mouth.

"Umm," I mutter.

"I'll take it from here, Hudson." Landon thrusts his arm between us, causing us to separate.

"What are you doing?" I ask, irritated, yet my body melts.

Landon eyes Hudson, waiting for him to back up.

"Look, man, I paid—"

"If you know what's good for you, you'll leave now, Hudson." Landon's eyes burn with a brightness that has Hudson clenching his jaw.

"Yeah, sure, man," Hudson finally replies, running his hand over the back of his neck. You can tell he's intimidated by Landon. I can relate. The way Landon walks in a room and just instantly takes charge without having to say a word, it can be overwhelming.

"What do you think you're doing?" I clip.

"Dance with me," Landon insists, his eyes hooded.

"No," I snap stubbornly, crossing my arms.

"Yes," he commands, grabbing me by the hips and turning me to where my back is to his front. He deepens his hold on my waist and slams my backside against his groin. His cock is hard, poking me with its excitement. I glance over my shoulder at Landon. The corners of his mouth curl into a smirk, and my heart skips a beat. *It's impossible for me to stay away from him. I'll never become immune to his charm.*

He shifts his hips side to side, the smell of him filling my lungs. My body ignites, feeling the heat from Landon's chest on my back.

I lift my arm, placing my hand on the nape of his neck, and loll my head back on his hard chest. My brown eyes exploring his emerald ones, he peers down at me. The way he looks at me, it's as if he can see past the scars and walls I've put up. Like he sees the real me. Which is unnerving, because *I* don't even know who I really am. He trails his fingers down my arm, the touch tickling the sensitive flesh under my arm.

I roll my hips against him, lowering myself then sliding back up, my ass teasing his already-hard length. He brushes the side of my temple with his nose, the sound of him taking a deep breath making me smirk.

"You're incredibly sexy," Landon rasps, his tone raw. "You only dance with me like this, Charlie. Your body is mine, for me to feel, for me to take. Mine," he growls in my ear, pushing his hips hard into my backside. My name slips from his mouth like a prayer, and I moan in response. "I'm not usually a jealous man, but you've made me one." He presses his fingers into my hips harshly. "I don't like it," he growls again, jerking me from my lust-filled state.

"Landon!" I open my eyes and see a pale Roman standing in front of me. He looks like he's seen a ghost, staring at Landon with wide eyes. I grimace, not sure why Roman is looking at Landon in such a way. "A word." Romans lifts a brow before walking off.

The song suddenly ends, and Landon lets go of me. My body weeps for his warmth and touch. I turn and find Landon looking out at the crowd, his jaw ticking.

"Go to your room, Charlie," he demands, his tone suddenly harsh.

"What?" I ask, shocked. "You can't just send me to my room like some child!" I yell, not caring who hears me. *Damn it, I did it again. I let myself become consumed in his charm. I'm so weak.*

Landon turns, leaning down to where our faces are mere inches from each other.

"I can, and I will. Now go to your room," he whispers seriously, his breath hot against my face.

"Fuck you," I grit, my jaw clenched with anger, my chest lifting and rising from my harsh breathing.

"Do as you're told, Charlie, or I will personally escort you to your room and lock you in there myself," he threatens, his brows narrowed. I stare off into the ballroom and find Jayden with Roman.

"I will make it to where you don't see her for a while if you don't go peacefully," he continues.

I close my eyes and sigh. This feeling in my chest, is it admiration or hate toward Landon? Either way, it's painful.

"Fine," I whisper.

I head toward a laughing Jayden and Roman. I smile at Roman and pull Jayden by her elbow toward me.

"Hey, I'm going to go to bed. I'm not feeling well," I tell her, lying through my teeth. But if I tell her the truth, she'll cause a scene and Landon may not let me see her again. As much as I hate this, I'm in

Landon's house, and he has the cards.

"You sick?" Jayden questions, looking me over.

"The food's just not settling well. I'm going to go to bed." My eyes drift to Roman, nervously brushing his hair back with his hands and adjusting his shirt. I cock a brow and grab Jayden by her elbow, pulling her into our own little circle.

"What are you doing with him?" I whisper. She looks over her shoulder and grins wildly before looking back at me with bright eyes.

"He's perfect. Laid-back, sloppy, and sexy to boot. Plus, he really seems to be into me."

"He's Landon's brother," I inform her, letting her know the sin he's capable of.

She smiles even wider, her cheeks flushing against her tan skin. "That must be where the confidence comes from. Blackwell."

I shake my head. My friend is gone. She's been love-struck. I glower toward Roman, telling him everything I can't say out loud with my stare. A 'you hurt her and I'll kill you' kind of stare.

"We'll talk about this later." I kiss her cheek and hug her hard before pulling away and making my way toward my prison.

LANDON

My jaw is clenched so tightly, I'm nearly crushing my teeth. Seeing Hudson all over her, seeing her kiss him, it fucking unleashed a surge of jealousy. Realizing my choices, I decide I can't do this anymore. My mother would tell me to go for Charlie if she were still here. I can still hold my promise to her. I can have the estate *and* Charlie, make her the madam of the estate. My father wrote the rules of not being with our escorts, but I'm in charge now.

I look over, watching Charlie explain why she's leaving to Jayden. I hated being a prick to her and sending her to her room, but I can't control myself around her. I feel accusing eyes stare at me from the side. Looking over, I see my father glare at me, an eyebrow arched and his arms crossed. He pats a client's shoulder and heads my way.

"Fuck," I whisper. I know he witnessed me sending Hudson on his way and nearly dry-fucking Charlie on the dance floor.

"Landon," my father greets. He jerks his chin toward the patio,

silently telling me to follow. I blow out a breath of annoyance and do as requested. Stepping outside, I hear the bugs of the night singing, and the heat instantly makes me sweat. "Why did Hudson leave, and where is Charlie going?" he questions, digging a hand in his pocket.

I swallow hard, not sure if I should tell him the truth.

"I don't like the way you look at that girl. You know the rules. No sleeping with the girls. She needs to go," he states sternly.

My head whips in his direction. "That is for *me* to decide," I inform him. "And why aren't we allowed to be with the girls again? Oh, that's right—"

"This is *my* estate. I worked hard for it, and I will not watch it burn to the ground over some whore!" he yells, blood vessels protruding on his forehead. I grind my teeth, infuriated that he called Charlie a whore.

"You *worked hard* for it? What exactly did you do?" I roar back, stepping up to him. He opens his mouth to speak but shuts it quickly.

"You were just given the throne. Your father didn't even test if you were worthy. Daddy's little boy," I sneer.

"Have you been drinking, Landon?" He tries to change the subject.

"But me, what did I do? What did I have to do to show I was worthy?" My hands are clenched with anger.

"I needed to know that—"

"That what? I was as fucked-up as you were?" I interrupt. His eyes go wide, and his chest lifts with a heavy breath.

"What is going on out here? Everyone can hear everything you two are saying," Roman explains, walking outside, Jayden by his side.

"Party's over," I clip, pushing past my father. This, right here, between my father and I, couldn't have made things clearer for me.

CHARLIE

I lie in bed watching rain splatter against the window as light thunder sounds from above. *Huh. It's the first time I've seen it rain since I've been here.*

My eyes become heavy as I watch the streams of rain cascade down the glass, taking me into a deep sleep. I hear my door click open and shut, waking me somewhat. I lazily look over my shoulder and see a big, black figure walk toward my bed. The smell of freshness and spice consumes me, telling me it's Landon.

"Landon?" I mumble, half-asleep.

He pulls back the blanket, revealing me in nothing but a skimpy cami and panties.

"What are you doing?" I whisper.

He doesn't answer me, just swoops his arms under my frame and picks me up, placing me against his bare chest. His skin against mine is hard and warm.

"Where are we going?" I whisper, wrapping my arms around his neck and inhaling a large whiff of his scent.

"My room," he finally responds. I want to go to Landon's room, I do, but I can't. I'm not strong enough to keep up with pretend and reality.

"I can't, Landon," I admit, but my words don't stop him. He strides out of my room and down the hall toward his. "Landon, I said I can't," I repeat, looking at his face. He keeps his stare

forward, not giving in to my rejections. "Do you hear me?"

He slowly turns his head, pinning me with those hunted eyes. "I heard you, and I'm not listening." My mouth gapes open, and my heart stammers.

He opens his door, the sound of Sam Smith's "Lay Me Down" playing. I look around his room but can't see anything it's so dark. I see a balcony, curtains drifting in and out of the room with the storm, and a bed in front of that. With the moon hiding behind thick, thunderous clouds, there isn't even a glow of moonlight to light the way. He shuts the door, slowly plants me on his bed, and places his hands on each side of my hips, his face level with mine.

"Landon, please. I can't do this anymore," I whisper, closing my eyes. The proximity of his large frame is already making me doubt the words leaving my mouth.

"Can't do what?" he questions, his minty breath brushing against my face.

I open my eyes, seeking his in the dark.

"I can't pretend."

Landon hangs his head and lets out a heavy breath. To be his one minute but not the next, I can't do it. I'm not that strong.

"Landon, what do you fear?" I ask, running my fingers along the scruff of his jaw. His head lifts in my palm and tilts to the side. Not containing my urges anymore, I run my nails through his hair, the feel of it sliding between my fingers making my body come alive.

"What is your biggest fear? What do you fear in life, Landon?" I repeat. He doesn't respond, just stares at me. I take the opportunity to open myself up a little. I shouldn't, I know that, but what do I have to lose?

"Mine. My fear..." My bottom lip trembles with nerves for what I'm about to say, what I'm going to admit to. I know if he wants to, he could use it against me. "I'm scared of not feeling the things I feel when I'm with you ever again."

Landon lifts his hand and grabs the nape of my neck, pulling my forehead to his.

"No more pretending," he mutters, his voice deep and raw. My breath hitches, and a tight knot forms in my stomach. What I'm feeling right now could be compared to someone who has gone their whole life looking for a cure to some intense sickness... and they just stumbled upon the remedy.

Our lips find each other in the dark, greedily seeking the other's as he lays me flat on the bed. His eyes hold a raw hunger as he looks upon me sprawled along his bed.

He dips his hand between my legs, his fingertips lazily trailing the inside of my thigh and awakening a dozen nerves.

"Tell me you're not done." My eyes lazily open as my fingers grasp his long hair. "Tell me you're not finished with me, Charlie," he rasps. His tongue tastes the skin along my inner neck, and my eyes flutter from the incredible sensation. I can hear the hurt in his voice. When I told him I was walking away, it bothered him.

I close my eyes and whisper. "Not done."

"All in," he mutters. "Remember?"

I nod and bite my bottom lip. "All in," I repeat.

"Do you want this? Do you want me?" he questions. I can't see his face, but I'm sure he has an arrogant smirk curling his lips. He moves his hand toward my apex, causing my body to hum with anticipation. He skids the pad of his finger along my wetness, causing me to bite my lip with the agonizing torture he's causing.

"Yes!" I moan deeply. I'd agree to anything I'm so wound up.

He slowly slides a finger into my heat, the feeling divine, causing my mouth to gape open as my eyes clench shut. He hooks

his finger, caressing the bundle of nerves that make me feel like I just came on the spot. An erotic mewl escapes my mouth, catching me by surprise.

"I can feel your greedy little pussy clenching my finger," he states, his voice husky. He slowly slips his finger out and I open my eyes, finding heavy-lidded ones pinning me where I lie.

He parts his lips, his eyes never leaving mine, and darts his finger into his mouth, sucking it clean of my juices.

I can't move. I can't respond. I just pant, watching him.

"You are the sweetest damn thing," he whispers.

His hands slide up the side of my body, taking my top with them. He hisses between his teeth and grabs one of my breasts with his large palm. He darts his head down and slips a nipple into his mouth. With the warmth from his mouth on my skin, my body arches against his and my core clenches.

I run my fingers through his hair as he places tender kisses along my tits and down my rib cage. He dips his nose into my belly button and chills race up my spine. My body twists and curves with his. Our bodies respond to one another like they've silently been talking to each other the whole time Landon and I have been denying our attraction. The respect he's showing me, the care he's showcasing has my heart and mind racing all over the place.

He grabs me by the upper arms and pulls my body up, turning me and laying my chest on his bed, my back facing him. He runs his hand down my spine, making me sigh loudly and arch my head backwards, my hair spreading across my back. He caresses my ass cheeks, his fingers so close to my heat but not close enough.

Nudging my legs apart, Landon places himself between my thighs. I look over my shoulder and see him sitting on his knees, his cock in his hand, sliding it up and down. He glides the head of his dick against my leg, leaving a trail of wetness behind. He centers himself at my opening and in one quick move, he thrusts in. My hips meet his mid-thrust, and I moan loudly as he stretches me. He lowers his body, his hard chest lying on my back as he thrusts in and out slowly, his weight nearly crushing me into the mattress. He brushes my hair to one side before he grabs both my hands and places them above my head, his sweaty palms never leaving mine as he fucks me while tenderly kissing along the nape of my neck. His lips make love to my skin as his length pounds into me, causing me to moan against the mattress.

"You're mine, and I'm yours. I'm your client now, forever. You hooked me from the day you ran into me, Charlie," he whispers into my ear. My only response is a whimper. "Now you're stuck with me, and I can promise you that you'll never feel alone again." He nips my ear, and I sag into him like a cat seeking attention from its owner.

My core pulses with pleasure. I'm not ready to come, not ready for this to be over, but my body has other plans. He untangles one of his hands from mine and slides it down my arm. Pushing it between me and the mattress, he grabs my breast while he picks up the pace. I hear his teeth grind as he rests his sweaty forehead on my shoulder, the sweet tempo of his hips recklessly pumping into me, finding its ecstasy.

The storm once building in my core fires back with a force so strong I can't breathe. I clench my eyes and my mouth falls open as I moan with my climax. Landon roars as he pounds relentlessly, spilling into me.

He pants hard, his breath tickling my face. My chest heaving as I try to catch my breath, my body is nothing but a mess from Landon devouring my senses.

"You asked what I'm afraid of. What I fear." He pants and I nod, my body sweaty and sticking to his.

"I'm afraid of becoming my father," he mumbles, his deep voice vibrating against my back. "Ruthless, arrogant, no respect for women," he admits. "I'm afraid of letting my mother down."

"Why don't you just leave the estate?" I question.

"I want to, but I can't."

"Why?" I whisper.

"When my mother was sick, she was sent away because my father couldn't bear to watch her die. When I went to see her one weekend, she said I'd changed. I told her I was fine, but she insisted that she knew me, and knew there was something wrong. I told her I wasn't interested in working the estate. She then grabbed my hand and made me promise to take the throne next. She said my father ruined the credibility of the estate, made a mockery out of the Blackwell name."

"You said she was sick? What was wrong?"

"She had cancer." His tone is grave, and I touch his arm for comfort.

"My mother loved the estate. She was truly the Madam of the place. Before my father inherited everything, working at the estate was only for those who were skilled, and our clients felt privileged to be on our list. Pimps around Vegas feared us and cursed our name. But my father used our girls, put them against each other, had parties to the point we had more than several girls overdose on many occasions. We had cracked-out escorts with STDs spreading around the estate and to our clients." Landon looks at me, his face hard. "I've worked very hard to bring our estate and the Blackwell name back to its rightful worth."

"So you were telling me the truth. You took me to show the

pimps around Vegas that you meant business?" I question, everything beginning to make sense.

"At first, yes, but then when I saw it was you... I knew I couldn't make you a working girl." He cups my chin and pulls me close, our lips almost touching. I was right; Landon isn't the dark asshole he tries to make himself out to be. He's actually endearing, and holding a promise to his mother. I don't think a man could be any more loyal.

"From the moment you ran into me in Vegas, I've been drawn to you," he whispers against my lips.

"I hated you for taking me away from Jayden, but how can I now?" I brush my lips against his, my eyes staring at his with a raw emotion.

"You couldn't stay mad at me," he replies arrogantly as he presses his lips to mine, rolling me on top of him.

"What about us?" I mumble against his mouth, nipping his bottom lip

"I'll figure it out." He moans, grabbing my hips and pulling me on top of his length. My head falls back, and I groan with satisfaction as Landon takes me for another round.

CHARLIE

I wake to the sun shining brightly and my body sore. Sitting up, I look for Landon, and discover I'm back in my room, naked and in my bed. I smirk, thinking about last night. Happiness is gluing my cold heart into something warm and whole this morning. I crawl out of bed, the ache between my legs reminding me of him, the things he said to me, what he said to me. I want to believe that we can make us work, that there might be something there, but from what Landon says about his father, I'm not sure if that will happen.

My eyes widen when a thought hits me. *The folder with Evans written on it. I forgot all about it.* I run to the clothes thrown on the floor, shimmying on some short-shorts and a white shirt that hangs off the shoulder. I open the door, looking both ways before racing toward the pot in the hallway. My heart pounds in my ears that I may get caught. When I reach it, I look around, making sure nobody is near before I grab the folder. I hide it under my shirt and run back to my room quickly, my heart slamming so hard against my chest I can barely breathe. I shut my door slowly, making sure not to make any noise. Once closed, I slide against it, falling to the floor with the folder.

I bite my lip nervously, scared of what is in it. It could be nothing; it could be some other woman named Evans. I let out a nervous breath and open it, lifting it upside-down and letting the contents fall to the floor. There are a bunch of pictures and some papers. I pick up a piece of paper and see men's names and figures. It's a client list, and payments. I frown. *It can't be me; I haven't had but one client so far.* I toss it to the side and grab the picture. Surveying the photo, I see Miller, but he looks much younger, and a woman. A woman who looks just like me. I frown and flip the photo over, my heart a painful ache against my chest. 'Gala of 2005, Miller and Maria Evans.' My mother. I drop the photo, my breathing becoming chaotic. I grab another picture and see more of my mother and Miller. Tears drip from my eyes and fall along the photos.

I clutch the piece of paper that was in the folder and look it over, searching for her name somewhere. There it is, at the bottom. Maria Evans. *My mother was an escort.* My chest heaves. I'm sucking in large amounts of air, but I'm still not catching my breath. I grab another piece of paper on the floor and look it over.

It looks to be some kind of doctor form. My eyes trail along the information of white female, age, hair color, and cause of death is a gunshot wound to the head. My nose flares. It's a coroner's report. *How did Miller get this? He's powerful, and he has connections. Did he have something to do with my mother's death? Why would he hide these in the back of his desk if he didn't?*

I let out a loud cry and kick the pictures and papers, trying to crawl up the door to get away from all the evidence linking my mother's death to the estate.

I close my eyes and rock back and forth. How? Why? My mother is dead. My lips tremble with sorrow as the news of my mother permanently being gone hits my soul. I used to curse her for being absent when things were rough in foster care, but she didn't leave me. She didn't kill herself, and Miller knows something. The way my body reacts in fear when he's around me, it's alerting me of danger, even if I didn't know it.

I stand on shaky legs and grab the photo of my mother. She was so beautiful. *I look almost identical to her. It's no wonder Miller looks at me the way he does.*

My legs make their way down the stairs on their own accord, as if my journey to Landon's office is on autopilot. Tears still stream down my face as I stare at the photo. I push Landon's office door open and head toward his desk mindlessly. Laughter comes from a room adjoining his office and echoes. I pull open the drawer and my eyes land on the gun. I reach in with a trembling hand, gripping the heavy metal. The office door swings open, but I don't look away from the weapon resting in my palm.

"Charlie." I slowly take my gaze from my hand toward the voice, finding none other than Miller.

"Whoa, what are you doing with that?" he questions warily.

"Admit it," I seethe, rounding the desk on shaky legs.

"I'm sorry?"

"Admit you killed her!" I scream, tossing the photo at him.

He leans down slowly and picks the photo up. Inhaling, his head tilted down, his eyes trail from the photo to me, looking vindictive.

"So, it was you who was in my desk," he states, his tone of fear gone.

"Admit it," I repeat.

"It's a small world, isn't it?" He chuckles. I lift my head with his comment. He admits he knows her, but did Miller kill her? The only thing I can remember from that day is that tattoo of wings. My eyes dart to Miller. He has a tattoo on his back; I remember seeing a piece of it.

"Take your shirt off," I demand, aiming the gun at him.

"Now, why would I do that?" He raises an eyebrow.

"I need to see it. I need to know it was you before I kill you," I threaten, thrusting the gun toward him.

The side door that contained the laughter opens, but I don't look away from Miller.

"Charlie!" Landon hollers.

"Oh, fuck!" Roman shouts.

"What are you doing, Charlie?" Landon questions cautiously.

"He killed my mother!" I yell, sobbing. "I was only nine, but I remember the tattoo of wings," I cry.

"She wants me to admit to killing her whore of a mother," Miller confirms, giving Landon a look I don't understand.

"You," Landon whispers, taking on a confused tone as he stares at me like he's just now seeing me for the very first time. I ignore it, my only mission centered on Miller and his tattoo.

"Take your shirt off. Now." I cock the gun like they do in the movies, loading a round in the chamber. The clicking of it placing a bullet marked for my mother's killer echoes through the room. I gasp, it actually worked.

Miller looks over at Landon and Roman, then he slowly starts to unbutton his shirt. My hands begin to sweat, causing them to slip from the gun. He pulls it off his shoulders and tosses it onto the floor beside him.

"Turn," I growl. Miller swallows and spins, holding his arms out,

the ink on his back on full display. My eyes widen, and my mouth parts as I shake my head. It just says 'Blackwell'.

"That can't be," I mumble, dumbfounded. "No, it was you!" I reaffirm, pointing the gun at him. Landon walks by his father's side and I swing the gun toward him, not sure what he's doing. My nerves and inner conflict are making me erratic.

Landon slowly starts to unbutton his white dress shirt, his head lifted.

"What are you doing?" I ask, pointing the gun between him and his father. Landon pulls on his sleeves and yanks his shirt off. He slowly turns, showing big, black wings staining his back. A strangled cry leaves my mouth, my knees threatening to buckle as I take in the wings that haunt me. My eyes catch one white feather on the bottom. *That doesn't match my dreams, though.* My legs shake and my blood rushes to my chest, trying to keep up with my racing heart.

"No," I whisper, shaking my head.

Landon turns and looks at his father.

"See. I didn't kill your mother." Miller looks at Landon and smirks. "He did."

Tears flood my eyes. "Is that true?" I question, my voice cracking with emotion.

"It's complicated," Landon starts.

"Yes or no. Did you kill my mom?" I scream, my throat hurting.

Landon lowers his head and swallows.

"Yes," he whispers. My body goes numb. The only feeling I register is the ache radiating in my chest. I lift my head, my chin trembling with emotion as my finger pulls the trigger. A loud bang echoes through the room and a bullet slams into Landon, causing him to fall to the floor.

The sound takes me out of my shock, and I scream and drop the gun. *I shot him. I fucking shot him!* My ears drown out all sounds. All the hollering from Roman, Miller, and Veronica. Silence. Everything slows down, my vision wobbling as I take in Landon's family panicking.

Roman, Miller, and Veronica all rush to Landon's side in what seems like slow motion. I see blood creep out from under Landon, and I sob, my body shaking as I cry loudly.

"I didn't mean—" I swallow hard and look toward the door. I glance back at the Blackwells and see Roman on his phone. At that point, I know I need to run. I look back down at Landon, not moving. I strengthen my legs and sprint out of the office, out the front door and toward a black car parked in front. I climb behind the driver's side and pray there are keys inside. My hands search the steering wheel, and when my fingers find them in the ignition, I cry harder with the relief.

Starting the car with trembling hands, I peel out of the driveway and race toward Jayden.

I just killed Landon. My mother is dead. I have to run. Those three things are on repeat in my head as I drive toward the city.

•••

I head to the strip where the sidewalks are littered with people going in and out of casinos and shops. I park the stolen car on the side of the road and get out, knowing I can't drive the car to my place or pass the heart of Vegas without a cop seeing the stolen vehicle.

I shot Landon, probably killed him. I close my eyes, the look of shock racing across his face as he fell to the floor flashing behind my eyes. *I didn't mean to shoot him. I was in shock, my finger reacting without real thought.* My heart aches knowing I might have killed the only person in this world I deeply care about, maybe love. The heat of the day instantly warms my skin when I step out. A woman with a tube top for a shirt and designer-looking jeans slows her stride, her eyes scanning me from top to bottom before her lip curls in distaste and she walks on. I furrow my brows at her reaction and look down at myself, curious at what she was looking at when I find myself in a camisole and PJ shorts, no shoes. I'm standing out like a sore thumb.

"Fuck," I whisper, running my hand through my hair in agitation. My eyes catch a door swinging open in an alley way, a guy in an apron and chef hat swinging a garbage can over his head and emptying the contents into a dumpster. Without another thought, I sprint down the alley. *I can't walk along the strip in this; I'll cause too much attention for sure.* I run. I run until my head throbs, my clothes are soaked with sweat, and my feet feel like they've been thrusting against razor blades. I run until I finally reach the shitty apartment I shared with Jayden.

My chest wheezes for air while I slowly climb the stairs. I open the door, which isn't locked, and find Jayden curled up in her bed, sound-asleep. The smell of home soothes my panicked state. The house is a mess. There are clothes thrown everywhere and empty boxes of food all over the floor.

"Jay," I pant, tripping into the apartment. Jayden pops up, her hair sticking up everywhere and eyes half-closed.

"Hmm."

"Jayden. We gotta, we gotta—" I can't seem to spit the fucking words out.

"Charlie? Oh, my God, are you okay?" She hurries out of bed and grabs me by the elbow to steady me.

"I'm in trouble, and I have to get out of town. I have to hide." I heave, sitting down on my old bed, trying to catch my breath.

"What happened? What do you mean?" Her eyes are wide, her head shaking back and forth in confusion.

I swallow hard, my dry tongue sticking to the roof of my mouth, and I choke. I slowly tear my gaze from the dirty floor to Jayden's panicked eyes and let out a breath of air.

"I killed Landon," I rasp.

"You *what!*" Jayden snaps her body up straight, covering her mouth with her hand in shock.

"I think. I don't know. But the Blackwells will be after me. I know it."

"How do you *think* you killed someone? You either did or you didn't." Her eyebrows furrow with confusion.

"I did. Now, I have to hide. I don't have time for this shit!" I yell, standing up and rushing to my closet.

I grab a sports bra and my stretched-out Harley Davidson shirt, putting them on quickly before grabbing some ripped shorts.

I risk a glimpse over at Jayden, finding her by my bed, her face still the image of shock.

I snap my fingers, grabbing her attention. She nods and licks her bottom lip.

"Mick, he'll save us," Jayden reassures, like everything is magically fixed.

I purse my lips and lift a brow.

"You're still holding on to that 'you're safe with me' bullshit? Because he didn't do a damn thing when Landon took me," I remind her.

She huffs out a tired breath and places her hand on her hip. "I

don't see a lot of other options right now, do you?"

I shake my head and grab some flip-flops. "No, I don't, unfortunately."

Jayden grabs some clothes off the floor and starts putting them on, making me realize she's been naked this whole time. I was just too determined to get some clothes and run to notice it.

We hurry out of the apartment and avoid the main alleys and streets to get to Mick's. The whole time, Jayden is staring at me, a million questions sitting on the tip of her tongue. And I'm looking over my shoulder, paranoid a Blackwell is tailing us. Along with my paranoia, I feel guilt. Sorrow. *I killed Landon, the man I care about.* But that man, the man I thought I finally had figured out, is actually the man in my dreams who haunts me. He killed my mother. To hate and to love are two polar opposites, yet I feel them both right now.

"Here we are," I whisper, striding into Mick's office.

"Fancy! Rarity!" Mick greets, sitting behind his desk, wearing a dark purple shirt with a gold chain. *He looks like a stereotypical pimp today.*

"Fancy needs help," Jayden spits outs, making me rub the nape of my neck nervously. *She couldn't ease into the conversation?*

Mick sits back in his chair and steeples his hands, his forehead wrinkling as he looks at me.

"Is that right? And why does Fancy need help?" Mick questions, his tone taking a hint of concern.

"I just—"

"She killed that rich fucker," Jayden interrupts. I slowly turn my head and glare at her.

"Fuck. No!" Mick shouts, pointing at his door dismissing me.

"But—"

"No. I am *not* getting involved with the Blackwells. Especially if some whore is dumb enough to kill one. You!" He points at me. "Get out and run. Run far away," Mick instructs.

"You owe me," I grit. I lower my head and glower at him, but he just chuckles and shakes his head.

"And why do you think that, sweetheart?" Mick laughs.

"You said I was safe. You said this was my family, but you didn't lift a finger to save me." I point at my chest and lean over his desk. "*I* saved me. I did what I had to do. Therefore, you owe me," I snarl.

Mick takes in a large breath, his face turning sympathetic. Like something you would see on a puppy begging for food.

"I'm sorry, Fancy, but I can't." He shakes his head. "Landon is making a statement by taking over the Blackwells, and I'm not about to jump on that ride. The best I can do is give you your cut from working here." He rubs his hands over his head and continues to shake it back and forth.

"I might know someone who can lower the rent on a place, get you in there till you can figure something out—"

"Deal," I interrupt.

He opens his drawer, pulling out a bag of some sort, and throws a bunch of hundreds on the table.

I grab the money and shove it in my pocket as he picks his phone up to make the call about the apartment.

I glance at Jayden, who is still looking at me strangely.

"What?" I finally ask.

"How did you do it?" Jayden whispers as Mick talks on the phone.

"Do what?" I reply vague.

"How did you kill him?"

I swallow, my heart sinking in the pit of my stomach as I think

about it. The gun pulling back as it fired. The loud bang. The blood. Landon's face.

"I shot him," I mumble, closing my eyes. *How did I miss the tattoo on Landon's back?* I close my eyes, and images of Landon and me together play behind my eyes. Us at the hotel, but the little bit of red lighting cascading into our room wasn't enough to see with. When I was on his desk in his office, he still had his shirt on, and when we were in his room last night, it was too dark to see anything. The evidence was right in front of me, and I missed it every time.

"Daaaaamn," Jayden remarks, pulling me from my thoughts.

"Done. Go out, make a left, walk six blocks till you get to a hotel that reads Hawns. He'll take care of you," Mick directs as he points toward the door. "Now. Get out now," he insists, his voice serious.

"Thank you," I reply, turning to leave.

"Rarity, you need to leave and never come back here. Do you understand?" Mick questions,, cocking his head to the side.

"Why?"

"You have been running the streets with Fancy, who killed a Blackwell. I don't need to chance that someone saw you two together, and is tailing you," Mick explains, his tone hard.

"I'm not leaving her by herself anyway" Jayden responds, walking out behind me.

"You don't need to come with me," I tell her, but only because I feel like that's what a good friend would say. In truth, I'm terrified right now and pray she comes with me.

"Screw you. I'm coming." Jayden reaches down and grabs my hand, giving it a squeeze.

"We're in this together," she mumbles.

LANDON

My chest aches, and my head throbs painfully. I open my heavy eyes, finding everything blurry. I blink a couple times, trying to clear them when I see Roman sitting in a chair across the room. His shirt's untucked, and he's in jeans. I look down, finding myself in my bed, a patch placed over my chest, just below my shoulder. Reminding me that Charlie shot me.

I close my eyes and take a deep breath. *It's her. How could I have not put two and two together? No wonder I've been so drawn to her; I knew who she was.* My body recognized her before my brain registered who she even was. The thought that she actually had the balls to shoot me runs amok between the pride I have for her and the fucking anger radiating in my chest.

"About time you wake up." Roman yawns. I open my eyes and try to sit up. My chest instantly smarts with the stretch of muscle, causing me to wince.

"How long have I been out?" I question, glancing toward the

window. It looks like the sun is just coming up.

"A day." Roman stretches and walks toward my bed. "How ya feeling?"

I glance up at him after finally getting in the position of sitting up.

"Like I've been shot," I inform dryly.

"You deserved it."

I whip my head up and glare at him.

"Why'd you do it?" He lifts a brow in questioning.

"Do what?" I mumble, looking my wound over.

"Kill that woman?"

"I'm not getting into this right now," I groan, resting my head along the headboard in exhaustion.

"I know Father had an affair with a woman with the last name Evans. I know the Evans woman was why Dad made the rule about not sleeping with the escorts, too." Roman walks back to where he was sitting and grabs a folder. The rule came from Charlie's mother, to be exact. She was the whole reason behind it.

"What are you rambling about?" I ask, irritated.

"Be honest. Did you sleep with her? Did you sleep with Charlie Evans?" Roman stands by my bed, looking at me with an unreadable look.

"Does it matter?" I shrug, my chest blazing with a warmth of pain.

"It does." Roman slaps the folder in my lap and grins. "I know for a fact she didn't have any clients. Well, none you didn't send on their way, anyway."

I open the folder, finding the girls' weekly health checks from the doctor as Roman continues.

"So, if you look at that, you will see why I ask if you've slept with Charlie."

My eyes roam the paper, finding all the girls with a negative sign for everything. But one plus sign stands out amongst those negatives, catching my attention. I furrow my brows and follow it to the escort's name, finding Charlie.

"The doctor said everyone checked out, but that one girl in particular had a rise in HCG."

I follow the positive sign up, looking for what Charlie has when the word hits me like a ton of fucking bricks.

"Pregnant," I whisper.

"Pregnant," Roman confirms. I drop the paper and close my eyes. *Charlie told me I was the only one she slept with without protection. Shit.* It couldn't just be that I slept with an Evans, that I cared for an Evans. No, I got one pregnant.

"You got an Evans pregnant, Landon. Do you know what Father is going to do when he finds this?" Roman points at the paper and scoffs.

I swallow the lump in my throat. *I know exactly what he's going to have done.*

"He's going to have her and the baby killed," I whisper, my chest not just aching from the bullet wound anymore.

"Do you love her?"

My eyes snap to him in shock.

"What'd you just fucking ask me?"

"Do. You. Love. Her?" he repeats.

I sigh, resting my head against the back of the bed. *Love. Does that even exist? Am I capable of love?* I don't think I've ever seen love to know what it consists of.

"'Cause if you do, you better go find her now. Father has the whole cavalry out looking for her," Roman scoffs, shaking his head.

My body goes rock-solid, my eyes widening.

"What?"

"Father has everyone we know out looking for her, demanding her back here alive. He's even got the police we have in our pocket on it."

"Why didn't you fucking start with that?" I yell, throwing the blankets off my legs.

I hurry to my closet and throw some jeans on. I rip a black dress shirt off the hanger and thrust one arm in the sleeve, wincing when I shove my other in it.

Looking over at Roman as I hurry and put my shoes on, I find him smirking at me, clearly amused.

"Something funny?" I snap.

"You love her. You love an Evans." Roman laughs.

"Fuck you," I sneer.

CHARLIE

Jayden and I follow the directions Mick gave us and finally arrive at Hawns. It's another motel, and it's not any nicer than Mick's. It's rundown, with chipped white paint. The motel doors are painted an ugly blue color, and half the roof is missing shingles. It looks to be the exact layout even. *It's only for a few days, just until I can figure out my next move.*

I grab Jayden's hand and head toward the manager's office.

"You must be Fancy," a black man mumbles as he lights a cigar. He has a thick, black ponytail and is wearing a floral t-shirt, one you would find in Hawaii.

246

A cloud of smoke climbs upward as he pins us with light blue eyes.

"I'm Fancy," I agree, the hairs on my neck standing on end.

He gives a salacious smirk as he continues to roll his cigar into a flame, puffing out a thick smoke.

"Right. Well, I owe Mick one, so you can have room 23 for two days tops. Then you owe me seventy-five dollars every day following." He cocks his head to the side, surveying Jayden and me. His bright blue eyes turn a shade darker as a vicious smirk curls his upper lip.

"You working girls?"

Jayden snorts, and I roll my eyes.

"No," I sneer, turning to leave.

"Right." He smiles wide. "Here's the key, baby." His tone deep and rough, he hands Jayden a key.

"Thanks," Jayden snatches the key from his grip and follows me outside. "What a fucking creep," she hisses, handing me the key.

Room 23 is up the stairs. As Jayden and I make our way up, I find them unsteady and creaking with every step. Once inside the room, it smells of cigarette smoke and stale fast food. There's a small TV sitting on an old dresser that looks to have grime and food all over it, and one queen-size bed in front of it. Whoever stayed here last didn't take the trash out obviously, and the bed is unmade and looks disgusting.

"I'm not sleeping on that." Jayden points to the bed, a red condom sticking to the sheets.

"Oh, gross." I scrunch my face. "Let's get bleach and trash bags. If we're going to stay here for a few days, we need to disinfect this room."

"I think we'd do better if we got a match and gasoline." Jayden

coughs, waving her hand in front of her face to try and escape the rancid smell of the place.

I laugh and grab her arm. "Come on, we got this."

Three hours later, Jayden and I fall onto a perfectly made bed with clean sheets, the smell of Lysol and bleach strong yet inviting.

"Mick has a much better work ethic," I state, making Jayden laugh.

"For sure. This guy is a pig," she adds.

"If he's a hustler, I hope the rooms he pimps his girls out of are in better condition," I respond. She turns over on her side, propping her head up with her hand. A question's clearly on the tip of her tongue.

"What?" I ask, turning my head to look at her glowing face.

"Why'd you shoot him?"

The mention of Landon makes my chest feel like it was just impaled. *I wonder if Landon is alive. Is he at the hospital? In a morgue? Looking for me?*

I take a deep breath and fiddle with fingers.

"He killed my mother," I whisper, not sure if she even heard me. Just hearing the words myself they sound unnatural.

"What?" she gasps. I prop my head on my hand to get a better look at her.

"My mother worked at the Blackwell Estate." I sigh, frustrated that I don't know anything more. "I don't know. All I know is for some reason, Landon killed her." I furrow my brows and shake my head. "There's so much missing from the puzzle. I'm so confused. I mean, why did he kill her?" I'm just thinking aloud at this point. "I was there that day she was killed, but I just can't make out what happened," I mutter, running my hands through my sweaty hair.

"You really can't remember?" Jayden rubs my arm in comfort.

I shake my head and groan in irritation.

"I mean, I remember some, most of it just coming back to me in the last few hours, actually. I remember I was taken to a hospital for sick people, where they think you're crazy. They wanted me to tell them everything about my mom, because they had nothing. But all I wanted to do was forget. I was in pain. All I wanted to do was look for an escape. Forgetting it did that." I peer up at Jayden, my eyes filling with tears. "Looks like I got my wish, though, 'cause I can't remember a damn thing. I have no idea why Landon would kill her."

"You love him?" she questions, turning on her back and looking up at the nicotine-stained ceiling.

"I'm not sure. Well, I mean my mother loved me. I know she did because I can feel it. But it was so long ago, and I've forced myself not to remember so much. I'm not sure if I remember how to love."

"Those who fall at their weakest cannot be judged. It's what they do to bring themselves back up that says who they are. I know you'll get through this, because you're the strongest person I know."

I look down at her, surprised with how real she just got. My chest warms that she thinks so highly of me. Jayden yawns and snuggles closer to me, so I wrap my arms around her and snuggle right back.

"I missed you," she whispers.

I look over at the window, the sun just starting to set. I'm exhausted, and my stomach is in knots and has me feeling queasy.

"I missed you, too," I mutter, closing me eyes.

●●●

Looking at the soap scum claiming the tiles in the shower, I think of Landon. The way he made love to my body just days before. The words he spoke to me, sounding like he meant them. The ache in my chest worsens, making my lips tremble. I miss him. His rude mouth, and his hot and cold behavior. I long for it all. When I said I felt alone before, when I said I had hit rock-bottom before, it was a lie, because the way I feel right now is so much worse. Water cascades down my body as I shake with emotion.

"I- I killed him," I cry quietly. I hurt, but I'm not sure where the source of pain is coming from. All I feel is this dull ache spreading through my body as I think about what I've done.

My legs give out and I fall into the tub, my knees aching as they slam into the ceramic. I know I need to get back up and figure my shit out, decide my next move, but I just don't have it in me. All I want to do is just cry, sleep, and cry some more.

I dry off and put on the clothes I wore yesterday. They don't smell too bad; I've had worse. I stop where I'm standing when I hear voices in the other room. My heart thuds against my chest in panic. Scared that Jayden is out there by herself, I open the door, still towel-drying my hair.

I step around the corner, heading into the main room when I freeze, my body reacting in pure panic. My hand drops the towel, my breathing comes in short spurts, and my body trembles.

"Landon," I croak.

"Charlie," he grits, his tone hard. I swallow, dumbfounded. *He's alive! I didn't kill him!* My heart thuds with joy, but my body pulsates with terror. *Is he going to kill me?* I glance to the bathroom door and back to Landon. It's my only escape, locking myself in the bathroom while Jayden runs for help. He cocks his head to the side, like he knows I'm up to no good. Without a

250

second thought, I bolt toward the bathroom door and shut it. Just as my fingers go to push the button on the knob to lock it, the door thrusts open with so much power it nearly throws me into the tub.

"You can't run from me, Charlie," Landon barks, slamming the door behind him. His size takes up every free inch the small bathroom holds. He looks good, like damn good. He has on a black dress shirt and jeans that hang deliciously low. I've never seen him in jeans before, come to think of it. I shake my head and look the other way.

"You can't hide, either," he growls eerily.

"What are you going to do?" I ask softly, feeling behind me for something to sit on.

"What *should* I do, Charlie? You fucking shot me."

I sit on the rim of the tub and look at his hard, forest eyes.

"You killed my mother," I fire back in response. I watch Landon's Adam's apple bob as a look of hurt crosses his face. His eyes squint at the corners as his forehead wrinkles, sorrow taking over his face. *How is he upset about killing my mother?*

Landon runs his hands over his face, masking his emotions.

"We don't have time for this right now. We have to go." Landon holds his hand out, waiting for me to take his.

I scowl, looking at his hand. The hand that spilled my mother's blood.

"I'm not going anywhere with you," I snarl. Landon blows out an irritated breath and looks at the ceiling like he's praying for control.

"If you don't come with me right now, you'll be killed." I wince at his words, fear striking me in the chest. "I found you very easily. My father's men will be here shortly. I'm sure of it," Landon explains further.

251

"Your father?" I question. *I'm confused; is he threatening me or his father?*

"Not here. Not right now, Charlie. It's not safe." Landon grabs my hand without my permission, and I try to resist.

"Why should I trust you?" I yell, anchoring my feet to the bathroom floor. Landon turns quickly and pins me against the wall, his hand slamming just above my head.

"Have I hurt you yet?" His breath brushes across my face. "If I was going to kill you, I would have done it already."

I huff at his remark. "Is that supposed to make me feel better?" I sneer.

"I don't care if you feel better, Charlie. I really don't. Not right now. Right now, I care if you live. I wouldn't be out here risking my ass to save you if I wanted it any other way."

I inhale a shaky breath, the severity of his tone telling me he's telling me the truth. Or he's a damn good liar.

"Where are you taking me?" I ask, looking into his deep green eyes speckled with brown. My head screams not to give in, but what if he's right? What if he's not the one I should fear? Landon once told me my body would tell me when something is wrong way before I know. When I met Miller for the first time, my body all but held up little red flags that screamed he's a bad guy. But when I'm with Landon, I don't get that feeling at all. If anything, it seems like Landon was placed on this Earth merely to protect me.

"You promise you won't hurt me?" I whisper, still looking into those intense eyes.

"If that's what it takes, then yes, I promise."

"And my mother?" I continue to bargain, wanting to know more about what happened to her.

"I'll explain it all later, but if you don't come with me right now, you won't ever have the chance of knowing, Charlie."

I close my eyes and nod. He grabs my hand and rushes me out of the bathroom. I pass Jayden sitting on the bed, chewing her nails anxiously.

"Jayden," I cry out as we head for the door. I thought she'd run for help, but she's just sitting there, dazed. Is she scared, or does she trust Landon?

"Wait," I plead, trying to pull from Landon. He stops but doesn't let go of me.

"Go, Charlie. Go with him. For some reason,"—she flicks her gaze to him, then back to me—"I believe him." I nod, knowing what she means. With Landon's intense stare and the tone of his voice, it's hard not to believe him. At least I know I'm not doing this just because I may be falling for him. I use my other hand to pull her close, taking in her cocoa scent and programming it to memory in case we're both wrong. *In case Landon does indeed drag me back to the estate and...* I can't even finish that thought.

"Be safe," I whisper in her ear.

"You, too," she whispers back.

Twenty Two

CHARLIE

I sit in Landon's beautiful black car. The smell of leather from the seats is strong, and it curves to my body like they were especially made for me. We drive out of the city, leaving the lights of Vegas behind us. The sun sits high in the sky without a cloud in sight, making Landon turn the air conditioning on. The tension in the car is so palpable you could poke it with your finger. I want to turn and demand why he killed my mother, demand to know who he really is and what he's hiding, but I'm simply scared of the truth. I don't know who to trust, what to fear. I curl into myself and stare out the window, my back facing Landon.

I hear him shift, and the warmth of his hand suddenly envelops mine. I turn my head, looking at his palm grasping mine. It's so big compared to my hand, so warm, and the gesture is tender. My hand tingles from his touch, the feeling shooting up my arm and to my chest.

"Everything is going to be okay, Charlie. I promise," he mutters, squeezing my hand. *Does he not have any resentment toward me after I shot him?* I squeeze my eyes shut, pushing back the tears.

The car turns into a suburban area, and I sit up straight in the seat to look around. There are houses of every color and every size, spaced accordingly to give one another privacy. They seem fancy, with the palm trees and cars that look brand new sitting in some of the driveways. Landon turns the wheel and pulls into the driveway of one. Its roof is tiled in some cream color, and the frame is made up of some stucco tan hue. The lawn is made up of palm trees, rocks and bushes, matching a lot of the properties around Vegas. The garage door opens and Landon pulls his car into the space with ease, the sound of the motor vibrating off the walls once we are inside.

"You hungry?" Landon asks, turning the car off. I tilt my head slightly and look at him with an arched brow. *Has he lost his mind? That's what he says? That's what he leads with to break the silence?*

"No. I'm just tired," I mumble, opening the car door. I hear Landon sigh as he steps out.

"Charlie, we really need to talk." He looks at me with such pain it takes me aback. I cross my arms, rubbing my hands up and down my forearms, trying to soothe myself. All I wanted before was to be with Landon, have that normalcy. But now, knowing what I know... I'm not sure that's what I want anymore.

I nod and shut the door. *Talking is the first step in figuring out what the hell I want next, though.*

Walking inside the house, it's huge. The ceilings are high and the space is large, but it's clean. There are no empty food boxes, or mail sitting on the counter.

"You live here?' I question, surveying the place.

"Sometimes. Not often, though," Landon admits, tossing the

keys on the counter.

Walking into the kitchen, there is a white tiled island with matching counters behind it, stainless steel appliances of the best quality placed accordingly. I explore the space, venturing into the living area. A massive U-shaped couch made up of white cushions occupies the space, a large TV placed on the wall in front of it and a fireplace beneath that.

To the left of the living room is nothing but windows and a sliding glass door. Looking through, I see little twinkling lights from the city as the sky starts to cloud over. My eyes trail to the right of the room and find wooden stairs. I make my way up them, Landon following behind me.

I pass more windows and closed doors, my eyes set on the one door that's open at the end of the hall. Entering, I find a large bed with white sheets, and a large floor-to-ceiling window in front of it overlooking the city of Vegas from afar. It's like this house is tucked out of the eye of Vegas, just watching from its own safety. There are shelves lined with books, and of course a TV directly across from the bed.

I sit on the bed, the blanket so cushioned I sink. I vaguely smell Landon's freshness and spice waft around me from the fabric.

He's staring at me, the intensity making me shift uncomfortably. I slowly trail my tongue along my bottom lip and risk looking at him. He's squatting, his elbows resting on his jean-clad thighs. His face is unreadable as he pins me where I sit.

"What?" I whisper.

"Charlie, I don't even know where to start." He looks down and blows out a tired breath. I shrug and purse my lips.

"You can start with why you killed my mother," I suggest, my tone coming off snappier than I intended. Landon's brows furrow, his jaw ticking as he takes in what I said.

"Your mother, Maria, was a turning point in my life," he starts, his eyes leveling with mine. "Growing up, I envied my father. He had power, control, money, and women at his feet. He was like a king. There was nothing he couldn't have and not a damn thing he couldn't talk himself out of." Landon's face turns hard as he points to his chest. "I wanted that. I wanted to be on top. I wanted to be the king of the estate."

He shakes his head and looks at the wall. "Roman and I fought about who it would be. Who father would chose to reign over the estate. Every Blackwell gets the throne until one of his heirs proves to be of quality. Hell, Roman and I couldn't piss without making it a competition." He chuckles and looks at me, but I don't laugh.

"What does this have to do with my mother?" I ask, irritated, my fingers clawing at the sheets in anger.

"Your mother was one of our escorts, Charlie. One of the best, actually. She was very quiet, didn't give much detail about her life, and my father had his sights on her. My father cheated on my mother regularly, but it didn't seem to bother her so it didn't bother me. I think she had her own partaking in cheating, but I'm not sure."

I nod, not knowing what else to do. I just want him to keep talking, to tell me more about my mother.

He continues. "One day, my father brought me to the side, loaded a gun and slid it across his desk toward me. He said, 'Landon, today is the day you prove that you're the worthy son. The next in line to become king of the estate.' I didn't know what he was talking about. I was only sixteen. Holding a gun at that age, and given my time to shine, I was up for anything."

257

He stands and runs his hand over his head, giving it that messy look. "He took me to your mother's apartment, not far from where you live now." Landon shoots me a quick glance before he stares out the window, placing his hands in his jeans pockets. "When we entered, Maria was frantic, sweating even. But man, she was truly beautiful." He whips his head around and smirks at me, like he is staring at my mother again. I close my eyes, tears threatening to spill as he continues.

"She screamed for us to leave, that she wasn't returning to the estate. My father roared that she was his indefinitely since she was pregnant with his child. She got this evil look across her face and said she had an abortion." Landon steps over to me and squats in front of me again, my hands digging into the sheets the more he tells me what happened that day. A piece of me still doesn't want to know.

"I've never seen my father so angry. He was blistering red, his body shaking with rage. He lashed out at her, told her an Evans would never roam this Earth again. That she killed his seed, and he'd see to it that her DNA never disgraced this Earth with its presence, starting with her. That's when something caught the corner of my eye." He grabs my clawing hand from the sheet and squeezes it. My heart races and sweat is forming on my forehead. It's like watching a movie, the climax happening right before you that has you by the seat of your pants. You know it's going to end badly, but yet you sit there watching with a racing heart.

"I saw you hiding under the table, looking right at your mother, fear written across your face like you'd just realized the devil was real. I saw my father reach behind him, going for his gun while walking toward Maria. If he made it just one step more, he would have seen you, Charlie, and not only killed your mother, but I know he would have killed you, too. So I did what I thought was right at the age of sixteen. I pulled my gun out, stepped in front of the table you were hiding under, blocking you from my father's view, and…" He pauses, squeezing my hand harder. "I shot your mother."

I pull my hand from his, a sob escaping my mouth as I stand. My body thunders with blistering rage, and I feel like I might vomit. I cover my mouth with the back of my hand and close my eyes. My mother flashes behind my eyelids, then ominous wings.

"Nobody even knew Maria had a kid," he mumbles. Knowing my mother protected me from the estate when I was a child causes admiration to bubble in my chest. I wonder if she feared Miller, or if she knew he was capable of evil. *I bet that's why she aborted his unborn child.*

"The tattoo on your back, I saw it that day. But I don't remember how."

"When I stepped up to block you, it made me closer to your mother. Blood splattered on me, and Father told me to take my shirt off and wipe my face with it. Our car was parked right outside, so nobody would notice if I was wearing a shirt or not. So I took it off, cleaned myself, and we left."

I shake my head, not wanting to believe anything he's saying.

"Do you know what kind of Hell you put me in? What life you placed in my hands?" I yell, pointing at him with resentment.

He stomps forward, his jaw ticking as he grabs me by the shoulders. "I fucking saved you. If it weren't for me, your shitty life wouldn't have ever happened.

"In fact, I've been saving your ass since the day I saw you hiding under that table. If I wasn't in that alley, who knows what those college pricks would've done to you. Taking you from Mick, taking

you off the streets, all of it." He waves his hand in front of his face as he continues to justify his actions. "I don't know what else you want from me," he mumbles, his head hung low.

"Knowing the truth, knowing that my mother is really dead – it hurts." I sob.

He grabs me by the shoulder and pulls me into him, hugging me. His arms are strong as he cocoons me into his taut chest.

"I just can't believe you somehow made it back to me," he mutters into the top of my head. "I went back when I could, but you were already gone."

I close my eyes and fist his shirt, images of cops and first responders popping behind my eyelids. The looks on their faces when they found me under that table. How I wouldn't talk to any of them, or let them touch me. The ride in the back of an ambulance with a gray wool blanket wrapped around me as they took me to the hospital, and eventually to the psych ward. I open my eyes, and I can't decide if I'm angry, hurt, or grateful. I have a right to all of those feelings, but they're all swirling inside of me at the same time, making me feel dizzy.

"Talk to me, Charlie," Landon whispers, sweeping his hands along my back.

"I—" I choke. I'm not sure how I feel, or what I think.

He edges back, looking at me with concerned eyes. I look in his eyes, tears running down my cheeks.

"This is too much for one day. Let's get you in bed." He grabs the bottom hem of my shirt.

"No!" I yell, shoving his hands off me. I'm done feeling sorry for myself, for my life, for everything. "You killed my mother, Landon!" Without thinking, I raise my hand and slap him across the face. Anger, sorrow, and vengeance all being released as my palm stings. His head whips to the side. His jaw ticks as his cheek fumes a red hand print. He slowly slides his gaze back to me, his eyes burning with fury. I swallow the unease forming in the pit of my stomach and point at him with rage. "One day you're loving and the next I find out you're a murderer! How do I know you won't do as your father orders and kill me?" I tilt my head to the side, and glare with all my might. "Tell me how I'm supposed to trust you?" I whisper. "How am I supposed to trust the man who has my mother's blood on his hands?"

Just as Landon opens his mouth to respond, a loud crash sounds from downstairs. My chest constricts with fear, and Landon's face hardens. He puts his finger over his lips, silently gesturing for me to be quiet. I nod, my nostrils flaring from my harsh breathing. He slowly walks to the dresser, and carefully pulls open a drawer. He clutches a shiny black gun and I cover my mouth with my hands. *How many guns does he have?* He points toward the bathroom. I nod and scamper to the bathroom. I peer my head around the doorframe watching as Landon slides up against the wall and peeks around the corner into the hallway. In one swift moment, he vanishes. My stomach sinks not having him in the room with me anymore. What if the intruder comes in here? What if they were sent from Landon's father? Sweat builds on my forehead as the minutes tick by. The silence is so loud my ears ring, and images of my mother hushing me and urging me to hide wobble in my mind. I clench my eyes as hard as I can to clear the memories, and shake my head. I can't just stay in the bathroom and hide. I have to do something to help Landon.

"Landon!" I whisper loudly. My hands tremble at the thought of something happening to him.

I tiptoe out of the dark bathroom into the bedroom, I take a step toward the dresser when something catches my eye near the door. I choke with fear. A large person dressed in black from head to toe and pointing a silver gun at me stands right before me. I open my mouth to scream but nothing comes out. This is it, this is the end of my shitty life. I'm going to die. Landon steps behind the intruder, his gun raised and fires. I cover my ears and wince from the loud bang. Blood scatters along the floor and the person falls on his face. I glance from the dead body to Landon, and sag with relief.

"Landon!" I cry, emotion bubbling in my chest that he's okay. He steps over the body and wraps an arm around my frame hugging me. All the anger and resentment I may have had flees my body. If Landon wanted to hurt me, if he was anything like his father, he would have let me die tonight.

"Are you okay, babe?" He looks me over. His tone's sincere as he searches my body for injury.

"Yeah, you came just in time," I whisper. "You—"

"Saved you?" Landon finishes my sentence and raises an eyebrow. "I told you the day I took you back to that hotel room, I wouldn't hurt you. I meant it." His tone is dry, and has me swallowing the lump in my throat. "I was sixteen when I killed your mother for Christ's sake. I was a damn child and did what I thought was right. I saved you." I stand in awe. *Landon has saved me since I was a nine-year-old little girl.*

"You..." I whisper. "You're right. You saved me," I admit. Landon's hard face and tense body relaxes instantly, his face taking on a softer look as he frowns. Landon may have killed my mother, but he did it to save me. He just saved my life again. Landon leans down, and pushes the black ski mask to the person's forehead.

262

Judging my tonight's events, I know Landon is not innocent in any way, but I can tell by the pain in his voice that he did not want to harm my mother. He was merely a child doing what he thought was right at the time. I bet if he defied his father in any way that day my mother died, Miller would have killed Landon too.

"Niko," Landon mutters. "I knew it would be him. He's the only person that knows about this place." Landon stands and places his gun on the dresser. The dead guy looks about Landon's age. His face is pale with bright freckles along the bridge of his nose.

"Will there be others?" I question.

"Possibly, but I doubt it. The only reason Niko knows about this house is because he was with me when I got the keys from the real estate agent. Niko and I used to hang out a lot when we were younger. He became caught up with my dad over the last couple of years. When he heard I was not on my father's side, he went on his way. Looks like he went right into my father's pocket."

An hour and a half later, the room is cleaned of Niko and any trace of blood. The way Landon cleaned any trace of DNA is almost terrifying.

"Where did you put him?" I question, sitting on the edge of the bed.

"In the ground," Landon replies quickly.

I bite my bottom lip, and nod.

"Let's try and get some sleep. I fixed the door Niko kicked in and set the alarms this time, they will sound if anyone so much as steps on the front step."

I stand to take my shirt off that has some spots of blood on it. Lifting the shirt over my head, Landon's fingers trail under the cup of my sports bra, his touch tickling my skin, reminding me I'm

alive. He tugs the fabric, pulling it off me, my nipples peaking when the sudden fresh air sweeps past them. My eyes flicker to Landon's, finding his hooded as he stares at my small breasts.

He grabs the back of his shirt and yanks it over his head, revealing his toned abs and that sexy V leading down into his pants. My gaze catches the square white patch on his chest from where I shot him. I tuck my bottom lip between my teeth and trail my finger over the cotton patch.

"It was an accident," I whisper, my eyes peering up from under my lashes.

"I'll live," he responds, his tone raw.

He unbuttons his jeans and shuffles them down using his feet before tossing them in the corner. I can't help but take in every inch of him as he stands in his black Calvin Klein's. I crawl in bed, and shift to get comfortable on my side of the bed. I instantly feel my eyes grow heavy. Landon tucks his hand around my hip, trying to tug me closer to him but I pull away. I just need a moment to myself to comprehend what's going on in my head. But he isn't having it. He grabs me by the hips and pulls me toward him, tucking me into the curve of his body, the smell and heat sweeps from his to mine. His fingers trail up and down my spine tenderly.

"You know how I said I saved you?" His chest vibrates against mine as he speaks. "Well, you saved me, too." I tilt my head back and look at him in confusion. He stares down at me, his eyes full of sincerity.

"If it weren't for you or your mother, I would have become my father. I would have followed in his footsteps and been a monster. But after what I did, after saving you, I wanted nothing to do with the Blackwell estate."

I sigh and tuck myself into him once again. Hearing my

mother's life wasn't in vain, that it had impacted his life, offers me a slither of relief.

"You saved me, too," he repeats softly into my hair. I close my eyes and let my dreams take me.

•••

I wake with a start, lightning cracking in the sky and illuminating the bedroom. My eyes fall on Landon who is fast asleep, his chest slowly rising with every breath. I lie back down and watch him. His face seems so soft and at peace as he sleeps. His closed eyelids twitch, making me wonder what he's dreaming about. I know I was troubled, had a shitty life growing up, but he killed someone at the age of sixteen. I can't imagine how that would stain a person's soul. His eyes suddenly open as he gasps for air. I jump, startled by his sudden reaction.

He places his hand to his chest, panting for breath.

"Are you okay?" I whisper, lying next to him. He nods and swallows. "Bad dream?" I question, propping my head on my hand.

He turns and fluffs his pillow under him. "Yeah," he mutters.

"I get them all the time," I reply, searching his face in the dark.

"Oh, yeah? What about?" His forehead wrinkles with question.

"Wings. *Your* wings, to be exact. But you have a white feather on your tattoo. The white feather's not on the wings in my dreams."

Landon tucks a hair behind my ear. "That's because I got it after that day. It represents you."

"Why me?" I narrow my brows in confusion.

"I got the black wings to represent my imperfections. A symbol of my ominous ways as a Blackwell. A rogue son going against God

and turning into something powerful and dark. But after I saved a little girl, I realized I didn't want to be the villain; I wanted to be the hero. That white feather reminds me that something good resides within me. I'm not my father one-hundred percent."

I can't help the throb between my legs, knowing I impacted Landon's life so much he got a tattoo representing me.

"How are you feeling?" he questions, his voice muffled with sleep. I wince, taken back by his question.

"Um, fine, I guess." I shrug to emphasize my words. "My mind is still wrapping around everything, but I'll live."

"There's something I need to tell you." He sits up, bending his knees and resting his elbows on them, tangling his hands in his hair.

I sit up as well, nervous as to what's about to come from his mouth. Just the way he's acting tells me it's going to be bad.

"I got the paperwork from your blood work." He turns his head, his fingers still in his hair. "Have you slept with anyone without protection since we met?"

"No." I shake my head slowly, my heart picking up its pace.

He takes in a sudden breath and blows out a long exhale. "The results said you're pregnant, Charlie."

Adrenaline spikes in my chest, and my heart feels like it stopped beating. My body heats to an inferno and my brain becomes mush. "Wh- what?" I stutter, blinking rapidly, hoping one of the times I open my eyes I'll wake from this dream. Landon untangles his fingers from his hair and grabs me by the arm, yanking me into him. He places me between his legs and pulls my back onto his chest.

"You're pregnant. You're carrying my child inside you," he whispers, trailing his hands down my arms and to my abdomen, laying claim on my stomach.

My lips part with disbelief. *I'm carrying a Blackwell inside me. A Blackwell and an Evans, two feuding households, and they've joined together to make one little heartbeat.*

"Are you sure I'm pregnant?" I tilt my head up, not sure what the doctor has told him exactly, what the paperwork entailed. *Could it be a mistake?*

He runs his hand through his hair and clenches his jaw.

"I have some pregnancy tests in the car, just to make—"

"Get them," I interrupt, pulling from his lap. I need to know for sure. *I can't be a mother. I can't even take care of myself.*

When he heads out, I move toward a door and feel along the wall for a light switch, turning it on to find a large bathroom. A glass shower and a tub, which could hold at least five people, fill the room, but all I'm looking for is a toilet right now. Stepping toward it, the corner of my eye catches my reflection and I stop. I look a mess. My hair is mussed, and I have tan lines claiming my skin. I turn and look at my stomach, which still looks the same – flat. My boobs are still small. *Aren't you supposed to get big boobs when you're pregnant?*

"Here we go." Landon sets a glass of water on the counter as he empties a plastic bag. Four boxes of pregnancy tests scatter along the surface, all a different brand. I grab a box and tear it open with my teeth, ready for answers.

I sit on the toilet and pull a pink cap off one, a cotton swab sticking out from the end of the stick. I'm assuming I piss on this end. I shove it between my legs and catch Landon leaning against the doorframe with his arms crossed.

"Are you just going to stand there while I pee?" I ask, suddenly feeling shy.

"Yeah, why not?" He shrugs, the muscles in his arms rippling as he chuckles.

"I can't pee with you standing there," I interject, scowling at him. He pushes off the doorframe and untucks one arm, turning on the faucet before leaning back against the doorframe.

I shake my head and try to concentrate. *Who knew peeing would require so much focus?* Listening to the water in the sink, I finally relax and pee.

I pee on all of the sticks, and now Landon and I are hovering over them as they sit on the bathroom counter. One finally shows a plus sign, the others slowly following suit. They all show positive, some lighter than others. I grip the counter and close my eyes. It's for sure. I'm pregnant.

"I can't even take care of myself." I choke with emotion, looking at the tests.

"I'm here, Charlie. You'll never struggle again. You're mine, and I told you that you'd never be alone again." He steps behind me and nips the top of my shoulder.

"Is this why you saved me? 'Cause I have your child in me?" I question, looking at his reflection in the mirror.

"No," he blurts quickly. "I saved you because I love you. Because you're mine and that baby is mine. I *will* protect what's mine, and I'll kill whoever steps in front of that."

He loves me? I want to respond, but I can't. I'm in shock, and I want to be sure I truly love Landon when I say it. I don't want to think I love him, or might love him. I want to know that the ache in my chest and the lust in my body is because I undeniably love him.

"Let's feed you. I know you haven't eaten." He grabs my hand and pulls me from the pee sticks on the counter. It doesn't seem to bother him that I didn't say 'I love you' back, which is a relief. I can't dive into that right now.

"I'm not hungry, really," I protest, trying to head back toward the bed. He turns his face hard, his jaw defined in tension.

"You *will* eat, damn it. Starving yourself is not an option, so go get a shower, and I'll meet you in the kitchen, Charlie. End of." His tone is so brutally harsh it has my eyes wide. Gone with the sentimental shit and back with full-force Landon Blackwell. As he strides out of the room, those ominous wings with the one white feather stand out against his golden skin. His back is ripped with muscles. The wings don't scare me nearly as before, not now that I know what the white little feather stands for: redemption.

Twenty Three

CHARLIE

I look at the fresh fruit sliced perfectly into a glass bowl, and my mouth waters for it. I grab a piece of watermelon and take a bite, its juices running along my chin and down onto the counter. Landon chuckles, making me look at him. A piece of me deep down hates the fact that Landon killed my mother, but I know he did it for me. I love him, regardless of any of it. I know that without a doubt now. If I didn't love him, it would be easier to walk away, to fight him. However, that is the current situation. I love him, and the heart wants what the heart wants.

"I can see why our trainer, Harron, was so appalled when he taught you how to eat with etiquette. You eat like an animal." Landon laughs, taking a large bite of his apple. He has the top of his hair pulled into a short ponytail, the other half down since it's too short to put into a ribbon. His jaw is sprouting that delicious stubble. He tears into the apple, his sharp jaw flexing as he chews. It causes my sex to throb with a craving so strong I have to clench my thighs.

I still can't wrap my mind around being pregnant. I'm not sure how I feel about it. I'm not mad, not happy. Maybe it hasn't hit me yet, the reality that I'm going to be a mother, be responsible for another life.

I shrug. "That guy was a pompous ass anyway."

Landon dips his brows and nods. "He was; I agree."

Thunder sounds from outside, catching my attention. The pool lights shine brightly from within the pool just outside the double glass doors.

I turn and smile wolfishly at Landon. "Wanna go for a swim?"

"Now?" Landon's eyebrows raise.

I shrug and look back at the pool. "Why not now?" I could go for a swim to relax my mind.

"It's getting ready to storm," Landon points out.

"So?" I stand from the chair and walk backwards. I didn't put on any clothes, so my body is bare for his hungry eyes.

Landon's eyes grow heavy as he tosses the rest of his apple onto the counter and follows me out. I dip my toe into the water, testing its temperature, but before I can push my foot in any further, large hands grasp my hips and turn me. Landon smirks as he grips both of my thighs and lifts me. My legs wrap around his waist and my hands tangle behind his head as he smirks and walks us into the lukewarm water.

Landon raises his hand and brushes his thumb along my bottom lip, his green eyes holding the warmth of a forest fire.

His excitement pushes into my butt cheek, and my nipples ache as they caress his hard chest.

"I admit, having a child right now is not ideal. But a Blackwell and an Evans having a child together is the beginning of something

epic. Besides, you were meant to be mine nine years ago."

"It's like God was testing us, seeing if we would find our way back to each other," I whisper, my eyes watching his mouth, that sliver of a scar shining against his lips. "How did you get this scar?" I gently rub my finger over the silver line. Landon smirks.

"Roman and I were fighting over a girl. I didn't like the girl. I just liked pissing him off." Landon chuckles, and I smile.

His eyes trail to my lips and he dips his head, taking my mouth without a second thought. His tongue massages along mine. With the taste of apple lingering on his tongue, I moan into his mouth and tangle my hands into the bottom of his hair. He angles his hips just right, the head of his length pressing against my sex. My body sparks with excitement, my heart thudding against my chest in anticipation.

The skies open up and rain comes pouring down, droplets diving into the pool water all around us. His large hands edge themselves up my thighs and pull them apart wider, and he pushes himself inside me. I close my eyes and part my lips to let out a satisfying sigh. I loll my head back as Landon fills me with his hard cock. His teeth scrape along my jaw, a raw moan vibrating his chest as he slowly thrusts into me. Thunder sounds from above, and rain pitter-patters off my head and shoulders.

His hands slide from my bottom and push against my back, the action smothering my chest to his. His jaw is clenched and his eyes take in every inch of my face. Pressure builds in my core with the way he looks at me, like the storm around us isn't even happening.

"If I could take it all back and make your life easier, I would." He pants, water splashing between us as he thrusts his length inside of me. "I would take it all back and become my father, just so you didn't have to suffer one day of being alone."

I bite my bottom lip to keep from getting emotional, but a sob escapes anyway. Like a fire claiming a wick, my heart vibrates in my chest. I feel alive to the fullest, and I know at this moment I want nothing more in life than to be with Landon.

"I really want to hate you. But I love you," I whisper, not taking my eyes off his. Landon smirks and thrusts his hips harder.

I moan loudly in response to his cock hitting me just right, warmth building in my lower half and buzzing its way through my limbs.

"I love you, too," he groans, dipping his head and sucking my nipple into his mouth as he drives himself into me over and over.

Warmth flares in my core, and my eyes clench to the point of seeing stars. My legs squeeze around Landon like a vise as I teeter on the edge of pleasure. I scream out as I fall over the cliff of release. Lightning ignites the sky and thunder booms as I ride my wave of satisfaction. Landon buries his head into my neck and growls, his body pulsing and tensing against mine as he follows his own release. Rain clings to my eyelashes as I try and catch my breath, Landon glancing at me from under his own. We should move, the storm around us becoming more hostile by the second, but we just cling to each other, not wanting to part.

"What are you going to do about Miller?" I question loudly so he can hear me above the rain.

"Whatever I have to. I'll kill him before I let him get between us."

LANDON

"Holy shit. There's no way I can take that. Look at that thing!"

Charlie's face twists like she's physically in pain as she eyes the prenatal vitamins in my hand. I smirk at her dramatic response to a couple of pills.

"I can hold you down, make you take them," I offer. Charlie rolls her eyes and holds her hand out, knowing I'll do just that. In fact, holding her down and showing her who's in control is not a bad way to start the morning, in my opinion. I still can't believe this is the same little girl who was under the table nine long years ago. I never thought I could care for another. I just didn't care to before. Nobody came along that I felt like I needed to pursue. No woman interested me past a one-night stand. Nobody but Charlie. It's like she said, it's as if fate was trying to tell us something the whole time we had been together. We just weren't listening.

She pops them in her mouth and takes a sip of water. She looks amazing this morning. Her dark, curly hair is down, and her cheeks are flushed from the round of sex we just had, which ended with us tangled in the bed sheets and falling on the floor.

She runs her hands through her hair and sighs loudly. She's nervous, not that I blame her. Taking her back to the estate where I know my father will be is risky, but I won't hesitate to protect her from him, even if it kills me. Miller and his bimbo are out of the Blackwell estate as of today, peacefully or otherwise.

"Stop worrying. Everything will be fine."

She snaps her head toward me and huffs. "Just leave me here. Come back and get me when everything is over," she whines.

"I told you, I don't feel comfortable leaving you alone. Not when my father has hired men to capture you. You're coming with me," I growl. I find her hand and pull her from the bed, give her a kiss on the forehead, and smack her ass. I'm not surprised Niko came to the house last night after Charlie. When my father puts out an order, it's a challenge among our most ruthless men. When I saw the person holding the gun at Charlie, I didn't hesitate. I killed the motherfucker. I didn't know it was Niko, but the ending would have been the same even if I had. I will do everything in my power to protect Charlie, to prove to her I am what she needs.

"Let's get a move on."

I slide my hands through my hair, slicking it back, and head toward my car to start the journey back to the estate. I set the alarm system and leave with Charlie.

During the drive to the estate, Charlie shifts and messes with her hair nervously. She keeps looking down at her stomach with an unreadable expression. I'm not sure if she's accepting the pregnancy or still on the fence. I admit, it's a fucking shock. There are pieces of me that have me scared out of my mind to be a father, but if I was going to have a child with anyone, I'd want it to be with Charlie.

Parking at the estate, I can tell everyone is on high-alert. Osborn is standing at the front door, along with some other no-named guards here and there.

"Osborn," I greet, shutting my door. I hurry my step and open Charlie's door, helping her out. Her face is pale, and her eyes dart around the yard.

"Landon." Osborn takes my hand and slaps my back.

"My father in?" I ask.

Osborn nods, his sunglasses blinding me from the glare of the sun reflecting off them. I open the large door and find my father yelling at a man in a police uniform at the top of the stairs. I lift my chin and exhale, my hand finding Charlie's as we charge forward.

"Last time I checked, Miller, you weren't running the show anymore. So why am I even talking to you? You can't benefit me in

any way. What I'm doing is a favor to your father," the cop sneers, his hand on his gun.

"What's going on?" I question, turning to shut the door but stopping when I find Osborn following me in.

"Landon." When the cop turns, I recognize him as Arlen, his caramel-brown curly hair sticking out from under his black police cap around his bright freckled face. He's built like an athlete and has been a client of ours before he was ever on the force. I head up the steps, and Charlie squeezes my hand. I turn my head and find her eyes wide as saucers and staring past me. Following her line of sight, I see my father looking right at her with hunger in his eyes. *I'll deal with him in a minute.*

"What can I do for you, Arlen?" I ask, shaking his hand.

"As I told your father, we cannot locate Charlotte Evans. We–" He stops and lifts his index finger, pointing at Charlie. "Is that—" His brows furrow.

"Thank you for your time, Arlen, but it's been handled," I interrupt.

"I see. Well, good. My men and I can get back to our job then." Arlen looks over his shoulder, glaring at my father before trotting down the stairs. I wait for him to leave before I turn to address Miller.

His face is still blistering red. He's in his red robe, his dark silk sweats showing from under it. You can tell he's not slept with the large bags forming under his eyes.

"You betrayed me," he spits, his fists clenching. I don't respond.

"An Evans. You let an Evans into my household after what her whore of a mother did to me." His lip curls, and his eyes squint with insanity.

I sigh.

"Maria got pregnant by you. We all knew she was here for money, and she had dreams, goals. We all knew that. Getting pregnant by your bastard baby and getting stuck here as your side ass wasn't going to happen," I remind him. Maria was a quiet person, but that was something she did tell everyone. She wanted better.

He turns, running his hands over his face. "She killed my blood. There is no explanation that could justify that!" he shouts, pointing at me. "But to make it worse, she had a daughter." He twists his face in anger, looking directly at Charlie. My body tenses as anger fuels my veins. "And she was alive this whole time." His face goes lax as he looks at me. "Did you know she had a daughter? Because she never told me. She didn't tell anyone."

I swallow, my tongue feeling thick in my dry mouth.

"I did," I respond strongly.

His head whips up and his jaw clenches. He wasn't expecting me to answer, nonetheless admit to knowing Maria had a daughter.

"I saw her hiding under the table that day," I continue, rolling the cuffs of my sleeves.

"You what?" he hisses, blood vessels protruding on his forehead.

"You were out of line that day. Out of your mind, to be exact. You would have killed a nine-year-old little girl," I fire back.

"Damn right I would have. And I will," he sneers, pointing at Charlie. Hearing him threaten her makes me want to snap his neck.

"No, you won't," I seethe, stepping nose to nose with him.

"I will, and I will do the job myself this time, seeing how incompetent you are. I should've made Roman the head of the

estate. At least he has the balls of a Blackwell," my father states.

"I'm good. I don't want the position," Roman adds, stepping up the stairs in his usual messy attire.

Father looks down and scowls at Roman.

"You won't go near Charlie," I tell him, my tone serious.

Father laughs, his bellows echoing through the estate.

"Oh, please don't tell me you've fallen for the whore. After everything I taught you about them. Let my mistake be a lesson, son. They don't care about us Blackwells. They just want what's better for them." He chuckles, his eyes watering from his amusement.

"Fuck you," Charlie clips, her body puffed out in absolute fury. I grab her hand and pull her behind me. I don't need her to make him any angrier than he is.

"So, Charlie is just okay with you killing her mother in cold blood," he states loudly, trying to look around me.

"I told her how if I hadn't, I wouldn't have been able to save her from you."

My father sighs loudly and looks to the heavens. "Oh, how my son has deceived me," he mutters.

"What I should have done was turn the gun and killed you that day. It would have saved everyone a lot of grief," I grit.

"It's not too late," Roman clips, standing next to Charlie.

"Screw you. Screw all of you. You don't know what power is, what control is." He points at all of us.

"Baby?" Tara walks out of the hallway, concern written on her face as she makes her way toward us.

"You need to leave." I take a step forward, ready to throw my father out the door if I need to.

"What?" He stops, his eyes wide.

"Why?" Tara cries, draping herself across my father.

"You need to pack your things and leave the estate. I can't have you here anymore. You've done enough damage to the Blackwell name." I lower my head and glower at him. "Besides, I'm sure Charlie will feel uncomfortable having you under the same roof." Now, I'm just trying to piss him off. I'm past the point of caring.

"You will *not* kick me out to move that… that…" He stutters on his words, his tone becoming flustered as he points at Charlie.

"I will, and I am," I interrupt. I stomp forward and clutch his arm, pulling him, ready to throw him out the fucking door in nothing but his robe. Tara screams and starts slapping my back in a fit of rage. It doesn't surprise me, Tara is obsessed with my father. She'll do anything to protect him.

"Don't you touch him!" Charlie shouts, grabbing Tara by the hair. Tara suddenly stops her belligerent slapping. I look over my shoulder to see where she went when Father roars, flinging his robe open and pulling a black pistol out. His chest heaves as he points it at me. I let go of his arm and take a step back, my hands raised. I look over and see Tara and Charlie going at it. Tara is pulling Charlie's hair, her teeth baring with anger as Charlie tries to gain her balance on the edge of a step. I take a step toward them to break them up and help Charlie, but father shoves his gun in my face, stopping me. Roman raises his hands, too, standing right next to me.

"Tell Maria I'll see her in Hell," he growls, cocking the gun. My eyes widen and my body tenses before a loud bang rings out and I flinch. Realizing I'm not hurt and the sound came from behind me, I turn to find Osborn in position, his gun aimed right at my father. A loud thump sounds as my dad falls on his back. He's sprawled out on the stairs, eyes wide and blood pooling underneath him.

One bullet hole rests in the center of his forehead.

"Holy shit," Roman whispers, turning to look away from Father.

Tara screams loudly as she sees my dad on the stairs, shoving Charlie off her. She falls to the floor, crawling toward him and in slow motion, Charlie loses her balance from the violent shove and goes flying down the stairs.

"No!" I bellow, trying to grab her, but my hand just misses her and she tumbles down.

I rush down the stairs to Charlie, a bundled mess at the bottom step, and pick her up.

"Are you okay?" I ask, looking her over frantically, my heart racing in my chest. She holds her head and groans.

"Roman, call the doctor!" I demand.

"On it," he calls out with a shaky voice.

"I'll get this cleaned up. You get Charlie to her room; the doctor should be here quickly," Osborn instructs, hovering over my father. Without another question, I step over a sobbing Tara and head up the stairs. My heart is slamming against my chest in fear, my legs shaking with the possibility that I may lose my child.

I set Charlie on the bed and start tearing her clothes off. The sound of fabric ripping and shredding fills the room.

She has red marks all over her arms and legs. She's holding her wrist, and her lip is bleeding.

I thumb her lip, wiping the blood. Her eyes fill with tears as she looks at me like I'm her answer for everything.

"Am I going to lose the baby?" she whispers, tears spilling from her eyes.

I swallow and grasp the back of her head, pulling her into me.

CHARLIE

Landon had the doctor stay at the estate to keep an eye on me, but he said there was nothing we could do but wait. He was a middle-aged man with extremely cold hands. He said we would know soon if I'd lose the baby or not. Twenty-four hours later, here I am in a tub of warm water cleaning the blood off me as Landon sits on the edge of the tub and sponges my back.

I woke up and had to pee. When I went to the bathroom, I found blood spotting my panties. I instantly felt failure, and emptiness. I screamed and sobbed, waking Landon up. I didn't think I would miscarry, convinced the world wouldn't do that to me and Landon after everything we had been through. Landon called the doctor straight away. The   doctor examined me, and shook his head unsure. He said he would do an ultrasound in a few days to see if we had indeed lost the baby, but to keep off my feet until then.

"Charlie, talk to me," he rasps, squeezing the sponge of soapy warm water down my back, bringing me from moments ago to now.

"It's all my fault. I shouldn't have tried to pull Tara off you," I whisper, staring at the tub's chrome faucet. "But I saw her beating on you and I just reacted." I shrug, emotion filling my voice. Goose bumps race along my arms, and even with the warm water, I feel cold and empty. The injuries from the fall don't compare to the pain splicing through my heart.

"The doctor said the bleeding is too light to determine a miscarriage. Don't talk as if this is it, Charlie."

I let out a heavy breath and lay my head back on his legs. "You're just trying to make me feel better," I sniffle.

"It's my fault, too. If I was away from the stairs..." he clips, his voice dark. "I should have listened to you and left you back at the house."

I shift sideways and look up at him, his face taut and eyes holding sorrow. He's blaming himself, too. It hurts me to know that he thinks this is his fault.

I raise my hand and cup his jaw, the scruff tickling my palm.

"I wasn't sure if I wanted the baby at first," I admit. "I didn't know what to think. Waking up one day and being told you're pregnant is a shock. But now, thinking I may not have that little heartbeat inside me anymore, I know for sure that I do want the baby one-hundred percent." I start to cry.

Landon cups my hand and brings his head down, kissing the skin of my inner wrist. "Let's get you out," he whispers against my hand. He stands and grabs a towel from the counter as I place my hands on each side of the tub and stand on wobbly legs. Landon wraps my body in a large, fluffy white towel and directs me out of the water. Standing in front of the mirror, I watch him pat and dry my body with such care and love, I draw in a sudden breath. He begins to roll down his pants legs, and I slowly head into the bedroom with the towel still wrapped around me.

I look out the window, all the twinkling lights of Vegas shining in the distance.

"We'll make it through this, sweetheart," Landon whispers into my ear. I nod as a tear trails down my cheek. I lean against him, my body drawing strength from his closeness.

"What now?" I question. *Where do Landon and I go from here?* We may lose a child, but Landon lost a father too. I tried to get him to talk about it, but he does the man thing and says he's fine. That his father got what was coming to him. He also assured me that Tara paid for attacking me. When I asked what he meant, he said nobody harms a Blackwell and lives to see another day. I don't know if he took care of it or Osborn, and I don't want to think about it.

"You become the Madam of the Blackwell estate. That is, if you want to." Landon pulls me from my thoughts, and I frown. Me as the Madam of the estate makes the nerves in my stomach knot. I'm not sure I could handle a bunch of damaged women.

"I'm not so sure I'm the one for the job, Landon," I whisper, grief lacing my words.

"I beg to differ. You are *perfect* for the job. You know more about being in those girls' shoes than anyone." Landon strides behind me, his hands on my hips as he rests his chin on my shoulder. "Let's get you to bed. You need to rest." Landon turns me and presses on the small of my back, leading me back to the bed. The bed is made perfectly, the sheets seemingly brand new. Landon pulls the comforter back and helps me crawl in; they're crisp and clean against my sore body. He turns the lights off then climbs in after me, pulling me into the crook of his torso. The

warmth of his skin against mine is comforting and relaxing. It's all I could ever want.

"If fate hands us the worst, Charlie, the doctor said we could try to conceive again." My eyes widen and my heart sputters. I tilt my head back and search Landon's face in the dark. *We should wait. We shouldn't jump into a commitment so quickly, but my gut says to hell with what normal people do. When have we ever been normal anyway?*

"Is... is that something you want?" I question. I know getting pregnant was an accident, but actually planning to have a child is a whole other level of commitment.

Landon runs his hand along the crook of my neck and exhales.

"If we lose this baby, then yes. When we're both mentally and physically ready." He raises a stern brow at me. "Yes, it is something I want."

I nod, agreeing.

"All in?" he whispers, kissing my forehead tenderly. My lips curl into a smile, his 'all in' making me giggle.

"All in."

LANDON

Three Days Later

I sit at my desk, working some of the girls' clients for the week when my phone rings. "Landon Blackwell," I answer anxiously. Charlie is with the doctor upstairs. She said she wanted to be alone when she found out if we had lost our child or not. I refused, but the doctor insisted.

"Good afternoon, Mr. Blackwell. This is Aaron from wildlife conservation. I got a call that you had two gorillas you were looking to have placed in our reserve?"

I sit up straight and jerk my tie loose. "Yes, that is correct."

"Can I set up a time to come and look the gorillas over, observe them to see if they're fit for our program? I'm sure they will be. I would just like to see them firsthand." He chuckles and I give a half-laugh, standing to relieve my nerves.

"Yes, that would be terrific," I respond. "Next week sound okay to you?" I'm not sure if I'm free next week, but I can shuffle some

things around if I need to. Since Father's death, Roman and I pretty much run things together.

"Great. If you want to email me the directions and any information regarding Jaheem and Ebele, that would be great."

"Yes, of course."

"I'll see you next week then, Mr. Blackwell."

"See you then." I hang up, my back sweating. I've been trying to get them into one of these programs for what seems like forever. It's not that I won't miss them, because I will. I grew up running out to their cage and seeing them. But they deserve to be free, to be animals. Not prisoners.

The door opens and shuts to my office, catching my attention.

Charlie walks in wearing a long, sexy-as-hell black dress, her dark hair is let down and curling at the ends. When I was younger, my mother would dress in a black dress before she worked the estate. When I asked her about it, she furrowed her brows and said, "Every woman deserves a little black dress, Landon." Then she smirked and ruffled my hair. "Don't forget that, son."

"Have I said how sexy you look in black?" I smile wolfishly. Charlie's cheeks flush as she strides over to my desk. My cock grows in my slacks with the need to take her again. "We just got Jaheem and Ebele a home into a nice reserve, I think," I inform her with a big smile.

"Really?" Charlie lights up. She smiles and looks off. "That's crazy."

I lift a brow, curious at what she's thinking in that head of hers. "Why's that?"

"They're free, we're free. It's just an odd coincidence." I nod and smile, noticing she has her hand behind her back and a mischievous smile playing her face. I cock my head to the side, curious what she's up to.

"What?" I ask with a laugh.

She pulls her arm out and shoves her hand in my face as she squeals in excitement. I pull my face back to look at what she has in her hand to find a picture of some sort. I take it from her, and examine it. It's an ultrasound image. I forgot for a moment about her being with the doctor I was so excited about finding Jaheem and Ebele a home.

"Really?" I look at her with surprise.

"Mmhhm." She nods. "We didn't lose the baby!" I stand from my desk and make my way to her, pulling her into my arms. "I can't believe it. I surely thought we had lost it," she mutters into the crook of my neck. I scoff.

"Must be a boy then, tough like his dad." She rolls her eyes and slaps at my chest. I slide my hand along her abdomen, and smirk. "A Blackwell and an Evans, imagine that," I mutter. Relief floods my senses that we didn't lose it, that Charlie and I created something precious out of an act of love rather than creating chaos and damage in our wake. This baby is a start to a new chapter in mine and Charlie's life. He or she stands for something memorable.

Charlie beams with happiness as she watches my hand caress her belly.

"Imagine that," she repeats. "We actually did something right for a change, and it happened when we weren't even trying," she giggles. I shake my head, and pull my hand away. Trying to get a hold of my emotions.

"How's your first day going as the Madam?" I ask, trailing my fingers up her spine. Making Charlie the Madam was the best decision I ever made. She's perfect for the girls. Hearing the news, Veronica got pissed and left. I can honestly say things between the girls have become a lot less catty since her departure.

"Jayden is not taking the team cleaning her up well, and Roman is pacing outside the door like a dog in heat waiting for her. I just..." She closes her eyes. "I don't even know what I'm supposed to do," she huffs, sitting at my desk. It took some threatening and cash to get Jayden from Mick, but in the end, it was all worth it. Charlie seems much happier that Jayden is here. I offered Jayden a position to help Charlie out around the estate, but she refused. Jayden said there's a void in her life we wouldn't understand and she'd rather be an escort.

I grab Charlie's hand and give it a reassuring squeeze. Things between Charlie and I are smoother now that we don't have to fight what we really want, which is just to be together. We're better people when we're together than when we're apart. We both have something the other needs. She needs my strength to cure her pain and my presence when she feels alone. I need her love and that attitude of hers to put me in my place.

"Your job is to be there for the girls, make sure they follow the rules. A lot of girls come in here damaged, although you wouldn't know it by the fake smiles and how they constantly throw themselves at men. But mostly, that's an act of filling an emptiness," I explain, sitting on my desk. She runs her hand down my arm and smiles.

Charlie nods. "If there *is* something I know, it's that you have to relinquish it all before you can have it all."

I hold her arm and pull her back to my front, brushing the hair from her neck.

"Do you have it all, Charlie?" I whisper into her ear.

She turns her head slightly and offers a wicked smile.

"I'm getting there."

Acknowledgements

This book was so much fun to write. The research alone was amazing and I found myself nose deep into the world of escorts and pimps till the wee hours of the night. It's as fascinating as it is dark.

This book could not have been completed without my amazing team of friends though. Thank you Author JC Emery and your ability to listen to me ramble and plot at all hours of the night.

Thank you LM Creations for the amazing cover. BIG thank you to Alessandra Torre for the cover blurb. I tried my hardest not to fan-girl all over you, but you rock... so it was hard.

My editor at Hottree, you are amazing and worked so well with my tight schedule. Julie, can I just say THANK YOU for proofing Relinquish on your vacation (If that is not loyalty, I don't know what is).

My street team and Addicts group, you are the best, and I love every one of you. Rock Stars Of Romance, you fucking rock! Thank you much for an amazing release, tour, and cover reveal.

Max Effect, you rock at formatting. I always know I'm in good hands with your amazing talent.

I am forever grateful to my betas. This book had me so nervous being my first out of my MC series. Some read a couple of chapters, some read all of the book. Stephanie, Brie, Bel, Julie, Vickie, Courtney, Jennifer, Nancy, and Emily. You're opinion, and advice helped me in many ways. Thank you!

Most of all, thank you- the reader. This book would not be here without you and your support. I'm beyond grateful and hope to keep pleasing you with books to come!

Love

M. N. Forgy x

Also by M. N. FORGY

About the
AUTHOR

M.N. Forgy was raised in Missouri where she still lives with her family. She's a soccer mom by day and a saucy writer by night.

M.N. Forgy started writing at a young age but never took it seriously until years later, as a stay-at-home mom, she opened her laptop and started writing again. As a role model for her children, she felt she couldn't live with the "what if" anymore and finally took a chance on her character's story. So, with her glass of wine in hand and a stray Barbie sharing her seat, she continues to create and please her fans.

www.mnforgy.com

www.ingramcontent.com/pod-product-compliance
Lightning Source LLC
Chambersburg PA
CBHW070920260626
47162CB00007B/2739

* 9 7 8 0 9 8 6 4 1 1 7 2 4 *